We Bombed In New London

by Brian Gari

We Bombed In New London

The Inside Story
of the
Broadway Musical

by Brian Gari

Late Nite Comic

BearManor Media
2006

We Bombed In New London:
The Inside Story of the Broadway Musical *Late Nite Comic*

© 2006 Brian Gari

For information, address:

BearManor Media
P. O. Box 71426
Albany, GA   31708

bearmanormedia.com

Cover art and photo of author by Roberto Gari

Cover design by John Teehan

Typesetting and layout by John Teehan

Published in the USA by BearManor Media

ISBN—1-59393-051-8
978-1-59393-051-6

For my mother & father who lived it as well

My heartfelt thanks to:

Robin Kaiser, who was the first to suggest that I write this

Larry Hochman, who lent me the tapes that inspired the book

Derek Tague for leading me to BearManor Media

Ben Ohmart for his belief in this book

Because this book was originally typed on an archaic Commodore computer, I am especially grateful to my mother for retyping & editing the entire book from the only existing printout.

Table of Contents

Foreword

The story behind this Broadway musical is incredible. Every vignette I relayed to friends seemed to capture their attention. (Could it have possibly been the handcuffs and gags I utilized?) Anyway, each time I finished telling one more amazing escapade, the friend would ask, "Why don't you write a book?" When I would finally give it the least bit of serious thought, another friend would tell me I should move on and forget about this brush with The Great White Way. I had an album of the show that did well—why don't I just leave the past behind me?

On August 3, 1989, I received a call from the musical's brilliant arranger and orchestrator, Larry Hochman; he had remembered lending me audio tapes of *Late Nite Comic* about a year before and thought it was time to retrieve them. I had stared at these cassettes over the year, and, although interested in listening to them, I found the thought of reliving the musical this soon was a bit too much to deal with. Hochman's phone call made it essential; I must hear them before returning them. With each 90-minute cassette I slipped into my machine, new memories would pop up. Some were pleasant, some were not, but all were worthwhile. The experience of having a musical on Broadway (and your first musical, at that) is an experience I found worth telling.

From the very beginning I kept every scrap of paper associated with the project. I've been told I must be related to the Collyer brothers, but I always thought this memorabilia would be important in one way or another.

The journey I have assembled will be informative. But besides that, I hope you will find it heartwarming; joyous, yet disappointing; funny, yet infuriating. At the very least, it will be honest.

– Brian Gari
New York City

Chapter 1
Broadway Baby

I had never expected to write for Broadway; my influences were more pop/rock than traditional theatre. True, my grandfather was Eddie Cantor, and I absorbed those great songs he was associated with, but I still had a passion for the contemporary pop song.

My earliest memory was of my father playing Judy Garland's recording of "The Man That Got Away," and I remember singing along at age three on the phrase "the night is bitter." My parents certainly kept up with the Broadway musical (my father, in the forties, having been in the choruses of *A Connecticut Yankee* and *Sadie Thompson*). *My Fair Lady* was frequently on the turntable. I was truly a fan (and still am) of that score.

The first Broadway musical I saw was probably *Li'l Abner*. I still have the huge yellow button that says, "I likes Elvis…but I loves *Li'l Abner*!" However, the score that had the most profound effect on me was *Gypsy*. I saw the original 1959 Ethel Merman production. One family member or another was always playing the album and singing along at top volume. My sister was only four, but she was screeching like Rose or bumping and grinding like Mazeppa. In later years I found myself especially drawn to delicate ballads like "Small World" and "Little Lamb." Jumping ahead for a moment—when I had the idea to write the book for what was to become *Late Nite Comic*, I studied Arthur Laurents's libretto, because I saw this as the ultimate book for a musical and the one from which I should learn.

Getting back chronologically, as time went on, I grew more attracted to the Top 40, as most normal teens would. My first Top 10 record purchase was "Sealed with a Kiss" by Brian Hyland. (Note: The writers, Gary Geld and Peter Udell, were later to work with Philip Rose

1

on several musicals, including *Purlie* and *Shenandoah*.) My bedtime was nonnegotiable, especially on school nights, so I had to listen to my rock 'n' roll with a transistor radio under my pillow. Coming through would be the sound of disc jockey Cousin Brucie, screaming, "Here's 'Next Door to an Angel' by Neil Sedaka!" Sedaka's melodies were very inventive and bordered on Broadway. He had an enormous impact on my songwriting.

By 1964 the Beatles had arrived, and I wrote my first song—not a very good one, mind you, but certainly influenced by Lennon and McCartney's work for Peter and Gordon. With my mother's encouragement I went on to write more and more. Even though she had taught me to play piano, I dropped it in favor of the guitar. "Why the guitar?" you ask. (I was hoping that you'd ask!) Well, I had seen a film called *The Parent Trap* with Hayley Mills. She supposedly played guitar in the movie, so I told my parents I must have a guitar. You see, in my naïve pubescent way I thought that if I could play, Hayley would go out with me. In going to an all-boys' school at the time, seeing Ms. Mills on the screen was about all the sexual activity I was experiencing.

Anyway, I continued writing on the $8 guitar my parents bought me. (Oh, the calluses you get from an $8 guitar!) It wasn't until 1967, when I saw a TV special by Leonard Bernstein entitled *The Pop Revolution*, that I switched back to the piano. Beach Boy Brian Wilson was performing a new song called "Surf's Up." It was obviously a piano-rooted song, and I was floored. From that point on I wrote most of my songs on the piano.

It was also in 1967 that I got my first song published. Two years later it was recorded. And in two minutes it disappeared into obscurity. With all due respect to the song, it was on an album by an unknown group fashioned after the 5th Dimension, but they did not go up, up and away. I continued getting songs published and having them recorded here and there, but it wasn't until 1975 that things improved. I had made the rounds of every label as an artist, but was always turned down. I consistently read the trade magazines and found a new A&R person by the name of Ann Purtill at the Vanguard label. I had already been rejected by this "new" person at a prior label, but I got an appointment, and she liked what I brought her. Unfortunately, when she played it for the head guys, she was told to pass on it. However, she encouraged me to come back with more, and I certainly didn't ignore the advice. I returned the following week with a record I had made five years earlier. They signed me. The record was a novelty-type song and didn't show the kind of music I was really into at the time. They released it, but it didn't catch on. I begged them to let me demo my newer songs, and one, "Dance," caught their ears. Alas, it was too late; I had already been dropped by the label. Little did I know that "Dance" was to be the start of a major project for the Broadway stage.

Chapter 2
The Inspiration

It was June 30, 1971—a beautiful summer's evening in Manhattan. A young actress named Neva Small had invited my childhood friend Larry and me to a party. Neva had quite a résumé for a 19-year-old, including the Broadway show *Henry Sweet Henry*. There was a clique of actors from the Professional Children's School. I just missed being part of that group because I had gone to that God-awful boys' school. I was not part of the showbiz crowd, which boasted a very young Pia Zadora. It wasn't until my last two years of high school, when I switched to a similar theatrical school, that I was able to meet kids with the same interests.

Neva was living in a high-rise on West 70th Street, off West End Avenue. I didn't know her all that well, but I had recorded a demo of one of my new songs, "Bicycle Ride," with her. Larry and I were psyched for this party and wore our best psychedelic summer garb—well, at least I did. Larry always seemed a bit more relaxed with social situations than I was. Five years at an all-boys school didn't prepare me well for socializing with the opposite sex—and especially beautiful actresses and models.

Upon entering the apartment, I immediately zeroed in on a long-haired beauty in hot pants. Little did I know that she was zeroing in on me as well. I was trying to be cool, but probably not doing too well at it. Her name was Janet, and she was not an actress or a model. The Lincoln Center area of the party should have given it away: she was a ballet dancer—one with a very theatrical personality. Her long auburn hair and big eyes were a perfect setting for such a bubbly presence. There was one big problem, however; Larry had cornered her. I figured he got there first; he's the lucky one. But for some strange reason, Larry walked away. I strolled over, gathering up all my courage, and started a conversation.

We ended up talking for hours, and Larry was already involved with someone else. When he never came back for Janet's phone number, I asked her for it. It turned out that she was Neva's downstairs neighbor. Larry and I were about to go home to our respective houses when Janet, without batting an eye, asked if she could join me.

We had just walked into my apartment when the phone rang. It was Larry asking if he could get Janet's number from me. I was shocked. He'd had his chance and had blown it. Janet had me mesmerized. We stayed up all night talking. Then I put her on the front of my bicycle and drove her down West End Avenue, with the sun peeking through over Riverside Park. It was the most romantic first evening together imaginable—one that led to a five-year relationship.

Larry was livid when he came by the following day. He felt he had a claim on Janet, "asking" me if it would be all right to date her. I told him no—I was definitely interested in her, and he left my apartment in extreme frustration. I saw Janet almost every day for the next week. I adored her. Besides being beautiful, she was highly intelligent, and her winning personality just bowled me over. There were a few times when I didn't see her, and one day she came over crying. "I can't take it anymore!" she screamed.

"Take what?" I asked.

"Larry just doesn't stop calling me."

I was confused. Didn't I tell him I was getting involved with this girl? "What do you mean?" I questioned. It seemed that Larry dated Janet even after asking my intentions. Janet said she went out with him to show me what a heel he was. I'm sure there were some psychological reasons for her behavior, but the bottom line was that Larry was a snake. I called him over, told him off and kicked him out of my life. That wasn't easy to do. Larry was my buddy from grade school. He taught me to be more comfortable talking about sex. He was my friend. Now he was a traitor. I could forgive Janet; she was new in my life. I could not forgive my friend of twelve years.

Oddly enough, the first song I wrote about Janet was entitled "What's the Use?" It dealt with a really defeatist attitude—what good is it to write your number in my book when tomorrow you may be gone? It was certainly not the case for a long time to come.

About six months into our relationship, Janet's frustration with her career took a turn for the worse. She was going to quit ballet. She had danced with Eliot Feld's company while her roommate, Garielle, was signed to the New York City Ballet. She would tell me over and over that even though Gari (coincidentally, Garielle's nickname) was with a big company, it wasn't the place she wanted to be. Ballet Theater was her goal. A few injuries and too long a neck seemed to be the reason they would not accept her. She was at her wit's end. She had been dancing since she was eight, and she just couldn't take the rejection anymore. (She should have tried songwriting sometime!)

Her last ditch try was going to be the Pennsylvania Ballet Company. An audition was set, and she had to be on a train at the crack of dawn. Morning came and she overslept. Rushing out of the house, she discovered, when she got there—extremely exhausted—that she had forgotten to put on underwear. Someone lent her something and she auditioned. It was not the greatest. Her heart was probably not in it. We were in love, and the thought of losing each other was probably taking precedence over almost everything she was doing.

She finally received the result; she did not get into the company. I was sad for her, but in a selfish way I was also relieved. I didn't know how I'd survive without her. She was completely out of money, so she had to move and get some kind of job. The apartment she got was a room; my next door neighbor rented her a maid's room for $75 a month. I, of course, was still living at home, but now we were across the hall from each other. When she wasn't going to Katherine Gibbs secretarial school, she was with me. Then she landed a job with a Japanese business. A receptionist. A far cry from the glamorous life of a ballet dancer. Her devastation seeped into my soul forever.

Over the next five years we had the usual ups and downs of any relationship that starts at that young an age. We were basically faithful, although we both strayed once during those years. It was extremely hard for me to let her go to someone else. She eventually returned, but after a million songs had poured out of me. One of those songs I recorded and left on her doorstep. When I played back my phone messages that night, she had the record playing in the background and was telling me that we would get back together. We lasted another year.

At the beginning of 1976 (our last year together), I decided to write a real tribute to her and her lost dancing career. The song was called "Dance," and it described all the heartache I remembered she felt during that painful transition period. Although she was now in the publishing field (and becoming quite successful), I felt there was a part of her that still mourned

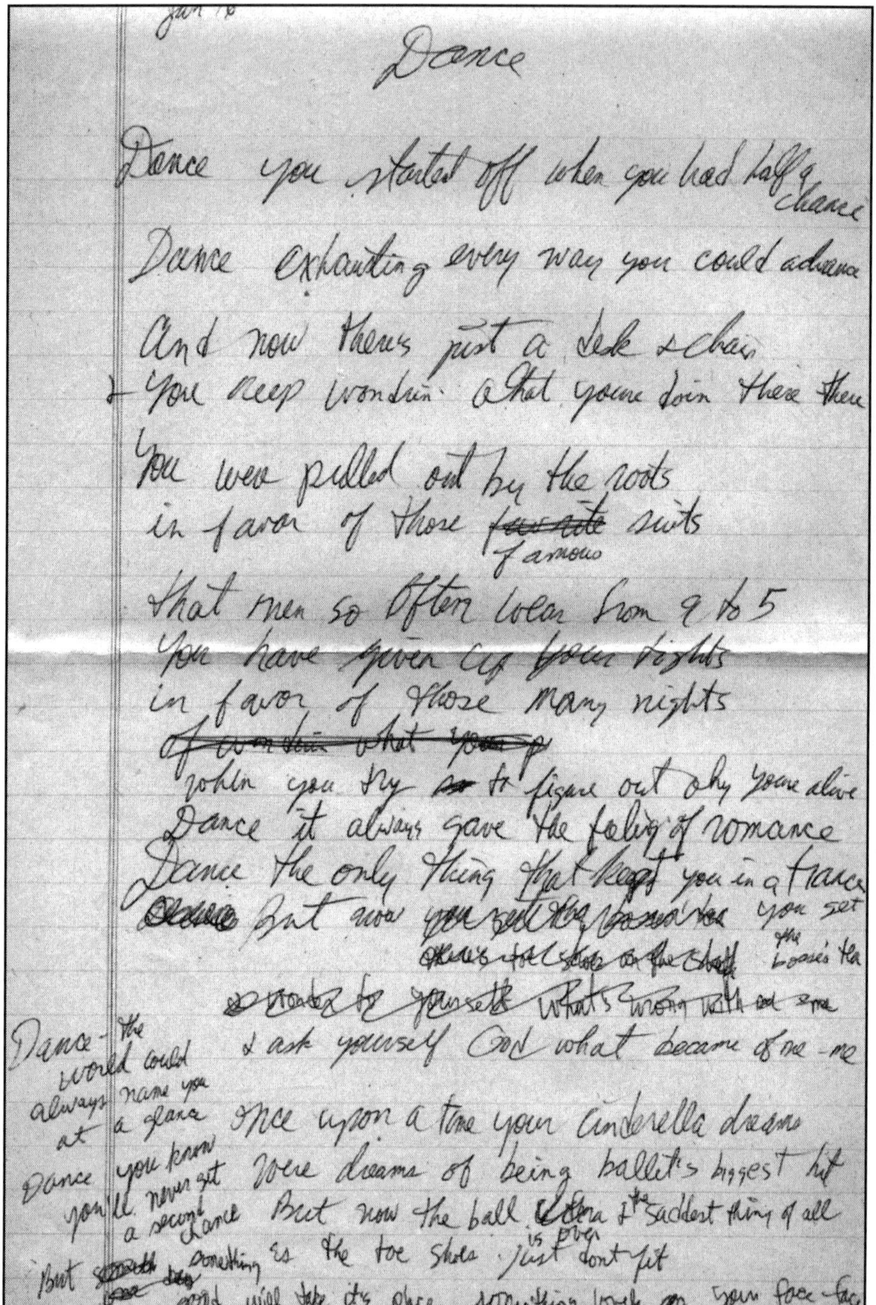

Dance

The original version, January 1976

My first Christmas with Janet, 1971.

the loss of her former life. Little did I know that I was to become part of that past as well. I was told much later, in therapy, that when someone has to make an enormous change in her life, very often everything else goes as well.

Janet never heard the song "Dance." Two months after I wrote it, I helped her move back downtown. I spent a few evenings there in her new apartment, but she was cold. She wanted to end this era in her life. She was definite. I was lost.

Chapter 3
The Comedy Clubs

In 1976 Alan Colmes was a radio personality who had stayed in touch with me ever since he was a DJ in New Haven and played my first record release. He had always believed in me and was now commuting between New Haven and New York. He headed the weekend shift of a country station called WHN. This meant he could make the rounds of the comedy clubs in the early evening with his stand-up act and do his radio gig at midnight. Considering the many hours he drove back and forth from New Haven, this was one dedicated (or perhaps insane) young man.

In April of that year he called me. I was still in bed…in the late afternoon…with the electric blanket on! I was, at best, a basket case. He came over and listened to my story about Janet, suggesting that we hit the club scene together. He could do his comedy act and I could do my songs. I quickly responded that I had never really done an act before. He insisted that I could and literally pulled me out of bed. I made us my greasy cheeseburgers and took off for God knows where.

Our first stop was a place on West 54th Street, right off 7th Avenue, called Al and Dick's Steakhouse. It had catered to theatrical folk for many years and was now on its last legs. The person who put us onstage was a man by the name of Ed Sommerfeld. We played to about three people and were not overly inspired. We returned only out of desperation, although Ed was decent enough to us.

In May we traveled a little further west—West 44th Street, that is. The Improvisation had a little more prestige (but a much more disgusting bathroom). I had a 45 in the stores at the time and thought I would have a little more luck getting some stage time. Boy, was I wrong! Chris Albrecht was in charge; he took my 45, thanked me and promptly put it on the top shelf of a cabinet. We were told to wait.

In those days the Improv had little booths for the acts to sit and chat. That's about all Alan and I ever got to do. We rarely got any stage time. Alan was at a real disadvantage, since he had to be on the air by midnight. A 2:00 A.M. slot was often allotted to him, but he would be gone by that time. It was a period of lots of energy and lots of frustration. The abuse we took was not to be believed. I bet the guys who gave out the slots had to look behind them when they left in the wee hours of the morning.

One day Alan called with good news. There was a club opening on the East Side, and we would be able to audition for it during the first week. It was called The Comic Strip. We had to audition in the daytime with no audience—not half as bad for the singer as it was for the comedian. We walked into the back room, and past some bad caricatures with off-center writing on them, and up to one of the owners.

Bob Wachs was a lawyer who decided to become a partner in this new comedy club venture. The only competition was Catch a Rising Star, which was about six blocks away. I played a couple of songs of mine (including one about Janet) and was told I could start performing—for free, of course! Alan was another story. Telling jokes to Wachs with no audience was not going to be the best audition, so they skipped it, and Alan was told he could work there as well.

I quickly became a fixture in the joint and worked with almost every singer who walked in. One night, when the regular piano player didn't

Alan Colmes, spring 1976.

show up, I said I could do the job. It paid $25, and I really needed the money. Imagine the singers' surprise when they handed me sheet music and found that I couldn't read notes! I got by anyway.

One evening I walked into the club and Lucien, the manager, told me a girl had come by earlier and asked for me. Her name was Janet, and she just wanted me to know that she wished me well. A chill went through me; I didn't know if it meant she wanted me to contact her or not. I never did.

The comics also utilized my musical ability. I played guitar for Alan on several parodies and piano for anyone who wanted anything! One comic, who had been lured away from Catch a Rising Star, was Larry Cobb. Larry was what you might call HOSTILE. His famous line to hecklers (or even borderline hecklers) was "I'll tie a rope around your dick and drag you down Second Avenue." It was even more graphic if his target was a woman. But there was a heart in Larry. Much of his hostility seemed to be a reflection of a childhood of extreme abuse.

He admired my work and asked me to write a song for his act. I was honored to be asked. I suppose he wanted comedy. What I came up with one cold February evening in 1977 was a one verse song entitled "Late Nite Comic." I invited Larry and a few of the other comics and waitresses over to hear the song. They all seemed very much moved by it. Larry's reaction was simply, "I love it, but you should do the song in your own act." I immediately expanded the song and performed it the next night. It became something of a theme song for all the comedians that got on late (and all of them did at one time or another.) Only one comic hated the song. I never knew why. One night, when I was about to go on, Richard Belzer, a Don Rickles-styled comedian, warned me not to do "that insensitive piece of shit, 'Late Nite Comic.'" I can only imagine that it must have hit too close to home.

With Larry Cobb at the Comic Strip 1976.

After the clubs closed, all the acts used to hang out at a Greek diner called the Green Kitchen. It was right down the block from Catch, so it had a potpourri of singers and comics. The original line of my lyric was "Stayed up at the Kitchen half the night," but I felt it was too obscure for the general public, so I changed "kitchen" to "diner." On September 15, 1977, I decided to demo some songs. I went into Chappell Studios, a kind of offshoot of their publishing company on the 32nd floor of 810 Seventh Avenue, and demoed four tunes, one of which was "Late Nite Comic." I utilized that version for many years as my official demo.

The original work sheet for "Late Nite Comic."

As my career progressed, I moved on to other clubs around town. Catch a Rising Star was the next logical locale. How I got there was typical. When Catch would run out of acts or one would not show up, a call was immediately placed to the black sheep club, the Comic Strip. I tried to remain loyal, but it really didn't matter; they weren't that dedicated to us, so when Catch asked for a singer, I appeared. And then I wasn't used. I was furious. If the expected act showed up at the last second, I was basically told to take a hike. This happened several more times until I finally said I wasn't coming over unless I was utilized. From that point on I worked steadily at Catch. One of my opportunities there was to be paid $10 for

performing at Catch a Rising Star. Notice who's looming above my head

four hours' work—answering their phones and taking reservations. It usually guaranteed that I'd be used for the opening spot, so it was a fabulous job. The opening slot paid an additional $5, and my transportation was my moped, so I was quickly becoming a very wealthy man.

During those four hours monitoring the phones, I was very often by

First page of my musical Song & Dance

myself, and I had access to the piano. I began to entertain the thought of writing a musical, and in between calls I grouped together ideas and songs that told the story of my time with Janet. There was no book, just a slight outline. When I found I needed a song for a scene I was recreating, I wrote one. There I was, running back and forth from the piano to the phones writing a new song. The song came out just as I wanted, despite the constant interruptions. I knew I had something. I titled the song "You Can Dance," and the show, *Song & Dance*. It was about—what else?—a songwriter and a dancer. This title remained for several years until I passed a Times Square record store and saw an import album of a show called *Song & Dance*. I was heartbroken.

The show would have to have another title. It would also have to have a book. This was still a lark, so I decided to try my hand at book writing. Day after day at Catch I would be writing scenes and putting reservation callers on hold until I either finished the scene or got caught by the owner. I was finally fired.

I continued performing at various clubs and met a new girl named Vickie, whom I stayed with for almost two years. She taught drama to the deaf and was interested in my musical, asking to read what I had with the possibility of co-writing it with me. The connection with my old lover was a bit much for her, and the collaboration idea was dropped very quickly.

In the meantime, the song "Late Nite Comic" was having a life of its own. It was submitted to a director, Miriam Fond, who accepted it for a revue entitled *You Won't Find That Here*, which debuted May 5, 1978, and was sung by Melinda Tanner. Shortly thereafter the late Jarry Lang mentioned to his friend Kaye Ballard that he had heard a great new song. She listened to a tape and immediately put it in her nightclub act, also performing it on several television shows. Eddie Bradford wrote the first arrangement of the song for Kaye, and she performed it on *The Merv Griffin Show* on August 14, 1978. When I saw Jon Peters (then involved with Barbra Streisand) on the panel, I thought Barbra would be calling immediately. Dream on! Nevertheless, it was still a thrill.

Somewhere, during this time, I heard that Kaye did a version with Sid Caesar in Las Vegas. If this is indeed true, I only wish I could have seen it. On September 4 she appeared on the Jerry Lewis telethon. I'll never forget her performance on that show when she said, "This is for you, Brian." A comic at the club, Glenn Hirsch, kidded me for weeks. Every time I would run into him, he would say, "This is for you, Brian."

Kaye's dedication to the song led to its inclusion in her engagement in 1979 at Burt Reynolds's Dinner Theater in Jupiter, Florida. She gave me a special credit in the program. A video tape exists of that performance, after which she was asked to do a syndicated TV special. An entire scene was written around "Late Nite Comic." It was taped in 1980, and I eagerly awaited its broadcast. It never arrived. It seems there were money problems, and the show was canned. Years later I finally got a copy of it. Perhaps it will air some day, but I'm not holding my breath.

A true believer in my music, Marc Malamed produced and directed a revue called *Remember These* in February of 1980. He loved the song and decided it would fit in. Marc coached a lot of singers, and Laurie Mosher, who performed the song, was one of them. There was no pay designated for the use of my song; after all, it was only a showcase.

Also in 1980 the Improvisation was having a 17th anniversary, and thought an album of their performers might be a nice touch—and maybe a nice buck when sold at the bar! I allowed them to tape me "live" with the house band and fellow performers doing "Late Nite Comic." It came out rather nicely and is probably still available somewhere (for a nice buck!).

An odd request came in 1981 from a writer by the name of Bruce Dobler, who was working on a book to be titled *Laugh Lines*. He had also heard the song (probably through the album) and wanted to use a section of it for his book. I never saw a copy.

In 1982 I got another call—this time from a young actor named Gershon Resnik, who had somehow heard the song and wanted to use it for his one-man show. It was not a musical, but rather a strange play he had named after my song. My demo of the song was played in the background. The only version I ever saw of this was in a loft somewhere in Soho on July 23, 1982 in 90-degree weather. There was no air conditioning, making it a very unpleasant experience, and of course there was no pay involved. It was performed again as a work-in-progress at the Raft Theater on West 42nd Street in February 1983.

Somewhere around that time I was desperate for some studio time. I called one of my first publishers and earliest believers, David Lucas, a top jingle writer, who had a studio. He said I should come by and play him some of my new songs. He had published my songs when I was 16 and always had faith in me. He loved my new songs—and so did his girlfriend, who was a filmmaker at NYU at the time. She was doing a short film for her class about comics. Guess what would fit in perfectly? They had me do

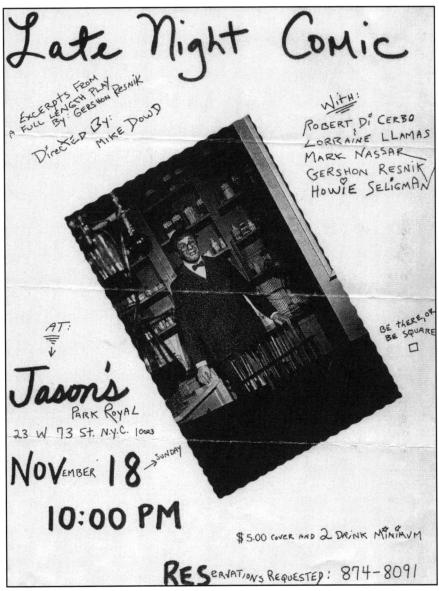

Late Night Comic

Excerpts from a full length play by: Gershon Resnik

Directed By: Mike Dowd

With:
Robert Di Cerbo
Lorraine Llamas
Mark Nassar
Gershon Resnik
Howie Seligman

Be there or be square

At:

Jason's
Park Royal
23 W. 73 St. N.Y.C. 10023

November 18 → Sunday

10:00 PM

$5.00 cover and 2 drink minimum

Reservations requested: 874-8091

Flyer for the unauthorized "Late Nite Comic."

a piano version of "Late Nite Comic," but with three lead vocals in unison. David was amazed; he couldn't believe how exact the vocals were. I wish I had a copy of that tape—and especially the film!

Meanwhile, my musical was still on hold and probably would still be if it were not for a chance meeting with my idol's agent.

Chapter 4

A Successful Marriage of Book and Score Is Like Any Other Good Marriage

I changed the names to protect the guilty. Truly, the subject matter was so close to home that I decided different names would be a good idea. My character was named Keith—just because I always liked the name. Janet's name was changed to Gabrielle for a more specific reason. I thought her friend Garielle had a nice name, so Gabrielle was just a variation on that. I also had a best friend in the story. He was a comic I named Alex Coleman. This, of course, was a variation on Alan Colmes.

I wrote the entire first act with a very brief sketch of the second. Some of the songs held on through Broadway, while others, in some cases sadly, bit the dust. I had a song called "Down the Hall," which described Keith's love for Gabrielle and the close proximity of their apartments. I had written a lullaby for Janet entitled "Janet, Are You Sleeping Yet?" It was unique because it was the only tune written on the guitar. In fact, I tuned all the strings differently from the norm and used a capo to make the key much higher. The result was a guitar that sounded like a harp. It almost made it to Broadway.

There was a song I wrote specifically for the scene where Janet (now Gabby) was auditioning for the Pennsylvania Ballet. It was a very intense, fast-paced song called "Get Me Off to Pennsylvania." I was sorry it didn't have a longer life.

The song I wrote at Catch a Rising Star was definitely included in this early version. "You Can Dance" had Gabby begging Keith to learn how to dance so that they could enjoy it together, but this was another energetic song that wasn't used later on.

21

"Late Nite Comic" was included because I thought it was a powerful song. I gave it to the character Alex to sing at the end of a very rough night at the comedy clubs. It was amazing how similar the scene was on Broadway to its original inception.

"Dance" was also in my original concept; Gabrielle was resigning herself to a life in the business world, so the song had some different words. I was so pleased that it survived all the way to Broadway.

The last song in Act One was a ballad called "You Won't Want It This Way." It took place when Gabby leaves Keith for someone else. This was patterned after the real-life separation we had. I had written it at the time and slipped it into my musical later on. I wanted the show to be emotionally realistic, which is why I included songs I wrote during the relationship itself. I always thought musicals needed that extra realism, and utilizing material that was truly written during the experience was my alternate approach to writing for Broadway.

It was not until late 1983 that I ever attempted to do something with this show. Jimmy Webb, who was best known for writing hits like "Up Up & Away," "MacArthur Park" and "Didn't We?," was a major influence on my songwriting—and perhaps on my life. When I was 16, I found out that most of his songs were written about one girl in particular. This romantic concept enthralled me. It was almost like *I Remember Mama*, where the young girl didn't write anything of substance until she wrote about her own family. Webb didn't care if his heart was on his sleeve; the song was more important. I collected everything he wrote and became known as the guy to contact for all obscure Webb songs. In later years, even Jimmy himself had me archive his songs.

When Webb moved to New York in the early '80s, I was in shock. I had no idea he would ever make that move from California. It turned out that Broadway was a great dream of his, and to achieve that dream, he felt he had to be closer to the source.

On May 30, 1982, I got a message from Jimmy on my phone machine. He wanted to get a feel for what he should do on a telethon the next day. We conversed for a while and agreed to meet. The telethon went fine (with or without my advice), and we met later at the Oyster Bar in the Plaza Hotel. Here I was with my hero. When I was asked what I would like to order, I was too nervous to think about food. Now anyone who knows me can vouch for the fact that I can eat my portion and theirs. In the course of our conversation Webb told me that I should get in touch with his publicist. It turned out that it was a man I knew from Webb's early days in California, Warren Seabury, actor-turned-publicist. He knew everything about everyone, and adored Webb, much of his knowledge about him probably coming from Webb's wife Patsy, who was Warren's best friend in those days. In 1970 I had gone to see the movie *Brewster McCloud* with Warren, Patsy and Johnny Green's daughter Kathe, and I hadn't seen Warren since.

I forget who got in touch with whom, but Warren distinctly remembered me and said he would be coming east very soon. He made several trips to New York and at one time even stayed in my little music room while publicizing Webb's career. He heard my songs and was very encouraging.

Yet another year slipped by, and Jimmy was involved in a cantata he wrote called "The Animals' Christmas." In December of 1983 Warren was in town again to publicize the event. All of Webb's New York associates were around, including his theatrical agent, Charles Hunt. Warren insisted that I meet him. The meeting was very casual and very short, but I did mention to Charles that I had a musical. Not expecting anyone to listen to a guy with no previous hits, I was surprised when Charles said he'd like to hear it. We set up an appointment for December 19, which he rescheduled for January 3, 1984.

I worked at a small piano in a tiny room off my kitchen, and it was not an ideal setting to show off a musical. Consequently, I asked my publisher, Ray Fox, if I could use his place—an apartment overlooking Central Park with a grand piano in the living room. He agreed.

At 5:30 Charles showed up from his office on West 44th Street, where he worked as an agent in the Fifi Oscard Agency, which specialized in actors and book writers. Charles sat down next to the piano, and after a little small talk, I played the first song. He seemed pleasantly surprised and asked me to play a second—and a third. After half a dozen songs and a brief storyline, he announced that he would get me a book writer.

"You mean you want this project?" I asked.

"Yes, and I think I have just the right book writer for you," he answered.

A few days later I received a phone call from a man named Allan Knee. I really wasn't that familiar with book writers, so it didn't seem unusual that I would not have heard of Allan's previous projects. My only concern was that he could write the story I had had in mind all these years. After a brief conversation we set up a meeting at my place (in the tiny room with the small piano).

On Friday the 13th of January, Allan appeared at my door at 3:00 P.M. I asked him if he'd like something to drink, and his reply was, "A little seltzer would be great." It became a staple of our future collaboration. There was hardly ever a time when I didn't see Allan with his bottle of carbonated water. Perhaps it was due to his workouts at the Y, which were often right before we would meet. (The extent of my workouts was walking from one end of my apartment to the other!)

Our first meeting was basically to get to know each other and for me to give Allan a rundown of what I wanted to do. I played him "Late Nite Comic" and "Dance," as well as several other songs, both those intended for the show and those that were not. I also gave him a copy of my script as a kind of direction. We discussed what was happening in our lives at the moment. He was working on some other plays and musicals, one with Cy Coleman.

I, on the other hand, had been asked a few months before if I'd like to fill in at a piano bar. I told the restaurant that I didn't think I was qualified, but the waitresses knew me and convinced the owner not to take no for an answer. I played every television theme I knew and all the Christmas songs one could imagine, and this was in the middle of summer! I was a hit and continued there and at a few other places as well. One was an Irish restaurant, and the only Irish tune I knew was "Danny Boy," and even that was because I watched *Make Room for Daddy* as a kid!

Allan absorbed these tales and laughed along. He went home and said he'd get back to me soon. About a week or two went by before I finally heard from him again. He had a rough treatment he wanted me to read. It was quite exciting to sit down and read the beginnings of a legitimate project. It was even more interesting when I realized what Allan had done; he had taken my lead character, Keith, combined him with the comic, Alex, renamed him David and made him a piano bar player who yearned to be a comic. I thought this was very appropriate. Comics and the comedy circuit were becoming hotter and hotter, and this could hit at just the right time. He also retitled the show *Late Nite Comic*.

The girl's character was still Gabrielle, but she had changed her name from one that she felt didn't suit her—Janet! I loved that for the realism alone. Her character seemed to be more ditsy than my version. It bothered me a bit, since Janet was not a ditz, just confused and frustrated. I thought it might work, however, because the musical had to have laughs. Were these laughs going to set females back several decades? Was this character insulting to women? I'd find out eventually.

It was two weeks after meeting Allan that another new phase of my life began. I was playing at a piano bar on Columbus Avenue and 83rd Street called Rare Form. It was not a regular job; I probably played there about once a week. Having been very close to marrying someone the previous year, I was generally down on serious relationships and had sworn I would not get involved for a while. Two women were at the bar chatting. On my break I went up to the bar for a soft drink. The bartender introduced me to both women. One was named Darla. I couldn't believe I had met someone with the name of a Little Rascal. I asked her to repeat it, since I thought I might have misheard. I heard correctly. We talked until my break was up. She was very beautiful, very thin and full of energy. She had come in with her girlfriend just to get out of the house. She had a boyfriend in Florida who was giving her

With Darla in happier times.

trouble, and she decided to stay in town instead of visiting him.

By the end of the night her girlfriend saw that we were becoming inseparable and bade us good night. It was January 29, very cold, with snow still left on the ground, but things were hot with Darla and me. I walked her to her apartment, which was just around the corner from the bar, and we kissed and talked for hours. She told me she was an actress and dancer and had just been in *A Chorus Line*. We exchanged numbers. It was Monday, and she said the earliest I'd hear from her would be Thursday.

At 11:00 A.M. on Tuesday the phone rang. It was Darla. We met for lunch and spent most of the afternoon and evening together. It reminded me of my early days with Janet. One night she arrived with the begin-

DRAMATISTS GUILD
COLLABORATION CONTRACT

MEMORANDUM OF AGREEMENT

between . .ALLAN KNEE . . . .

c/o Charles W. Hunt,FIFI OSCARD ASSOC.INC 19 W. 44th Street, NYC,NY 1003
. . Street

and . .BRIAN GARI . . . .

c/oCharles Hunt,. FIFI. OSCARD ASSOC Street19 W. 44th St., NY,NY 10036

members of the Dramatists Guild of the Authors League of America, Inc.

WHEREAS the parties hereto are mutually desirous of collabor-

ating in the writing of a musical play provisionally .entitled

"SONG.AND DANCE" . . .; and

WHEREAS each of the parties represents that he is a member in

good standing of the Dramatists Guild of the Authors League of America,

Inc.;

NOW, THEREFORE, in consideration of the mutual covenants herein

contained, it is agreed as follows:

1. That the parties hereto shall undertake jointly to write said play, provisionally entitled as aforesaid.

2. That copyright in said play shall be secured and held jointly in the names of .Allan Knee .and Brian Gari . . . . . .

. . . ., and that all receipts and returns from said play, or from any rights therein, and any dramatic, literary, photographic or any and every form thereof, whether specifically herein enumerated or not, shall be divided as follows:

To . . .Allan Knee . . . . per cent (.50%)

To . . .Brian Gari . . . . per cent (.50%)

Fifi Oscard contract.

nings of a cold. She stayed over and never left.

On March 6 Charles Hunt thought it was time for a contract to be signed between his client and me. What was sent to me was slightly disconcerting. The deal was 50/50. Ordinarily one might find this perfectly fine—two writers splitting the royalties. However, I found out that it was customary for the lyricist to get a third, the composer to get a third, and the book writer to get a third. Because I had written both lyrics and music, my share should have been two-thirds. When I mentioned this to Charles, he flew into a rage. His client had credits, but I had nothing. If I didn't sign this contract, I could take my songs and idea and walk. I was advised by family and friends that even though it wasn't fair, I should probably go with it. It was true that I didn't have any theater credits, and there was an agency ready to represent the show. Reluctantly, I signed. It was ironic that the contract still had my original title, *Song & Dance*.

Then it was back to work. Allan had a fuller script this time. This version had an ending with David being booked in Honduras and Gabrielle getting mixed up with stilettos and Latino choreographers. I thought this was far-fetched, even if there was the possibility that the scene could be a dream. It was the first of many endings for the show.

In April the first song Allan asked me to write specifically for his version was an opening number for David. It was to take place in the piano bar and speak of all David's yearnings to be a comic. I designed "Stand Up" to have the energy of an opening number. It did. It should never have been moved as it was later on in the Broadway previews.

The next obvious step was a theme for Gabrielle. I had to write something that would describe her, as well as give a slight hint of David's attraction to her. I wrote the song "Gabrielle" one night in June, picturing myself as David. I think Allan did as well, since he mistakenly called me that at times. I treated the song the way I composed any other song about someone I had just fallen for. I suppose it was even a song for my new love, Darla. I played it over the phone for Allan, and he was elated; it was just what he was looking for.

It was now July, and Darla and I were set to be married at the end of the month. We decided on July 29—exactly six months from the day we met. The wedding took place in my—now our—apartment, and all our family and friends were there. My good friend Don Ciccone, former lead singer of the Critters and one of the Four Seasons, was my best man. Michael Wolff, later musical director for Arsenio Hall, played "Here Comes the Bride" for

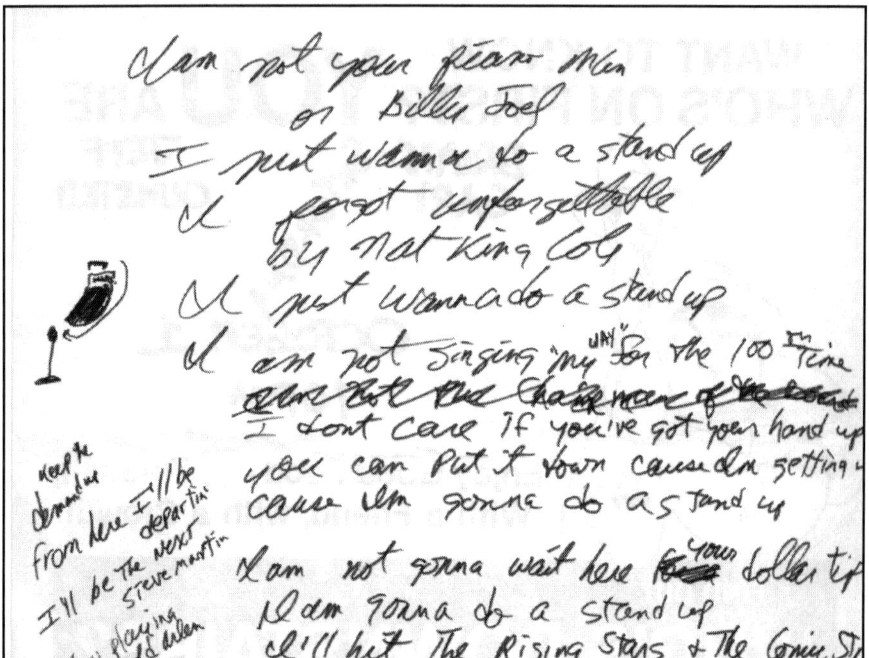

I am not your piano man
or Billy Joel
I just wanna do a stand up
I forgot unforgettable
by Nat King Cole
I just wanna do a stand up
I am not singing "my way" for the 100th time
I'm not the chairman of the board
I dont care if you've got your hand up
you can put it down cause I'm getting up
cause I'm gonna do a stand up

I am not gonna wait here for your dollar tip
I am gonna do a stand up
I'll hit The Rising Stars & The Comic St
cause I'm gonna do a stand up
I am tired of pianos get another guy
hire bass & drums
I dont care if you want you can
bring a band
But I'm comin out from the 88's
& I'm gonna do a stand up

keep the demand up
From here I'll be departin'
I'll be the next Steve Martin
I'm thru playing Harold Allen
I'll be the next George Carlin
I'm throwin out all my fake books
I'm gonna do a stand up
I'm gonna do a stand up
& I'll get that spot on a Friday nite
cause I'll always do
a stand up
fake books

Original work sheet for "Stand Up."

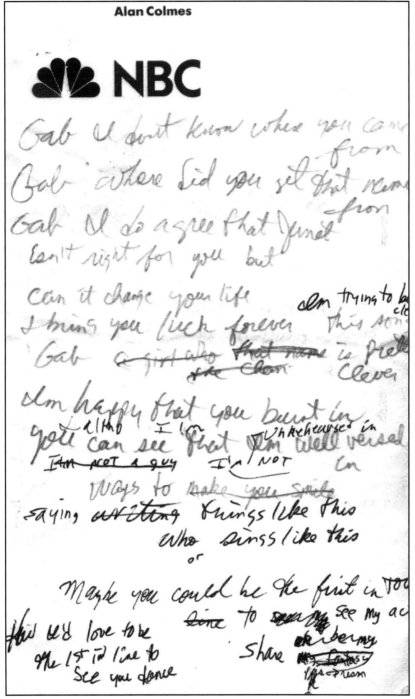

Original work sheets for "Gabrielle."

Gabrielle I don't know where you came from
Gabrielle where did you get that name from
Gabrielle I do agree that Janet
isn't right for you but can it
change your life
Gabrielle bring luck to you forever
Gabrielle you're really ~~very clear~~ a girl who won't say never
Gabrielle I ~~can't believe~~ in a way that you burst in
but your ~~quenching~~ such a thirst inside my head
you could quench this endless for love
let's start my love
Gabrielle you're really off the wall but
Gabrielle it's crazy if I fall but
Gabrielle you're the prettiest of dancers
you have given me the answers
I can tell Gabrielle

Original work sheets for "Gabrielle."

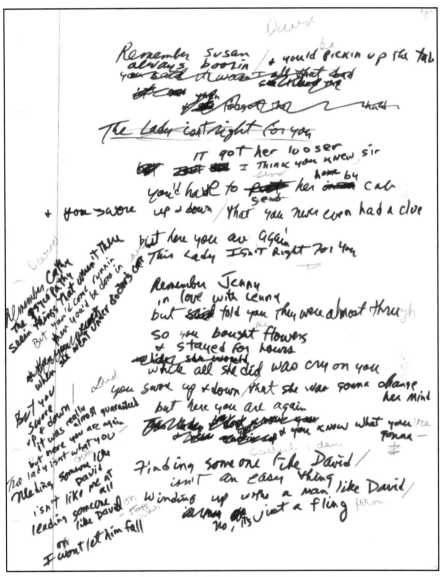

Original work sheet for "This Lady Isn't Right for Me."

Original work sheet for "It Had to Happen Sometime."

us. Allan Knee was there. I laughed during the vows; well, it was my first marriage, and I was nervous! Suddenly, I was being married and working on a musical.

August was a very productive month. Allan came up with a scene that had David frantic about falling so hard and fast for Gabby. He had a pal named Mike, who reminded David of all his past experiences and how dismal they were even though they started out rather promising. My assignment was to tell this musically. Again, "This Lady Isn't Right for You" was written in one night. I could relate to the story very easily.

The second song during August had been partially written before Allan ever mentioned the scene. The girl whom I had almost married was still in touch, and the finality of my marrying someone else touched off a song idea for me. "It Had to Happen Sometime" had been started as a statement to that girl. The original lyric went:

> I don't need to read your letter
> I know every word you said
> How you're very happy for us that we wed
> Well, It Had to Happen Sometime...

I didn't continue that version, as it was becoming something I didn't want to have to deal with again. I turned it into a vehicle for the show and finished it as a duet for Gabby and David.

Allan liked my lullaby, "Gabby, Are You Sleeping Yet?," but decided it would have more impact if it were sung to David and not by him. Consequently, it became Gabby's number.

In November, Gershon Resnik sent me another flyer; he was doing "Late Nite Comic" again. Allan flipped out and said there can't be two shows using the same song; I had to stop this guy. I did, and he was not happy about it.

The last song written in 1984 was "Obsessed." Allan asked me for a frenetic song for David in place of a comedy monologue. He felt that writing jokes was not his forte, so a funny song might do the trick. I had written a piece of special material for Kaye Ballard called "Don't Smoke." This opening song for her was to tell the audience in a humorous way to refrain from smoking during her act. Well, the song had a lot of words that came very fast. She wrote them on her hand! The song was dropped after one performance, because she couldn't

Original work sheet for "Obsessed."

sing the song and read her hand at the same time. I was annoyed, but saved the song for future use. When the opportunity came up for a crazy song for David, I rewrote the lyric and retitled the song "Obsessed." It was a Spike Jones-meets-Danny Kaye number and a favorite of Allan's. It remained in the show through the first few performances in New London, but was cut supposedly because the show was getting too long. It never appeared on a stage again until my 1990 revue entitled *A Hard Time to be Single*, where Michael McAssey revived it with a brilliant rendition.

There was a song I had written in 1978 called "I Wonder If I'll Ever Be a Father/Mother." I had written it on my way home from the Improv about the state of my life at the time. I knew it was a show piece, so I saved it for the musical. I thought it would have a good dramatic effect. It was one of the first songs I had played for Allan, and he made note of it. It was supposed to be the 11:00 number in Act Two, but it didn't stay in for long. I think there were probably too many ballads, so we both agreed to drop it as the musical got bigger.

Allan also liked a blues song I had written for a singing waitress at the Comic Strip named Robin Kaiser. I told him "Relax with Me Baby" brought down the house for her, and perhaps we could work it into the show. He agreed, and it was in. The scene would be a singles bar in which David would be surrounded by many sarcastic, tough women.

By the end of 1984 the lineup of songs was as follows:

ACT ONE
 Stand Up
 Gabrielle
 This Lady Isn't Right for You
 It Had to Happen Sometime
 Late Nite Comic

ACT TWO
 Obsessed
 David, Are You Sleeping Yet?
 Relax with Me Baby
 Dance
 I Wonder If I'll Ever Be a Father/Mother

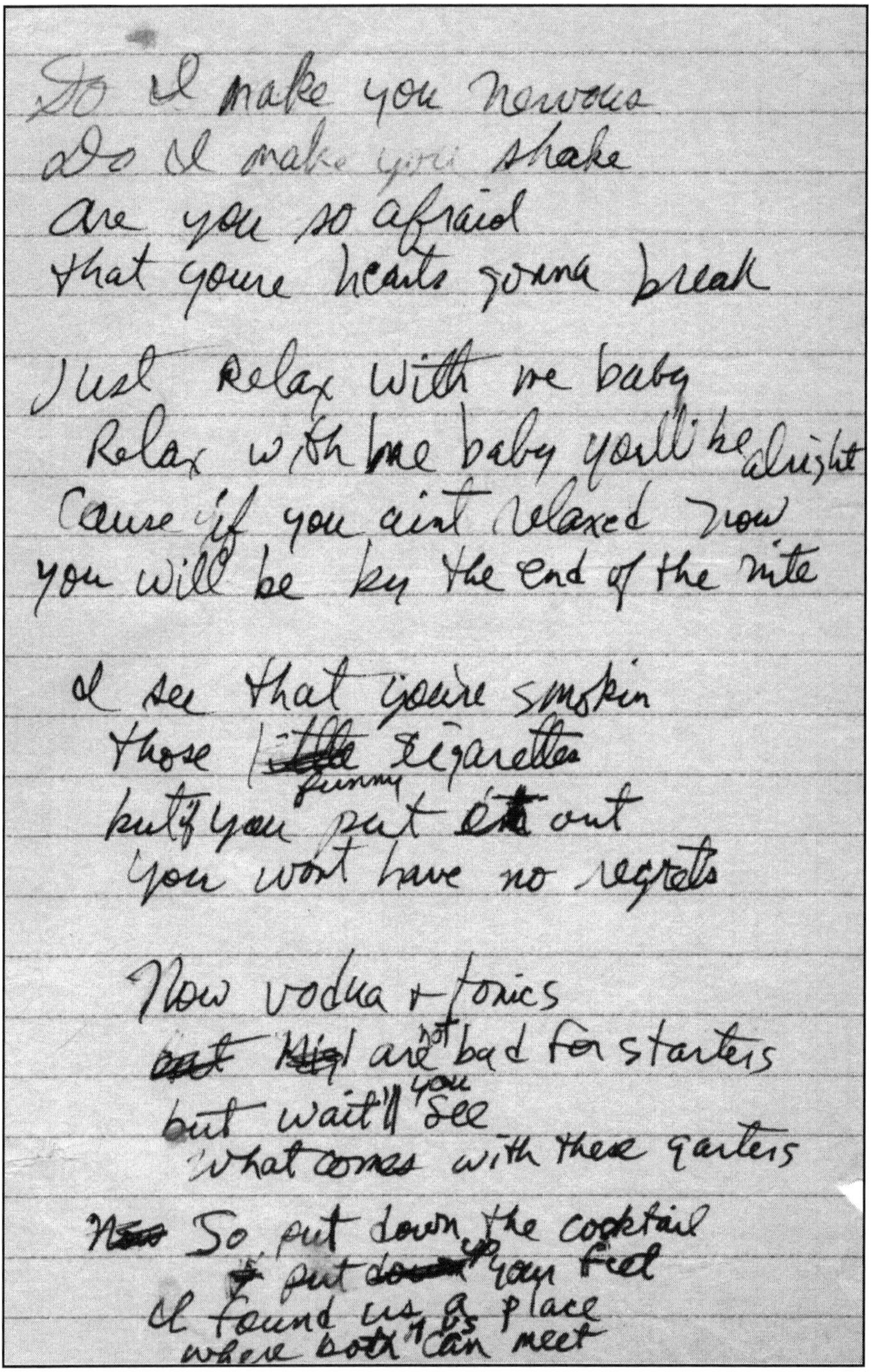

Do I make you nervous
do I make you shake
are you so afraid
that youre hearts gonna break

Just Relax with me baby
Relax with me baby you'll be alright
Cause if you aint relaxed now
you will be by the end of the nite

I see that youre smokin
those little funny cigarettes
but if you put em out
you won't have no regrets

Now vodka + tonics
are not bad for starters
but wait'll you see
what comes with these garters

So put down the cocktail
I put down you feel
I found us a place
where both I can meet

Original work sheet for "Relax with Me Baby."

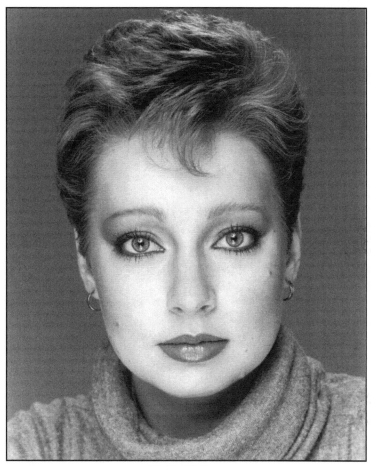

Robin Kaiser.

1985 arrived with a phone call from my buddy Alan Colmes. He was going to be doing a week at the comedy club Caroline's and asked if I would like to play piano on some comedy bits and open the show for him as well. He asked if $150 would be okay. I told him I would play anywhere with him for free for old time's sake. I did, however, graciously accept the $150! It was the last week in January, and I put together a set of a few songs from the musical, as well as a few of my other tunes that were not from the show. I know I performed "Stand Up" and "Late Nite Comic." Allan Knee, ever faithful, showed up, as did Darla.

One night, after one of the shows, Alan introduced me to his new manager. I looked up to see a man in a business suit, looking much older than I found him truly to be. Rory Rosegarten was a very sure of himself twenty-four-year-old. His eager and intelligent manner was very striking. He shook my hand and complimented me on my songs. He was impressed with the fact that Eddie Cantor was my grandfather and mentioned that he lived in Great Neck, where my grandfather had once lived. Then he handed me his business card. I kept the card and thought he might be a person I should get to know better. I liked him very much, but I didn't call him for nine months.

Allan, meanwhile, had done some more work on his second version of the show. He suggested, for this script, that I write a happy song for David to sing in the first act that would show that nothing in the big city could get him down. I had a song that I had also written in 1978 that had that exact feeling. I thought if I used that melody and rewrote the lyric, I would once again have transferred real feelings to the stage. "Nothing's Changin' This Love" remained in the show through most of the New London run.

Another song in this version was supposed to show how David got his material from real life. The title "Life Is Material" came directly out of Allan's script. I tried my best writing this piece, but it just wasn't that great. It stayed in for a while, but was one of the first songs to be dropped when we began refining.

By now it was summer, and Allan had another suggestion for a new song. He thought David should sing about how good everything else can be if the love is there. I came up with an up-tempo song called "I'm at My Best in Love." We both liked the song, but it didn't stay very long either. There wasn't really a need for the kind of material it turned out to be. However, it was also added to *A Hard Time to be Single*.

As I was having lunch in a coffee shop on 58th Street and Broadway with Robby Benson, his wife, Karla DeVito, and their manager, Winston Simone, a dancer/choreographer by the name of Lara Teeter stopped by our table to say hello. He mentioned that he would be choreographing a new musical called *Captain America*. Always on the lookout for jobs for my wife, I asked if it would be too late for Darla to audition. He gave me the name of Philip Rose and said she should make an appointment to see him. She did, and she remarked that he was very nice. It's amazing how this one time meeting would have such a profound effect on my future.

In September Allan had yet another spot for a new song. This time I was to tell how David was becoming a much better comic and was slowly moving out of the showcase clubs and into some paying jobs. It was not the big time, but it was much better than before. "It's Such a Different World" was a bitch to write. The rhyme schemes I had set up were incredibly complicated, yet a fun challenge.

It was at this time that I decided to get in touch with Rory Rosegarten

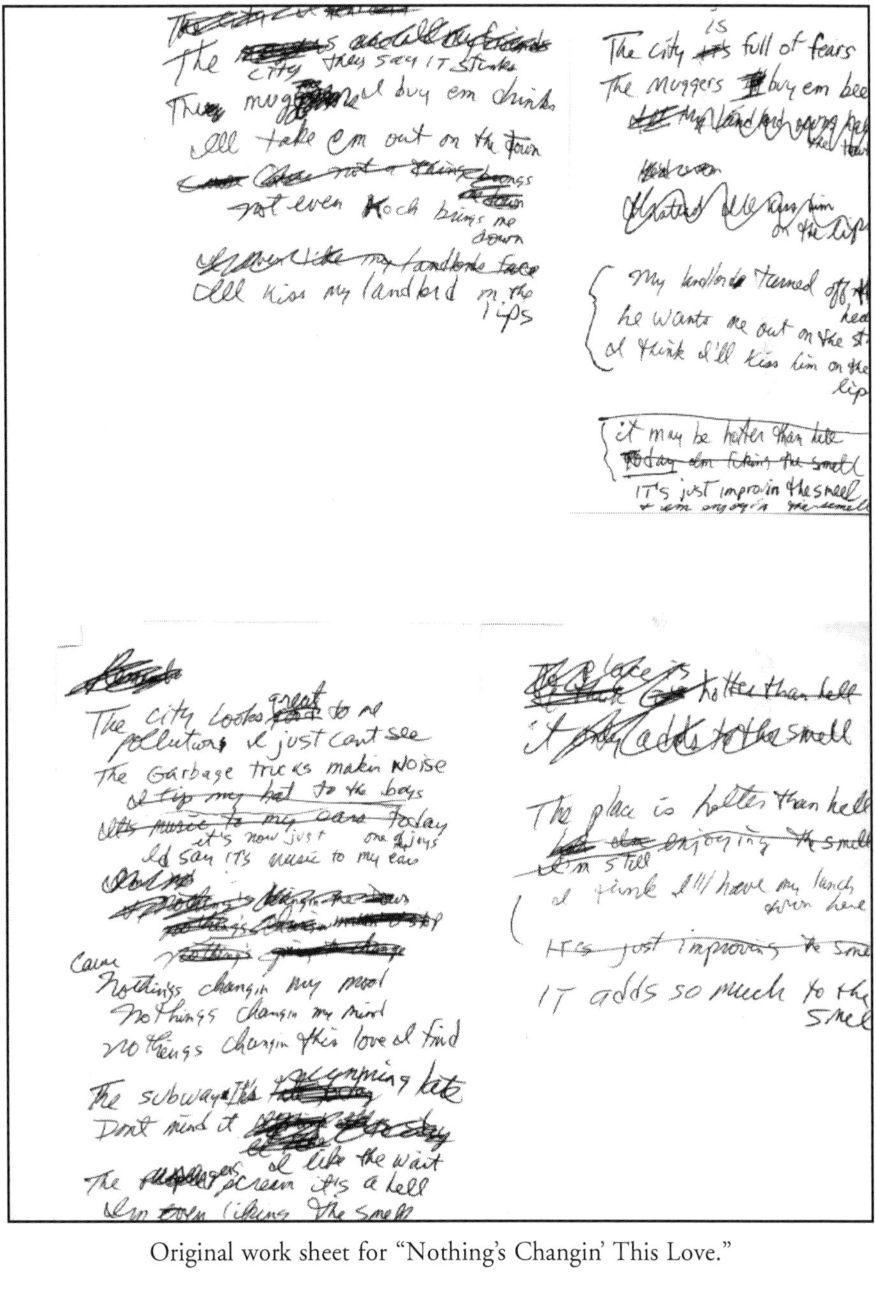

Original work sheet for "Nothing's Changin' This Love."

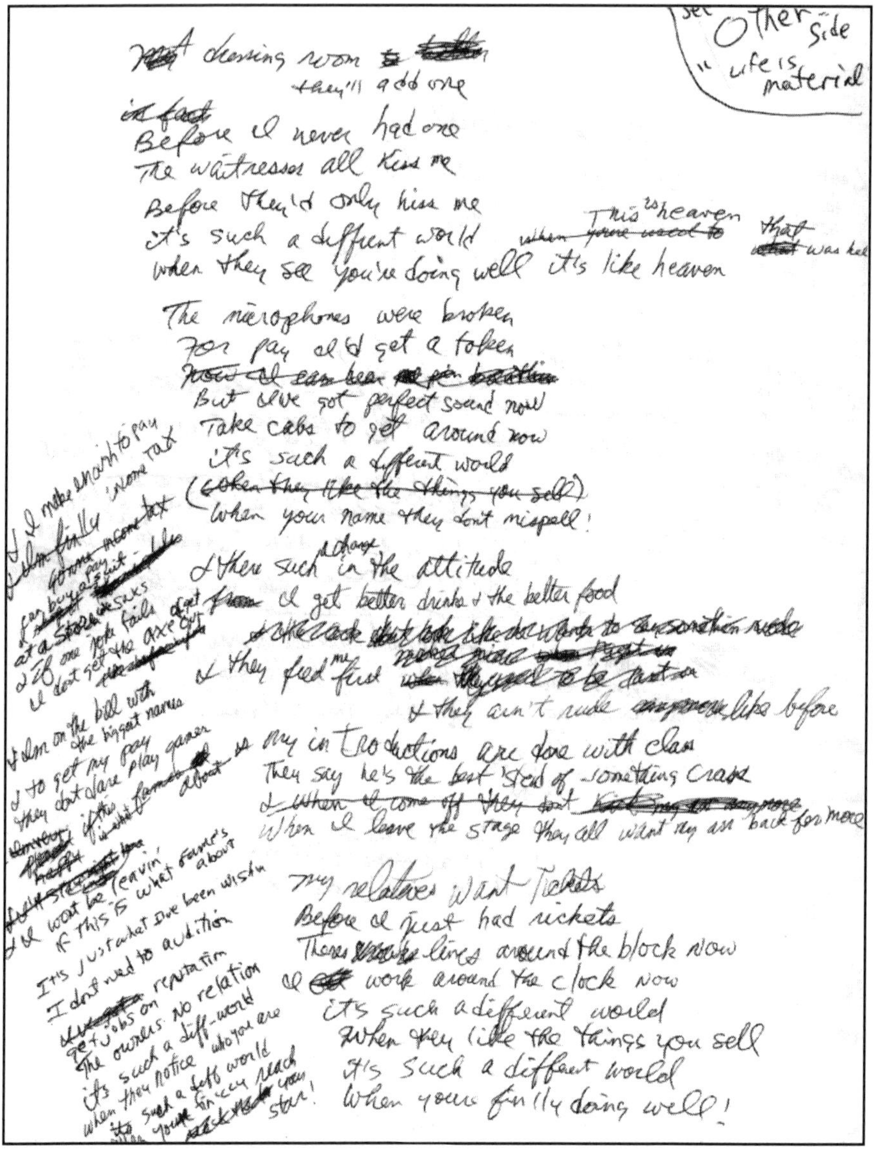

See Other side
"Life is material"

A dressing room
they'll add one
Before I never had one
The waitresses all kiss me
Before they'd only hiss me
It's such a different world
When they see you're doing well it's like heaven

The microphones were broken
For pay I'd get a token
But I've got perfect sound now
Take cabs to get around now
It's such a different world
(When they like the things you sell)
When your name they don't mispell!

& there such a change in the attitude
I get better drinks & the better food
& they feed me first
& they ain't rude like before
& my introductions are done with class
They say he's the best 'stead of something crass
When I leave the stage they all want me an back for more

My relatives want tickets
Before I just had rickets
There's lines around the block now
I work around the clock now
It's such a different world
When they like the things you sell
It's such a different world
When your finally doing well!

Original work sheet for "It's Such a Different World."

again—about another project. I knew he admired my grandfather, and I had an idea about a project concerning him. He was very enthusiastic and agreed that we should meet in his office in Great Neck. I mentioned *Late Nite Comic* to him, but he was not as interested in that as in a project about my grandfather. We became friendly and got together several more times.

Meanwhile, Darla got a call to do *A Chorus Line* again. Her performance as Sheila was impeccable, and the Long Beach Civic Light Opera company in California wanted her to reprise her role. I made arrangements to go out there in October to see her do it. It was a wonderful time. Darla was the most confident I had ever seen her. I saw the show every night and every matinée for the week. She was, indeed, excellent. The rest of the cast was wonderful as well, and I had the opportunity to meet one of the original cast members of the Broadway version, Kay Cole. I had heard how great she was in New York and was not disappointed in California. One night I played "Dance" for her backstage and was excited by her encouraging response.

When we returned to New York, Darla asked me about playing the lead in my show. She had been hinting about it for a while, and now she confronted me. I had to tell her that the leading lady had to sing an entire score and had to be in her early twenties. Darla was by no means old, but she was not twenty, either. I also felt that I had written a score for a very strong Streisand-type voice. Darla could not accept any of this. Fights began to occur almost every other week.

I had always intended to help Darla if I could. One time I remember hearing of an upcoming part on the soap opera *Ryan's Hope*. I sent Darla's picture to the casting people, along with a note that said I had seen this girl in *A Chorus Line* and thought she would be great on my favorite soap. I didn't reveal that I was her husband. That night she was called for an appointment with ABC. She didn't end up with a leading role, but she appeared on the show from time to time.

The funniest story, however, was when she had a small part on *All My Children*. I drove down to the studio, where many fans gather outside. I handed them Darla's photo and told them to be sure to get her autograph when she came out. Darla was in shock as a fleet of soap fans rushed up to her to sign their pictures.

The first song I wrote when I got back from California was forgotten almost as fast as it came. "Try to Be Funny" was a song in 3/4 time that wasn't half bad. It just didn't seem to excite anyone, including me. It was basically about getting through obstacles by laughter. It was pleasant at best.

In November Allan called me up with a new scene. Gabrielle needed more songs, and this could be a big one…in fact, he mentioned the phrase "think big." She wanted the very best for herself, aiming as high as she could. I wrote a song that even included an old-fashioned verse.

> "A lot of people don't like to make waves
> They settle for less than they should
> A lot of people will go to their graves
> And they won't possess what they could"

Allan and I both thought this could work well for Gabby. It was to be her first song. We even reprised it in the second act when Gabby comes back into David's life and seduces him. In my original concept of *Song & Dance*, I envisioned a scene where Keith went from music publisher to music publisher getting rejected each time. The song was one I wrote at age twenty, "Life Begins at Top 40." "No, I'm sorry we can't hear another song today…" was the opening line of that version of my tune. When Allan had David as a struggling comedian trying out at each club, I rewrote my catchy melody from 1972 and had the lyric reflect the rejection David received from each club owner. It was retitled "The Best in the Business" and turned out to be the earliest written, yet most appreciated song in the show.

Allan was now on his third rewrite, and the musical lineup by the end of '85 was:

ACT ONE
>   Stand Up
>   Gabrielle
>   Think Big
>   This Lady Isn't Right for You
>   I'm at My Best in Love
>   The Best in the Business
>   It Had to Happen Sometime
>   Late Nite Comic

ACT TWO
    Obsessed
    David, Are You Sleeping Yet?
    Relax with Me Baby
    Think Big (sexy version)
    Life is Material
    Dance
    I Wonder If I'll Ever Be a Father/Mother
    It's Such a Different World
    Gabrielle/Yvonne
    It Had to Happen Sometime (reprise)

The third rewrite eliminated a scene in which David had a break-down and ended up in a wheelchair in a sanitarium. I just didn't think the character would ever have ended up in such bad shape. Allan changed it to a more subdued mental illness; David would visit a psychiatrist. Charles Hunt had been calling about when he would hear what we had. With fifteen songs and a more complete book we thought it was time to unveil the show for Charles. At least we *thought* it was time…

Chapter 5
Rose's Turn

An appointment was set up at Charles's office for January 9, 1986. Allan and I were both nervous, but confident; well, at least I was. Allan always seemed to have a degree of pessimism hanging over him. He did, however, like my aggressive and more optimistic attitude. Little did he know—I didn't sleep very much the night before and was worried about my vocal performance. It was winter, when I always seem to get rundown enough to acquire some kind of cold that lands in my throat. Unfortunately, it often settles in when I need my voice the most.

The meeting was scheduled for the end of the day. Most of the other agents were either on their way home or trying to get their clients the last booking of the day. Charles was still in the middle of some other things when we walked in, but he managed to calm down in time for the unveiling.

I sat down at the piano. I had never used their piano before, but Charles said Jimmy Webb had just used it the week before. When I looked at the keys, I could imagine what had gone through Jimmy's mind. It was an antique piano in horrible condition. The keys were old and broken. It was also out of tune. I'd played on poor pianos before, but this was one of the poorest. I dreaded playing one song on it, let alone an entire score!

With some explanatory words to set up the show, Allan gave me the signal to start the opening song. From "Stand Up" right through the reprise of "It Had to Happen Sometime" there was nothing but a positive reaction from Charles. In between songs Allan would continue to tell the story. With bleeding fingers and a raw throat, I realized that I had made it through. I could see Charles was pleased. He held on to a copy of the book and said he'd call us shortly about the next step.

Allan and I walked onto 44th Street both stunned and relieved. We talked to each other on the phone that night and relived the performance. There seemed to be a hint of optimism in Allan's voice this time. He complimented me on my delivery of the tunes. We were anxious to hear from Charles again.

Charles called Allan first. He felt there could be some adjustments. They were logical, so Allan agreed to look over the script again. While Allan worked on a fourth revision, I started to demo some of the songs at home. My mother had bought me a small drum machine that had some preprogrammed drum parts. I was never very mathematical. In fact, I once had to go to summer school for math, so I arranged my songs around the existing drum patterns already set in the machine. I played piano, bass and guitar, and I did all the vocals—both male and female. At one point I thought I should have a more involved arrangement, so I sprang for a Casio synthesizer for $200 and found a nice string and brass section. Winter was never a problem for the small room in which I recorded, but in the summer, with no air conditioning, I literally sweated out the parts!

After a few weeks Allan sent over a fourth script to Charles. We were on pins and needles. After all, we needed Charles's enthusiasm to get us a producer. If we didn't have that, the musical would never have a chance. There was no response from Charles. I called him a few times, but my calls weren't returned. It was now April, and nothing was happening. I finally spoke to him. He said he had some problems with the script, but would send it out to a few people he knew anyway—to get a feel for the climate concerning this show. I found out later that sometimes my music would not be sent with the script. The feeling was that "if the book is good, then we'll listen to the score." Annoyed, I insisted that in the future all scripts would arrive with a cassette.

On May 5, 1986, the show was sent to Playwright's Horizon. I never saw a rejection letter, but there was no good news. Hudson Guild never even responded, and eventually admitted they couldn't find my tape! M2 Productions was also contacted, as well as the Jujamcyn people. All of them, I was told, turned it down.

Charles was not in a very good mood at this point. He avoided my calls like the plague. I finally got him on the phone, and he said I could do whatever I wanted with the show; he didn't have the interest anymore. I called Allan immediately. It seems they had also had a discussion. Charles told Allan that the show wasn't different enough. Couldn't it take place inside a jukebox or something?! Allan was extremely disappointed. After all, this was his agent speaking. I told Allan I was not going to let our work go down the drain. He had no idea how hard I was going to work.

I ran into Cy Feuer, a legendary Broadway producer, and he told me he would look at the project. I jumped on my moped and hand delivered the script and cassette. It was rejected on May 19. I asked Charles Hunt's secretary to give me a list of all the places to which the show had been sent. Of the four, only one rejection letter was in my possession. I followed up the rest to no avail.

Next, I contacted Joseph Papp's office. The comment was that although it was a well-written play, they wouldn't produce it. Liz McCann wasn't interested, nor was Francine Lefrak, whom I had once dated. She wouldn't return my calls. (Geez, we went out only once—was it that bad?)

I remembered that David Susskind produced musicals, so I took a chance and called his office. In my eagerness I had forgotten that he had produced one of the biggest failures in the last twenty years, *Kelly*. I got him on the phone and told him about my show. He wasn't on the phone more than ten seconds when he screamed, "I'll never get involved with musicals again!" I guess he was right; he died a very short time after my phone call.

My wife was sympathetic about the rejections and suggested that I contact the nice man she had gone to see about *Captain America*. She was doing her hair in the bathroom while I dialed Philip Rose's office. I got him on the phone immediately. He was willing to meet with Allan and me. It was set up for June 11 at 3:00 P.M. I kissed my wife, and we hoped for the best.

Philip's office was on 57th Street across from Carnegie Hall. Allan arrived early with a bottle of seltzer. I drove up on my moped and locked it directly in front of the building. It was a beautiful summer day, and there was a Merit Farms chicken store in front of the bus stop. You could smell the bus fumes mixed with the chicken. We rang the bell and nervously waited for someone to open the door. A lovely, friendly soul by the name of Lynda Watson greeted us. She had bright eyes and a lively personality. Although she looked quite young, she had been working for Phil for decades. She showed us into a small waiting area near her desk. The walls were covered with Philip's triumphs. *Purlie*, *Shenandoah*, *A Raisin in the Sun* and *Does a Tiger Wear a Necktie?* were among the posters. Some of them had been directed by Philip, but most of them were his productions. He had originally been a singer, but had slowly gravitated toward a career on the business side. In 1957 he found a song called "The Banana Boat Song" and put it on his own label, Glory. When RCA started distributing it, they figured they could do far better if they recut the song with Harry Belafonte and promoted theirs instead of Phil's distributed version. Philip sued them, but didn't win.

There was a rebel side to Phil. He had a passion for and a strong identification with black writers and artists. Growing up in a poor neighborhood of Washington, D.C., he took a job as a bill collector, going through all black neighborhoods. He told me he would be the only white man walking the streets, and it was obvious that if you were white in that neighborhood, you were the bill collector. Far from being fearsome, Phil found a rapport with these people, often giving them advice on how not to get so far in debt.

Many years later, in Greenwich Village, a young black woman named Lorraine Hansberry showed Phil a script. It was A *Raisin in the Sun*. Against all odds, Phil got the show on, and it became a big hit. He did the same with *The Owl and the Pussycat*, about which many were skeptical because of its interracial theme. Sadly, *Raisin* lead, Diana Sands, and Lorraine Hansberry both died very young. It was an injustice that seemed to stay with Phil to this day.

To get back to our appointment, a few minutes went by before a small man who appeared to be in his sixties emerged from an adjoining office. "Hello, I'm Philip Rose," he said, ushering us into the office. It was a rather small room with a large desk, a piano, a couch and a very noisy air conditioner. "I've told the building manager to come up to fix that, but they've yet to find the problem," he explained.

Allan and I sat down on the couch, while Philip pulled up a chair. We discussed the project for a short time, and then he asked me to play a few of the songs. One of the first was "Gabrielle." Philip seemed quite gracious and asked to hear a few more. I ran through a good deal of the score, which seemed to intrigue him a lot. He looked over the script and asked for a bit of background on both of us. Allan and I were completely prepared. He reminded Philip of how encouraging he had been some years back when Allan had just graduated from Yale. Philip smiled and was quite gracious. He asked us to contact him on Monday after he had had the weekend to read the script fully. Then he would be able to give us some kind of decision, and he would hear the rest of the score if he became interested in getting involved.

It seemed as if Monday would never arrive. I made the call at 10:30 that morning. Lynda put Philip on the phone. He asked if Allan and I could meet with him again—he was interested!

Chapter 6
I Never Promised You a Rosegarten

We met with Phil on June 18 at 2:00 P.M. I played the rest of the score, and we discussed the future of the project. Allan was actually getting excited.

I sat down at the piano and went through every song. Phil had no problem with what I played. He understood my style of pop/rock combined with traditional Broadway and thought it truly had a chance.

Allan and I sat down on the couch, and Phil pulled up his usual chair facing us. He said he would like to direct the show and would work on developing it with us on a daily basis. He then asked how much money we had. Allan and I looked at each other in shock. What did he mean? He explained that he must get his fee as director. We quickly responded that we had no money (my income for that month was $472). I was naïve, but not that naïve and thought the questioning of our monetary status was a bit of a hustle. Phil probably thought that if it didn't get produced, at least he would be compensated for his time. My feeling was that if he liked the show that much, he would get his money legitimately and not from two struggling writers! We made that plain, and he quickly got off the subject. He did go on to say that he was now directing exclusively and would not produce anymore. He would guide us toward producers, since he knew a lot of people, but he would not be a backer or raise money for this show. It suddenly dawned on me that I was close to being back at Square One. We thanked him and said we'd think about it.

Allan and I went next door to a health food place called Amy's to discuss this latest turn of events. We agreed that it might be helpful to have Phil's name associated with our show. However, we didn't know of many people who knew his directorial capabilities. His name had been associated with many shows, but not very often as a director.

I called my friend and publisher, Ray Fox, to ask his advice. He said that Philip's reputation was primarily that of a good hustler in the most respectful sense of the word. He could probably get this thing off the ground at least with his name value.

On Friday of that week I called Phil back, and he said he would draw up a brief contract. On June 24 Allan and I signed an agreement with Phil that the three of us were a team. This, Phil said, was to avoid the possibility of someone eliminating Phil if it got produced. Simple as that. It said that the three of us began our collaboration on June 18 and that the contract was to be in effect for two years.

Phil wanted to know if we knew of anyone who could possibly produce the show. I mentioned a young man named Rory Rosegarten and related that he was already interested in another project of mine, but that I would inform him of the progress here and see if he'd like to become involved.

I called Rory and told him that this show was really moving. He said he would consider it and that I should get a script and tape over to the Comic Strip, where he would be that night. I tried to insist that he hear the songs live, but he said he listened a lot in the car and would really rather have a cassette first. Reluctantly, I complied. I rode over to the Comic Strip and delivered the script and a tape. Within days Rory called back and said he was interested enough to meet with Phil, as he did have some reservations about the script. He lived and breathed the comedy scene, having many comedians as clients, and felt the script was not funny or realistic enough to reflect the showcase club scene. He would voice these thoughts on Monday in Philip's office.

Meanwhile, Philip was excited about finding an interested producer so fast. He pumped me for information about this young whippersnapper and told Allan and me to meet him on Sunday, the day before our meeting with Rory, to prep us for the important appointment. We would also work further on the development of the show.

I found out that Phil's birthday was later that week, on July 4, and wanted to come up with a great present. Allan showed up with a book about New York, since Phil was living in a landmark building on a landmark street. I, on the other hand, found a tee shirt store and had a yellow shirt with black lettering printed up that said "LATE NITE COMIC" on the front and "DIRECTOR" on the back. We gave him his presents a few days before his birthday, since it was the July 4th weekend, and he was going away early. He thanked us, but I never saw him wear that tee shirt.

Rory and I were talking constantly. His mother, Rita, was his secretary, and it turned out that she had heard my demos of the score. She was very enthusiastic and remarked that "Stand Up" was her favorite song. Rory told me he would like to bring it to a partner named Ted Goldbergh. He was a lawyer who was interested in hearing the score and seeing what this was all about. A meeting was arranged for July 22 at 6:30 P.M. at my mother's place, since she was centrally located, had a piano and was simply a great hostess. I invited my publisher, Ray Fox, and his wife, Jean Thomas, while Rory brought Ted. Philip and Allan were also there, of course. Allan gave his usual scene set ups and brief dialogue, while I performed the score. I gave it my all. This was a very important audition.

At the end I watched Rory and Ted embrace joyfully; they had decided to produce the musical. We were all elated. The next day Rory asked for more cassettes. I rushed to make about a dozen copies, while Allan worked on a fifth script revision. Rory still had reservations about the script.

On July 24 Rory's client and my friend, Alan Colmes, did a live show at the Comic Strip for which I was designated bandleader. Besides playing the guests on, I was to do one song myself during the show. That song was "Stand Up," complete with a band. It went over great. Philip and his wife, actress Doris Belack, were there, as well as Rory and his mother, who once again told me how much she loved that song. At the end of the night I asked the Comic Strip manager how the video tape had come out. He admitted that he had forgotten to turn on the VCR until after my song.

July 29 was Darla's and my second anniversary. The marriage was still having problems, and now that the show was being produced, Darla was pressuring me even more about who would have the lead. I told her it was a four-man decision—that I would never have the kind of power she thought I'd have, and I reiterated my feelings about her singing songs requiring such a wide vocal range. The screaming and yelling were beyond belief. At times I felt sorry that I couldn't help her. At others, I wanted a divorce.

On August 15 an agreement was drawn up among Allan, Ted, Rory and me. There was a separate yellow post-it on my copy. It read: "Brian, now let's go make a million bucks! Love, Rory." What a thrilling time!

Phil asked us who our lawyer was. My regular lawyer was on vacation, and the contracts had to be signed right away. Phil explained that this was very important so as not to lose the enthusiasm of our new producers. He recommended a lawyer in this area that he said was good. He would tell him to expect our call. Meanwhile, he would take care of his contract on his own. Our new lawyer looked over our agreement and said we could sign; how-

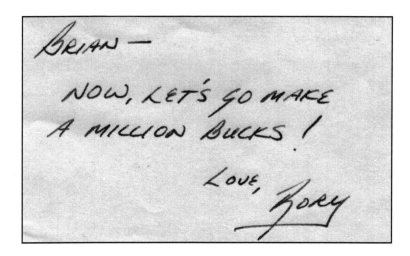

BRIAN —

NOW, LET'S GO MAKE
A MILLION BUCKS !

LOVE,
Rory

ever, he added in the following: that the agreement be contingent upon entering into a satisfactory agreement with Philip Rose. Once again, being a novice in the "business" of show business, I didn't realize that this was a rather strange addition for OUR lawyer to be writing into OUR contract.

Phil was working with us constantly. He had a knack for being able to refine both score and book. He went over every lyric of mine, and when something struck him as needing improvement, he'd ask me for a change. I changed almost anything he wanted. After all, he had the background. There was also a psychological reason; both Allan and I saw Phil as a father image, given his age. The need to please the older man was a positive factor in many of the changes in our work. It also caused problems. Allan would sometimes burst out in anger at this man. At times he was justified. At others, it was embarrassing. He would also end up apologizing. We'd sit in Phil's office, often ordering in sandwiches. Allan and I each got $250 option money from Rory and Ted. We were living on it!

One day Rory called me up with a startling announcement: Ted was no longer involved with the show; Rory would produce it himself. He had met some wealthy gentlemen, who were associated with New Jersey Senator Bill Bradley's campaign, and they wanted to hear the music. I rushed another cassette to Rory.

A few weeks went by without a word, but finally the call came. These guys were putting up more than a million dollars for *Late Nite Comic*. I thought Rory was a genius. I told him that he was singlehandedly making my career happen. We would do movies, TV specials, records! I asked him if he had an Off-Broadway theater in mind. He answered: "Off-Broadway nothin'! We're goin' big time…we're goin' Broadway!"

Chapter 7
Is It Funny Yet?

With all the excitement going on, Darla and I decided to head down to Florida for her father's birthday celebration and a much needed vacation. I never feel I'm due a rest until I have a hit, so I almost have to be forced to take time off. It turned out to be the last vacation Darla and I would ever take together.

Her parents had just moved to Jupiter from Palm Beach, and they treated us with their usual incredible hospitality. All the hospitality in the world, however, couldn't stop us from having another big fight. She was being considered for a reading of a new play, and I had a chance to talk to her about it in more detail in Florida. She would not only have to take off from her salaried job to do this nonpaying performance, but there was no guarantee that she would get anything further from this reading except that some casting people might see her in it. Up to this point, whenever Darla's expenses would go above what she was earning, I would cover the rest, but it seemed that this was occurring all the time, and I was starting to resent it. I was writing the show, composing pop songs, writing for a magazine, booking guests on a cable TV show and running messenger jobs just to cover our bills. I told her it might not be a good idea, and she blew up. She screamed that I wasn't supportive, was trying to screw her out of my show and hated her singing. Her parents and sister witnessed this outburst and even suggested that perhaps she might be putting a little too much pressure on me. As far as Darla was concerned, I was preventing her from succeeding. The trip turned into a nightmare. I had the feeling that this might be the last time I would see her family.

When we returned to New York, we decided that a dual therapy session might be of some use. We went to her therapist. She listened to my complaints about Darla not earning her share of the household expenses, and asked Darla how much extra she would need to be completely self-sufficient. It came to about $200 more a month. Darla was pissed. She screamed once again about how unsupportive I was, and I screamed about how I didn't think I had to cover all her expenses: dance classes, singing classes, makeup, transportation, pictures, résumés, dental…it was mind boggling! There was no way she could cover this herself on what she was making. She reminded me of all the money she made during *A Chorus Line*. In her mind this money seemed to cover every expense ten times over. She couldn't see the reality that the money was spent a long time before. Nothing was resolved.

By this time Allan was reworking the entire show with Phil's advice. It was actually the sixth rewrite. Rory was also having private meetings with Phil about the book. He finally put his foot down and said, "It's just not funny." A staged reading was arranged in Phil's office. Two actors were brought in to do the leading roles. The male came through Rory; his name was Steve Hytner, who was also working as a stand-up comic. I had been told about him through Lucien Hold, manager of the Comic Strip, about a month earlier. The female, Hannah Cox, came through Philip and Lynda. This was the first time I got to hear the dialogue as done by working actors. It was very exciting. Robin Kaiser had been asked to do another role. She sat on the couch next to Rory, script in hand. Rory was supposed to sit there and watch. Instead, because Robin was sitting right next to him, he was looking over her shoulder at the dialogue on paper. Robin was unaware of this, but Phil was infuriated. I particularly wanted Phil to hear Robin sing "Relax with Me Baby" in person. I thought it would be great if Robin, who had been in other musicals, did the song in the show. When she performed the song for Phil, he never looked up, and she was never called back.

At the end of the reading everybody left. Rory asked for a private moment with Phil. Rory was still not satisfied. Phil tried to convince him that all shows read that way; it's the way they're acted and staged that brings the laughs. Phil said he would prove it to him and actually went out and bought Rory several books of hit musicals to illustrate his point. Rory read them, but was still not convinced.

On October 17 Robin and I went into Safe Sound recording studios and cut a few piano/voice demos of songs from the show. I wanted to show off the songs with a decent studio sound. We recorded "Stand Up" and "Late Nite Comic" with me doing the vocal, and "Relax with Me

Baby" and a new song with Robin. I had just finished "Clara's Dancing School." The song was originally written in May 1984 about a lady named Clara who ran a record store on 106th Street and Broadway during my teen years. Even though I was happy with that version, I thought it could be reconstructed as a song about Gabrielle's dancing teacher. Janet had taken classes with a legendary woman of the dance world, Madame Pereyaslavec. She was tough, but someone the young dancers all looked up to. I rewrote the entire lyric with her in mind. Allan had liked the original so much that when I played him this rewritten version, he agreed it would not only be

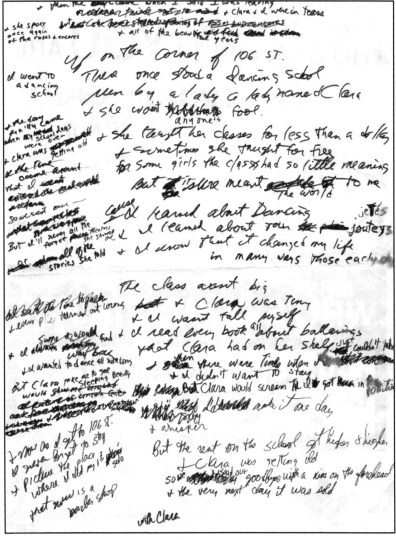

Original work sheet for "Clara's Dancing School."

ideal for the show, but that he could work it into a new scene immediately.

Phil loved the song and decided that "Think Big" would work much better later on as a song for David. We added in "Clara" as Gabby's first number and saved "Think Big" for later.

Another song that worked very well for me in my own nightclub act was one I had written in August 1980 while housesitting in Los Angeles for songwriters Joel Hirschhorn and his then-wife, Jill Williams. I remember sitting down at their piano one day, staring at Joel's intimidating Oscars for "The Morning After" and "We May Never Love Like This Again" and trying to write my own Oscar-winning song. At first I was going to write a depressing ballad about California, but I couldn't take it seriously, so I wrote a comedic song about the town called "I Live in L.A." When I came back to New York, I performed it at the Improv and found it had great potential. It really got laughs, which is a much sought after response when doing songs in a comedy club. Allan and Phil thought it could be rewritten for the show when David hears about Gabby's trip to Los Angeles. It would make fun of L.A. in a playful way and be retitled "They Live in L.A." The scene was cute and charming and had comedic value. It was a good idea. Rory knew the song and felt my contribution helped somewhat with his anxiety about the comedy content.

The first snippet of news that leaked out on the show was in a magazine about comedy, appropriately enough. In the fall of 1986, in an edition of *Comedy USA*, with Garry Shandling on the cover, there was an article on Rory. In it he mentioned "taking an option on a musical called 'Late Nite Comic,' which is slated for Broadway some time next year." I gathered up as many of these magazines as I could get my hands on. Just to see that in print was an unbelievable thrill.

On Thanksgiving Allan gave Darla and me two tickets to *Me and My Girl*. Broadway shows are so expensive, and here Allan just gave us free tickets. Even though I wasn't nuts about the show, I was extremely touched by his generosity. Whenever that show was the least bit boring, I would fantasize about what it was going to be like to have my music on a stage. Darla knew I was a million miles away. She understood.

December brought more meetings with Phil and Allan. Phil felt that the "Gabrielle" theme should come back in the traditional Broadway style. I saw his point completely. When Gabrielle asks to come back to David in the second act, I was to come up with a one verse version of "Gabrielle" that captured his vulnerability in allowing her to return anytime. I thought it would be a cinch. Little did I know how difficult it was going to be. It took me forever, because it would have to be the last verse, which had such an intricate rhyme scheme that I almost give up several times. Finally, I came up with:

> Gabrielle, you always have a place here
> Gabrielle, I love to see your face here
> Gabrielle, I'll always leave a light on
> No one else can bring the night on
> Half as well
> Oh, Gabrielle...
> What a bitch!

I am very proud of that simple little verse.

By the seventh rewrite Phil and Allan made some other major changes. First of all, the character of Mike was no longer to sing "This Lady Isn't Right For You." It was given over to David with a new first-person title, "This Lady Isn't Right for Me." "Think Big," in a shorter version, was now David's big Act One closing number. It seemed to have a lot more impact in this spot. The verse was now gone, but would be expanded later on. Phil also decided that "Stand Up" would be nice to hear again, so the last verse was repeated as a confidence number for David right after the melancholy "Late Nite Comic."

In December I was asked to write a cute song that would have David playfully trying to make Gabby jealous. It was called "She's in the Other Room" and sounded so much like my grandfather's signature song, "Makin' Whoopee," that I had to change the melody a bit. It didn't matter, as it never made it into any version of the show.

By the end of 1986 the lineup was now:

ACT ONE
   Stand Up
   Gabrielle
   Clara's Dancing School
   This Lady Isn't Right for Me
   Nothing's Changin' This Love
   The Best in the Business
   It Had to Happen Sometime

Think Big
Late Nite Comic
Stand Up (reprise)
ACT TWO
David, Are You Sleeping Yet?
Obsessed
Relax with Me Baby
Life Is Material
Life Is Material (reprise)
Gabrielle (reprise)
Dance
I Wonder If I'll Ever Be a Mother/Father
It Had to Happen Sometime
It's Such a Different World
Yvonne/It Had to Happen Sometime

For Christmas I had some pens inscribed with the name "Late Nite Comic" on them. I gave them out as presents to Rory, Phil and Allan. They all seemed to like them. I wish I had kept one for myself as a little momento.

Allan continued to work throughout the holidays on an eighth re-write. The new year of 1987 brought a very new script. This time there was a song loss. "Life Is Material" went to that great big musical in the sky. I didn't mourn the deletion. It had never grown on me, and I knew some-

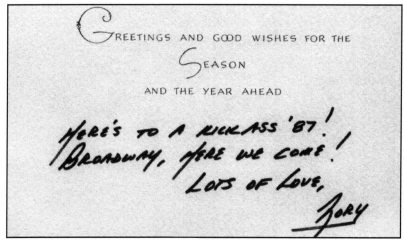

Rory's Christmas card.

thing was bound to get cut eventually. I was just happy it was this one. Also, the song "Dance" would now be a duet with David starting it off. Since he has rented out the Met for Gabby, it is logical that he would prompt her to dance. Once he started, she would continue the song as her own. I liked this change very much.

1987 also proved to be the end of my marriage. Darla took her therapist's advice and got a better paying job, but instead of seeing if this helped our situation, she announced that she had found another apartment. At first it was a relief. I had a wonderful distraction; the show was moving along, and I was very busy…not too busy to notice some suspicious phone calls coming in for Darla. A dentist she had met at work was interested in her. He even had the audacity to call her at our apartment. I believed there was nothing going on—yet. It was inevitable, though, that this would be Darla's first affair when she left. To be honest, I saw my career looking very promising, and even though I still loved Darla, I thought I could find someone who would not be as needy. That aspect, I believe, was the largest factor in the dissolution of our marriage. By February she had secured a mover. She was to move out a week before my birthday.

On February 15 Darla and I planned to see a musical entitled *Dazy* that Phil was directing and that Allan had helped finish writing. Phil had an ongoing relationship with the people who ran the AMAS Theater near Harlem, so that's where it was to have a short run.

Darla and I decided to borrow a friend's car and kill two birds with one stone. Her new apartment was near the theater, so we would move some stuff and then park the car and see the show. I had heard a cassette of the score, so I knew what I was in for…well, almost. It was truly pathetic. We were very anxious to get out. Perhaps we should have left early. When we got downstairs, the car window was smashed, and some of Darla's things that were still in the car were stolen. It cost me $100 in repairs—more than if we had actually hired the movers later that week!

By early April another idea was suggested; maybe the title should be changed. Phil thought *Stand Up* would be a better idea. Allan and I were not excited by this turn of events, but we went along with it—for a while. *Stand Up* would have numerous meanings. First, it could mean stand up for yourself; second, it would be the opening song, and third, it would refer to comedy. *Late Nite Comic* seemed not to include the part of the dancer, which was true. A new script, the ninth, was printed up. It now included "They Live in L.A." The ending had David playing a piano bar in Grand Rapids and running into Gabrielle there. Amazing in how many towns this show ended!

Darla called me often during this time. She wanted to know if we were going to get back together. I wanted to know what was going on with her and the dentist. It all seemed fairly useless. I couldn't see a future with her anymore. Rory encouraged me to get a lawyer. I had a show that could change my financial state drastically. He said there was a divorce lawyer who shared office space with him. I put off calling this woman for a month. Finally, I knew I had no choice. I met with her on April 22. She said she would draw up the papers, as my assets were very small, and Darla and I did not want very much from each other. When the papers arrived for Darla, she went crazy. It seemed that she had forgotten that to get a quick divorce, one must say that the other partner withheld sex. That was hardly one of our problems. My mother calmed her down and explained it was just a technicality to speed up the process. The papers were sent back to my lawyer in the hope of a speedy return. I didn't hear from my lawyer again for almost a year! To this day I do not know the reason for this lady's incompetence, but if my show had succeeded, I would have been vulnerable to any demands Darla might have had at that time.

I called the lawyer at her office and never received an answer. It was odd to discover that she had moved out of her apartment in the city, and Rory's brother had moved in, although she still shared an office with Rory. It took another lawyer just to get it all settled.

Also, in April, the Dramatists Guild had heard about the show and invited me to join. At this point I had no idea how important they would be for me. I didn't follow up on it for a while. The Guild helps the writer in all the legal aspects of his endeavor without actually representing him as his lawyer. They fight for him when necessary and look over contracts.

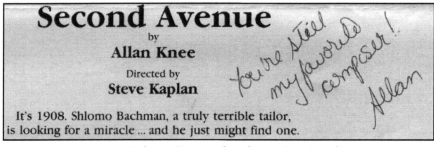

Second Avenue
by
Allan Knee
Directed by
Steve Kaplan

It's 1908. Shlomo Bachman, a truly terrible tailor, is looking for a miracle ... and he just might find one.

Kind words from Allan on a flyer for another play of his.

They are on his side. Still, I felt I had no use for their services—yet.

On May 15 the approved production contract was submitted by Rory's lawyer to the lawyer Allan and I had hired upon Phil's recommendation. Things were really starting to happen. Only Allan was a Guild member at the time, so the contract had to be read by the Guild as well as the lawyer representing both Allan and me. The contract was explained to us by our lawyer. In one section, about unusual subsidiary rights for Phil, he said we were getting many other "extras" from Rory and that we should accept this clause. Being particularly naïve and anxious to get moving, we trusted our lawyer's words. He was the kind of guy who, when questioned too much, got annoyed and intimidating, giving the impression that we weren't allowing him to do his job. The option money this time was going to be a lot better. We couldn't wait for that check.

It was also at this time that I decided to form my own music publishing company. Since I wasn't signed to any major company, I would be able to own my own publishing, which, if the show were a hit, would make me wealthy indeed. I also felt I should split the publishing 50/50 with my longtime supporter, Ray Fox. He had paid for all the initial lead sheets on the show and had advanced me various monies, so it was really due him. I named my company Tenacity, because it was a word once used to describe me by a record executive named Warren Schatz. He was going to sign me, but the company he worked for suddenly went under. I looked up the word and decided that was me!

After the Guild had time to look over the contract, a letter was sent back to our lawyer questioning a 3% royalty to Philip Rose for subsidiary rights. Our lawyer quickly replied that his clients felt it appropriate considering Phil Rose's input. The Guild was not satisfied; they called Allan and me in. Ron Sandberg, the wonderful former lawyer for the Guild, talked to us about this clause. We told him that supposedly we were getting other things in return for this minor addition. He said that this was just a standard contract. I joined the Guild on the spot. I couldn't understand why our lawyer would ask for such a clause—and on our time! He was adamant, but so was the Guild, which called in the troops. A meeting was set up with Guild representatives Mary Rodgers, daughter of Richard Rodgers and a well-known composer herself, and Lee Adams, lyricist of numerous Broadway musicals, including *Bye Bye Birdie*.

Allan and I were taken into the President's office and questioned. Mary asked what Phil did on the book. We said he helped make it cohesive. She asked, "Yes, but did he write actual dialogue?" Allan answered no. Lee asked me if Phil had written any of the music or lyrics. I immediately answered no. It was obvious that the Phil clause was a sham. He was just doing his job as director and had no rights to any additional monies. I will always be grateful to Mary and Lee for their kind advice. It is also indicative of the Guild's assistance. Incidentally, the clause was removed.

By the end of April I was asked to come up with an important song for Gabrielle. The notes I took from Phil and Allan were to describe the high Gabby gets when the world disappears—along with all of her problems. She is alone and doesn't need anyone. She's never coming down. We were already talking to a few people for the role, and Laurie Beechman had come by. I had known and loved her singing for ten years. She wasn't exactly the right type for Gabrielle, but just the thought of her singing my music was exhilarating. We had dated once many years ago, but she seemed different and more together now. I was also on another level. I went home and wrote "When I Am Movin'" with her in mind. The next day I played it for Phil and Allan. They were ecstatic. They called Rory to set up an appointment for him to hear it. It was unanimous; I had written a showstopper! It would come right before

When I am movin
Then when I'm in the air
I don't really care what's below
No one can hold me
No one can
There's not a reason to care
I'm high on my plateau

When I am movin
When I'm not held down
Then I go to town in the sky
Just me, not he, & I
(you)

(It's not
that u don't
love you)
I defy gravity
whatever that can be this no one is tellin me come down
Hell with reality & if you dare to try
get a good look at my thumb down

When I am movin
when I'm in mid flight
nothing is quite like it before seems
I'm not afraid anymore

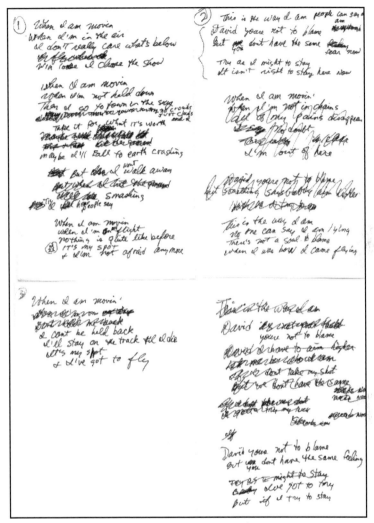

Original work sheets for "When I Am Movin'."

David's Act One closer, "Think Big."

Another song casualty occurred during this tenth revision. "David, Are You Sleeping Yet?" was deleted. It was disappointing to have a song that had lasted this long removed, especially one that had such a connection to my original relationship with Janet.

Phil and Allan suggested something else. Could I come up with an entirely different lyric to "Late Nite Comic" to incorporate David's feelings of lost love? It would be sung as a reprise after David and Gabby were back together for six weeks and she leaves him again. I loved the idea and wrote a completely new lyric that night to play for them the next day. Rory happened to be there

Original work sheet for "Late Nite Comic" reprise.

as well and was deeply moved. It became one of his favorite songs, although "Clara" always seemed to have a place in his heart. He then proceeded to ask a special personal favor; would I write a song that speaks his love for his own girlfriend? I gathered up his thoughts and wrote a song called "Wendy, We're Always Laughing." I demoed it and gave it to him the next day. He was on Cloud Nine and planned everything around it. He and Wendy had a lovely dinner and then he played the song on the cassette deck. I think we can all imagine what happened next. I only wish my songs worked that well for me!

Rory had just gotten word that we would have a ten-performance run in New London, Connecticut before opening on Broadway in October. He turned to me and said, "Either I'm gonna make it real big from this thing, or you'll see me on 7th Avenue and 53rd Street, handing out flyers for the Kit Kat Club!"

On May 22 the first official *Late Nite Comic* publicity ran in Enid Nemy's column in *The New York Times*. It centered around Rory's amazing ability to raise over one million dollars for the production. The following day Michael Burlingame wrote in New London's *The Day* that *Late Nite Comic* was coming to New London. It also erroneously reported that it would open later on at the Brooks Atkinson Theater.

With the addition of the "Late Nite Comic" reprise, the script was now ready to be submitted to actors, and casting would begin.

Chapter 8
Casting

The casting of actors and the casting of our technical/creative crew took place simultaneously. The open call announcement went out on June 19, while many appointments concerning the leads took place in Phil's office.

Phil's passion for doing black-oriented shows was no secret. After all, he was responsible for *Purlie* and *A Raisin in the Sun*, as well as numerous other involvements along the way. The question for Allan and me was inevitable. Phil sat us down in his office and asked us how we would feel about an interracial show. Presumedly, he was suggesting the casting of a black girl in the role of Gabrielle. He mentioned Debbie Allen. My liberal instinct was to respond affirmatively, so as not to suggest any prejudice. However, one should not have to feel as though he is being racist if he chooses not to go with an idea that might change the direction of the show. The additional conflict of an interracial situation on top of an already difficult relationship between David and Gabrielle was just not something I wanted an audience to deal with. Phil's immediate reaction was to remind me of *The Owl and the Pussycat*, the interracial romance to which the audience adjusted almost immediately. Allan and I were not overly enthused. Of course, within the week a young black girl was brought up to the office at Phil's request. She was very nice, but not right for the part. Phil said she *was* Gabby, and we were asked to see her again. We heard her act; we heard her sing. She was black, but not that talented. Phil said she was going to be a star and that we'd better grab her. He never let go, working with her on his own time, while we continued looking at other people.

Another aspect of Phil's taste was reflected in the body type. I had lived with ballet dancers; I knew that shape very well. The black girl, as well as dozens of girls Phil would bring up, did not look as if she could possibly be from the ballet world. Ballet dancers work extremely hard on their bodies. They can usually be spotted blocks away! It's not just their walk, but rather a slim, boyish shape. Phil would seriously consider big, wide-hipped women. I began to realize that he personally found this type to be very attractive. I did not find the look as believable for Gabby, and I put my foot down numerous times concerning both the lead and the chorus. Allan wasn't as concerned. He went to the ballet, but he hadn't been as intimately involved with dancers as I had.

Lynda Watson wanted to head up casting. Phil asked Rory to put her on an additional salary to do this job. He did. Rory, in the meantime, was seeking out possible stars for the roles. "How would we like Dudley Moore?" Rory asked. "Wouldn't he be a little too old?" Allan and I would answer. He was contacted and either couldn't or wouldn't do it. Other names that popped up early always seemed to start with "Tom": Hulce, Cruise, Hanks. It's interesting to note that Tom Hanks later starred in a film about comedians called *Punchline*.

The fine actor, Ron Silver, dropped by Phil's office one day; he and Phil were friendly. Silver was obviously backed up with other properties, but Phil gave him a script anyway.

I had my own list. Bob Saget was on an Improv comedy show, which I taped. He was musical, funny and charming. Rory, Allan and Phil watched the tape and agreed that he might be right. He was contacted and interested. Unfortunately for us, he got a TV series. I also suggested a great musical comic named Dale Gonyea. When they saw that video tape, they were really excited. I located him in Los Angeles and gave Rory the information. Rory told him we were interested, but that he would have to meet with Phil in New York. Dale paid his own way. His singing and playing were still great, but his acting was a little disconcerting. I still thought he was a possibility, but I was outvoted. We all went to lunch down the block from Phil's office at the New York Delicatessen. How hard it was for all of us to keep smiling when we knew he didn't have the part. That was some lunch. Dale and I have stayed in touch, and he's doing just great in English television and performing. I still think he has strong possibilities as a stage actor.

Dana Carvey was another suggestion of mine. I had met him many years before at the Improv. He was finally becoming a big success through his work on *Saturday Night Live*. Phil met with no luck in acquiring him, because he was about to make a film.

On June 14 I went to see Phil's wife in a one-act play. The other one-acter starred the well-known television actress, Sarah Jessica Parker. Phil flipped for her and wanted her for Gabrielle. Unfortunately, she had other commitments.

John Kassir, who played a comic in *Three Guys Naked from the Waist Down*, was someone Phil was pushing for, but for some reason we never saw him.

Meanwhile, we had to get started on our creative and technical crew. It was a given that Phil's longtime buddy Mort Halpern, stage manager extraordinaire, would be on the staff. He had done many shows for Phil and at one time had acted himself.

I was asked whom I would like to orchestrate. This was a dream question for me, since I have so many favorite orchestrators. Of course, my first instinct was to ask my talented friend Don Ciccone if he would like the job, but he declined on the basis of his lack of theatre experience. My friend Jeff Olmsted declined for the same reason. These are extremely talented musical people, but to do the orchestrations for a Broadway musical is a whole other ball game. Phil was quick to come down on me for suggesting any "record" arrangers; he insisted they would cover up stage voices in the wrong spots because of their lack of theatre knowledge.

I remembered Robert Dennis having done some lovely arrangements for then-producer Stephen Schwartz on a pop album by Jill Williams, and he was contacted. Phil wasn't overly excited. I had also asked Julie Budd's longtime arranger and musical director, Herb Bernstein. He had done Laura Nyro's first album, as well as arranging some of my all-time favorite hit records like "See You in September." I thought he might be ideal. Don Ciccone also suggested another member of The Four Seasons named Lee Shapiro. Lee and I had worked together in 1979 on some of my early demos, and I was very much impressed by his musical ability. Both he and Herb were interested. Both were capable of doing the job alone, although Phil thought the two might work well together. This almost happened until another name was suggested by Don—Larry Hochman. Larry had some theatre experience, yet was pop-oriented. This would fill both my needs and Phil's. It turned out that Phil had worked with Larry peripherally in the past. There was mutual respect, so Larry was contacted. The meeting went great, and I felt that if Phil thought he could do the job, then our search would be over. The only problem was—how would I tell my friends, Herb and Lee? It was very hard, but

Lee Shapiro and Don Ciccone.

I did. Lee probably didn't care that much, but Herb genuinely wanted to work on the project. He had had several meetings with Phil and brought tapes along to show what he could do. Phil's tape player left a lot to be desired. It was a boombox, not exactly something on which a musician likes to hear his music. I was always adjusting the volume and trying to figure out what channel was missing when I played demos for Phil. I begged Phil to upgrade, but I think it fell on deaf ears.

Phil knew Herb was good, but he wasn't going to take any chances. A tape of my songs was given to Larry to begin work. I also supplied Larry with the lead sheets that Jeff Olmsted had done, so as not to have any conflicts as to how the songs really were to be played.

Along with an orchestrator had to come a musical director and a dance/vocal arranger. Once again, I knew very few theatrical musical directors, so the choices came mainly through Phil. He wanted Linda Twine. She had done *The Wiz* and most recently, *Big River*, but she was unavailable because of *Big River*. Larry Hochman recommended a guy he had worked with during a dinner theater run of *The Wiz*, Greg Dlugos. Greg arrived at Phil's office to meet all of us and give his credentials. I played a couple of songs, including the new "When I Am Movin'." I immediately had an uneasy feeling about Greg. Perhaps it was his constant puns. His reaction to my music didn't seem to

Larry Hochman.

come from a genuine like of it, but rather a desire to add another credit to his résumé. He seemed more interested in pleasing Phil, since Phil was the "name" and had another Broadway show in the works called *Captain America*. I didn't realize how closely we would have to be working, or I probably would have listened to my instincts and not been so quick to say yes to the first musical director who walked into Phil's office.

Coincidentally, back when Darla was doing *A Chorus Line* in California, she had become friendly with D'lyse Lively-Mekka and her husband, Eddie Mekka, who played Carmine on *Laverne and Shirley*. She introduced Eddie to Rory, who ended up signing him to his management company. Eddie was very much interested in becoming involved with *Late Nite Comic*. He was best friends with a choreographer and dance instructor named Phil Black. Phil was considerably older than Eddie, but they worked well together. Eddie wanted to be the choreographer on the show. He asked Rory to consider him and Phil Black as a team. They even put together several routines and invited Philip and Rory to see them. They went through a lot of trouble to do this. For some reason Allan and I were not invited. Philip wasn't convinced, and Rory wasn't familiar enough with that area to take a stand.

Phil was also seeing other choreographers. A young guy from a ballet company upstate brought down his own dancers just to show what he could do. He was good, but Phil wasn't committing himself.

Dennis Dennehy had recently worked on a show called *Cowboy*. Phil was familiar with him and set up a meeting. They got along fine, and Dennis showed Phil his ideas. I liked Dennis as well, in the beginning. His attitude was hip and cool, and I thought we would get along as well. He was hired. Most important, however, was to hire a dance/vocal arranger who could complement Dennis's work and vice versa. James Raitt was suggested. He had been involved in Broadway's *Stardust* and was musical director for American Dance Machine for ten years. He would work hand in hand with Dennis, Greg and Larry. He was considered a perfect choice and hired. Also, Dennis decided to use a young dancer by the name of Danielle Connell as his assistant. This lady worked her buns off for us. She was a delight. She also had another job. One day she casually mentioned to Rory that she was doing *Oh, Calcutta*, the nude musical, on the side. She said she could get him in if he wanted. I overheard this, and being the voyeur that I am, I asked if I could go, too. I didn't know how serious she was about the offer, but I wasn't about to take no for an answer. She said she would leave me a ticket. Let me tell you it's a fun experience to see someone you know—naked! You don't have to have a relationship with them, but you get to see them totally nude. I had a great time.

In fact, I wrote a parody of "Gabrielle" for Danielle. It went:

> Oh, Danielle, the star of "Oh, Calcutta"
> Oh, Danielle, you made my heart go "flutta"
> Oh, Danielle, I couldn't really doze off
> When I saw you take your clothes off
> In the show. I'm really not a dead head
> Oh, Danielle, you truly are a redhead.
> Oh, Danielle, I really liked the story
> Now it's time to go tell Rory
> That I saw you dance
> Without your pants
> Oh, Danielle, you're really off the wall and
> Oh, Danielle, I really had a ball and
> Yes, Danielle, your singing was exciting
> Wanna thank you for inviting me as well
> Oh, thanks, Danielle.

A general manager by the name of Frank Scardino had called me months earlier. He had also known a friend of Darla's and was interested in representing the show. I mentioned his name to Phil, and he told me to refer all calls of that nature to him. I told Frank exactly that. He met with Rory and Phil, and a deal was struck. Frank had recently had a strong connection with the Jujamcyn Theaters, who also owned Broadway's Ritz Theater. He and Rory got along great and would meet almost every day after work for a drink. Frank was a stern, businesslike guy. He had a sense of humor, but was basically quiet. He had a slightly intimidating quality, but maybe when you handle money to that degree, you need to present that image. His company handled all checks, as well as salary negotiations.

Speaking of Scardinos, Don Scardino (no relation) had also been considered for the role of David. He had done *Godspell*, as well as many other Broadway and television shows. He was directing a lot and did not get back to Phil as far as I know. I thought he might have been a good choice.

On June 26 Harry Haun wrote about the show in *The Daily News*. Some of the papers read "producer Roy Rosegarten," while others were correct. I could tell that Rory was not thrilled. On the same day Rory and Phil went on Alan Colmes's radio show to announce that the musical was happening and that they were looking for actors. They actually asked people to audition over the radio. Rory stated on the air that "Brian wrote the original book and concept" and wanted to thank Alan publicly for introducing me to him. Phil added that he would be doing *Captain America* "after *Late Nite Comic* is a big hit."

We were getting our share of names to consider now that we were really going to be on the boards. Sean Young wanted the role. I had never heard of her, but Allan had just seen a coming attraction for her film *No Way Out*, and he said she was getting very hot. Allan and I were there for her audition. In person she did not impress me as the Gabrielle type. I had heard that she had extensive dance training, but she just didn't have the look that I felt would be Gabrielle. Still, she read the script. No comments were made on my score. I had no idea if she had ever listened to a tape or even if she could sing. Her reading was not great. She knew it as well. It's funny…with all the hoopla about this up-and-coming star, I just didn't feel she would have done the role justice. She called Phil again and asked for another audition; she really wanted this part. Phil called Allan and me and told us she was coming back. Allan couldn't make it, and it was lucky for him. This time she brought along one of the most untalented acting partners you could ever imagine. If Allan had heard what was done to his script, he would have split a gut. Phil told me later that she probably brought him along to show the contrast—that she would look much better next to someone so bad! It was embarrassing. She and I never made eye contact. When Robert LuPone was hired and told that Sean Young had auditioned, he made it plain that he never would have taken the part if she had been Gabrielle. It seemed that he had worked with her at one time and did not have a positive experience.

Phil told us that Jeff MacGregor, the current host of *The New Dating Game*, was coming in from California to meet with us. He wanted to prove that he could do more than just host that show. He had a great sense of humor and was certainly good looking. That might have been what was wrong; he was TOO good looking to be David. Nice guy, though.

I had been friendly with Peter Noone of Herman's Hermits fame. The staff was also interested because of his work in *The Pirates of Penzance*. Unfortunately, Peter took too long to get around to reviewing the project, and we had a deadline. He did like it, however.

An interesting coincidence was the submission of Scott Bakula and Alison Fraser. For some reason Alison never showed up for the audition, and Scott, like many of the actors we wanted, was committed to a TV series. However, the two of them did end up together—in a small Broadway musical called *Romance Romance*.

Comics were always coming by Phil's office; he kept insisting that we needed actors, not comics. Since Rory managed comics, he did suggest many of them. Paul Reiser was approached, but I was told he didn't like my score. That was odd, because I knew him from my Comic Strip days, and he was always complimentary about my songs. Paul Provenza was interested, and Phil liked him. In fact, it was the only time Phil ever went to see a comic perform during these auditions. It was at Caroline's at the South Street Seaport. Paul was great and could act, but he really couldn't sing the score well enough. Phil was hopeful, but soon gave up. Paul went on to star in a hit play about comics called *Only Kidding*.

A suggestion of mine was a comedian named Larry Miller. He and I had been friends since his first night at the Comic Strip. He worked his way into the club by bartending and playing drums. In fact, he played drums for me when I did "Late Nite Comic" during my sets. He has always been a fan of my music, as I have always been a fan of his comedy. Even though he certainly could act, the staff was concerned about his ability to sing an entire Broadway score.

An interesting suggestion for Gabby was Charlotte D'Amboise. I say interesting, because she is known as a wonderful dancer, and the role of Gabby was that of a not good enough dancer. I liked Charlotte, but once she gave it some thought, she told us that the role was just not something she could play, given her background. She later went into *Carrie* and then *Jerome Robbins's Broadway*.

A comic actor by the name of Don Stitt got an appointment with Phil. He was a short, blond guy, who also did some comedy in the club scene. He read for us for the lead. He wasn't exactly what we were looking for, so he was thanked and told to leave his picture, just in case. He was very high strung and really wanted that part, and he was not about to be forgotten.

A young singer/actor named Michael McAssey came in. He had performed my song "Late Nite Comic" in his nightclub act. He was also not suitable for the lead, but we did hold onto his picture and résumé as well.

I remember one girl named Bambi whose agent contacted Phil; he said, "You have to see this girl!" She was in from L.A. and would be in town only for a short time. She could have been right out of *Penthouse*. The mini-skirt was so mini that I think we could almost read the brand name of underwear she had on. Yes, she was the type! No, she couldn't act. Rory and I were drooling. She was definitely one of the most stunning to audition.

Veanne Cox came up to Phil's office. He had interviewed her before and now wanted Allan and me to see her. She read very well, with a kind of Laura Petrie quality (Mary Tyler Moore's character on *The Dick Van Dyke Show*) that was funny and charming. It was something that really gave the role life. Allan and I were impressed. We told Phil we thought she should be seriously considered. She was called back many times.

One day, as I was heading up Sixth Avenue on my moped, I ran into the late Robert Colby, who was a writer and publisher. He had published some of my earliest songs. I told him my great news about coming to Broadway. He asked me who the director was, and when I told him, his face dropped. "Why would you go with him? Everybody knows he's a terrible director," he revealed. He wished me luck and told me he hoped we'd succeed anyway. His comment was not to be taken lightly. He had been in the business a long time. Some of my nagging doubts about Phil's abilities had just been confirmed.

Since the show was well on its way, I brought up the question of a "based on an original idea" credit in the presence of Rory and Phil. Rory admitted there were many similarities, having read my original script. Phil was reluctant even to consider that I had written an earlier version. He conceded to meet with me at his apartment over the weekend to check out my claim. I arrived with the script in hand. Phil took it, flipped through it in less than two minutes and exclaimed, "There's nothing here that even remotely resembles the show!" I pointed out actual lines that were in both scripts. He refused to see it.

Allan was just as blind. When I brought up something as obvious as the name Gabrielle, he screamed, "I saw a girl with that name in a late night movie." I decided I was in a no-win situation.

On June 29 auditions started at the Minskoff Rehearsal Studios. We saw 50 Equity women and 50 Equity men that day. There were 21 non-Equity actors as well. I kept a complete list of all who auditioned. Pamela Blasetti was the 11th woman, and she got a call back. Lauren Goler, who was a friend

CHORUS CALLS

EQ., "LATE NIGHT COMIC"

6/29 at 10 AM & 2 PM; 6/30 at 10 AM at Minskoff Studios, 1515 B'way.

There will be Equity chorus calls for "Late Night Comic" at Minskoff Studios, 1515 B'way, 3rd fl. LOA contract. American Musical Theatre, Stonington, Conn., Charles Peckham, prod'rs.; Philip Rose, dir.; Gregory Delugas, mus. dir.; Dennis Dennehy, choreo. Rehearses Aug. 10. Contract runs for six weeks. Chorus call procedures in effect. Must have strong ballet and jazz skills.

Mon. June 29—Eq. male singers who dance, 10 AM.
Mon. June 29—Eq. female singers who dance, 2 PM.
Tues. June 30—Eq. female dancers who sing, 10 AM.

of Darla's, and who I thought would make a good Gabrielle, was number 29 and asked to come back. There was a girl named Mary Buehrle who I thought was really good. I remember her getting a call back and bringing us cookies. She didn't get the part, but I always wanted her to know how sweet a gesture that was. Susan Santoro, the 39th auditioner, was also good and asked back. A girl named Crista Moore I thought was a very good Gabby type; she was asked back, but didn't get the part. She did, however, go on to do many other musicals, including the revival of *Gypsy* with Tyne Daly.

The 23rd man to audition was Barry Finkel; he was called back. The 28th and 30th men to show up were Don Stitt and Michael McAssey, respectively. It was like—okay, you don't want us for the lead, how about the chorus? We want to be in your damned show. They were called back. The 43rd male auditioner was an extremely professional actor by the name of Patrick Hamilton. It was almost automatic that he had to be in our show in one role or another. He looked as if he just left the beaches of Malibu with his blond hair and tanned skin. His singing was fantastic. He was asked to visit Phil to read for the lead also.

The next day we saw 32 more men and women. The first was Kim Freshwater, and the second was Joyce Fleming; both were called back. Phil

particularly liked Kim Freshwater. She was tall and big. Once again, I saw Phil's personal taste being reflected in his casting. Kim was hardly the delicate dance type I saw as Gabrielle. Phil held strong.

The singing ranged from excellent to ridiculous. One girl sang with a record; others did opera. One guy did his magic act! Some, of course, couldn't sing at all. They usually blamed the piano player.

Kim Freshwater.

On July 10 *The New York Times* printed a blurb about the show, mentioning the producer, "Barry Rosegarten." Again, Rory was not thrilled.

It was now mid-July, and we didn't have any idea who was going to play the leads. Allan and I were getting a little annoyed at Phil's process. We would send him people who would be dismissed almost immediately or not seen at all. Allan would suggest an actor he had just seen, and Phil wouldn't follow up on it. Sometimes we would hear the phrase "they're Hollywood people." One such actress was Cyndy Gibb, who did a brilliant job playing Karen Carpenter. Lynda wanted her seen very badly, but Phil discouraged her. He disliked a lot of film actors, said they couldn't do stage work well. Maybe that's true in some cases, but it shouldn't wipe out the whole community. Lynda would interview some potentially good actors, and Phil would look over their 8X10s and not even give them an appointment. Some people would come up to Phil's small suffocating office and be dismissed before Allan and I even shook their hands. We demanded to see everybody. Phil was not happy. Allan and I just thought we should see for ourselves. I personally did not want to feel that some poor actor got screwed out of a part when all of us didn't get to see him or her.

A costume designer had to be found. I brought up the name Carol Oditz, who had done extensive work, including a previous show of Allan's. She lived in my building, so I told her to contact Phil. He couldn't decide soon enough, and she had to take another job. Instead, Phil hired Gail Cooper-Hecht, who had worked for him on the PBS version of *Purlie* and the recent *Dazy*. As Rory said, what does a comic wear—a jacket and a pair of jeans? Costumes were not a high priority.

Phil had decided to use Clarke Dunham as our set designer and Ken Billington as our lighting director. They respected each other's work, so it was a good team effort. The budget was very low, forcing Clarke to make the most of what he had to work with. The first rough plan was delivered on May 26. It showed four mini-turntables split in the middle by a large turntable that functioned as both an apartment, a club and a street. Clarke's daughter Pam became Phil's assistant.

Henry Luhrman was contracted to publicize the show. His office would coordinate all interviews for Allan and me and, of course, our producer. I pictured myself doing Regis Philbin's morning show and things like that, but it didn't quite happen that way. Allan and I got an interview with The *Sunday New York Times*—the Connecticut edition! I got to do a Columbia University radio show with Ezio Petersen. Ezio was great, but that was it! Rory's name was everywhere! "Boy genius who gets show to Broadway at 25" was the key phrase. I learned to live with that. He had to live it down.

I asked Rory about my father's doing the logo for the show. He had painted the portrait of Judy Garland that hung in the Palace Theater for many years, as well as having a painting hanging in the White House. In other words, he was no slouch when it came to quality artwork. Rory agreed to let him try. My father came to Phil's office with numerous versions of the logo. I thought at least one of them would be chosen, but I got the distinct impression that Phil did not want my family involved. Rory's father was in advertising, so it was inevitable that a name company would be contacted. In fact, R.J. Rosegarten is listed as the advertising consultant in the playbill. My father's work was rejected, and Grey Advertising was utilized. My father had worked hard on this project and received no compensation whatsoever. I felt really bad for him, but my hands were tied. Grey came up with the half moon and big comedy nose and mustache idea. It was professional. I didn't mind.

On July 14 we held more auditions. These included people who had been seen by Phil personally. The 10:00 A.M. group included actresses by the names of Dee Dee Kelly, Mary Ann Lamb and Aja Major. Dee Dee was another find of Phil's, and while she could sing well, she was overweight. Her legs could not be construed to be those of a dancer, and she knew it. She was not a dancer. Still, Phil persisted. He'd confer with Dennis Dennehy and ask him if he could do anything to help her. Rory agreed with me. She just wasn't believable. Phil called her back.

Mary Ann Lamb was a perfect Gabby type. She was cute and pretty and danced great. However, she was in *Starlight Express* and couldn't get out of her contract. Aja Major was from the American Dance Machine. She had come to Phil's office and was called back. She was also not the Gabby type, yet was called back again by Phil.

One beautiful girl I shall not name did her dance audition in a most unusual fashion. Rory's eyes lit up, and he grabbed my arm.

"Did you see her?"

"Yeah, Rory, of course."

"No, you won't believe what I saw!" I didn't understand what the hell Rory was implying. It seemed that this girl wore no underwear at all. She raised her leg, but I, unfortunately, had turned away for a second. I couldn't believe I missed it. Rory was dead serious. I could have kicked myself. She was gorgeous. Dancers seem to be a bit on the exhibitionist side, but this was a little more than I had expected.

Another girl, named Sharon Moore, was black. She couldn't sing, but she was a very good dancer with a good ballet background. Dennis took note of this.

I also thought Darla could at least get a chorus role if nothing else. She was, and still is, very talented and could have added a lot to the show. I felt it was only right that she have the job; after all, Phil himself might never have had his own position if she hadn't suggested him. I asked Phil for a specific audition slot for her. He was reluctant. I said that all I was asking for was not to make her stand on line at six in the morning to get a number. We could give her that much, couldn't we? He begrudgingly gave in.

At two in the afternoon the call backs began. Another black girl by the name of Judine Hawkins came by. Crista Moore returned, as did Lauren Goler, Pamela Blasetti, Susan Santoro, Joyce Fleming and Kim Freshwater. They sang their best and waited. Then they danced their asses off. The grueling steps that these struggling young actresses had to endure were beyond belief. And then there was the waiting for the cuts. Who would go…who would stay? I found that Phil and Dennis were having most of the say on the chorus choices. I got up and sat on the floor with the girls. They couldn't believe it. Here I was, one of the "decision makers," sitting on the floor with them. I just felt it was too much. I couldn't stand the tension, and wanted them not to feel so threatened.

During one dance routine, a girl fell. It wasn't so much the fall that had her in tears, but rather the gut feeling that that fall probably cost her the job. It did. She ran out of the studio. I ran out after her and held her while she cried. I told her she would get something else and that she was still very talented. I called her at home later on. She survived.

Toward the end Phil asked if there was anyone else waiting to be seen. Morty mentioned Darla. Phil looked at me and asked, "Are your cats out there, too?" I came very close to slugging him. I was separated from Darla, but he was not going to insult her. I played piano for her. She sang fine. She was then given the dance steps. In doing the routine she had to move out of the designated spot, because she was going to bump into the piano. This, I was told, cost her the job. Apparently this move was taken as wanting the spotlight; all she did was try not to crash into the piano. Phil conferred with Dennis. The answer was that she would not be hired. I asked why. Phil would only answer that she "just wasn't chosen." I told him that was not good enough. He just grinned. I was livid. I had to tell Darla, who kind of expected it from Phil. She said she knew he was giving her the audition just as a favor. She asked me why. I told her I didn't know. It broke my heart. I wanted to kill Phil. Rory went looking for me. He took me aside, because I was really loud about how I felt concerning Phil. He tried to calm me down. He explained that supposedly Darla said something to Morty when she was waiting that he didn't like. I checked this out with all the girls who were there, and they unanimously sided with Darla. They felt that either Morty heard wrong or Phil just used his buddy Morty as an excuse. I was going to fight for her further, but Darla told me she didn't want to be in a show where she wasn't wanted anyway. Things were never the same with Phil and me after that.

From these auditions we hired Don Stitt, Michael McAssey and Patrick Hamilton as the club owners. Patrick was also signed as the understudy to the male lead. Lauren Goler, Pamela Blasetti, Susan Santoro, Aja Major, Sharon Moore, Barry Finkel and Judine Hawkins would all be in the chorus, with Sharon as a featured ballet dancer, along with Mason Roberts, and Susan understudying the female lead.

The next day was a fiasco. It was truly a publicity gimmick. Rory had made the announcement that we still needed that elusive lead comic. Auditions were set up at the Comic Strip, and the media covered the event. The newspapers gave it a blurb, while WABC covered it for the news at 5:00. We saw 143 comics. Baseball caps with "LATE NITE COMIC" printed on them were handed out as souvenirs. It was really a farce, since there was already an actor we had seen that Phil wanted. Actually, I wanted him, too. His name was Robert LuPone. Phil was concerned that this massive audition might make LuPone uneasy. There was always that possibility that we might find someone better. LuPone was reassured that this was a publicity stunt. I took it pretty seriously, though, and kept a list at this audition, too. We saw everything from impressionists to ventriloquists to mimes! No one was called back.

While we were there, Patricia O'Haire from *The Daily News* interviewed Allan and me. I mentioned Larry Cobb as the inspiration for the song "Late Nite Comic." Allan was furious; he did not want me to refer to the events prior to our collaboration…at least not in print. I argued the point, telling him that it was factual. He didn't want to hear it. A picture of us appeared the next day in *The Daily News* under the title "Nothing to Laugh At." Allan was sporting a new mustache and was not laughing.

Don Stitt.   Michael McAssey.   Patrick Hamilton.

Lauren Goler.   Pamela Blasetti.   Susan Santoro.

Aja Major.   Sharon Moore.   Barry Finkel.

Judine Hawkins.   Mason Roberts.

I was warned about Robert LuPone; I was told that he could take over. I wanted to judge for myself. He did not look at this interview as an audition. Instead, he played around, read a bit and improvised on the piano. I found him to be charismatic. He charmed me. He sang "Happy Birthday" as his audition song. He played off another girl who came up. He had a comic flair, but most of all, there was an indication that he was a good actor. His credits were excellent. Zach in *A Chorus Line*, *Nefertiti* and Zach on *All My Children* were among many major credits. Phil was crazy about him. Allan was not as enthusiastic. He still thought we should keep looking. We did, but Phil was pretty much sold. So was I, if the truth be known. Actually, I never hid my feelings about wanting LuPone. He was the most professional we had seen. Rory was still looking. He was also feeling better that at least two of us were enthusiastic. Negotiations were started with LuPone's agent. It was becoming pretty definite that LuPone had the role.

On August 4 and 5 we were to hold more auditions at Equity. We were starting to panic, because we didn't have our Gabrielle. At one point Rory and Phil had discussions about the possibility of Bernadette Peters, but I thought it was unrealistic. Allan and I were becoming more and more angry at Phil for his audition process. We were seeing people who were absolutely wrong for the part, and no one was looking promising. Lynda was also frustrated; Phil would constantly undermine her suggestions, and many a good lead was ignored. Rory was putting pressure on Phil to fix the casting situation; he wasn't happy with Phil's process either. Lynda, it was discovered, was working another job two days a week, because Phil had made her a part-time assistant, and she had to survive.

One day I was supposed to drop something off to Phil and heard a huge fight going on behind Phil's office door. It was Phil yelling at Lynda that he could "handle Rory." I didn't stay to deliver the package.

Rory had to fly to California to supervise Alan Colmes's appearance on a comedy television show. While he was there, he followed up on a lead Frank Scardino gave him. There was a girl he knew named Teresa Tracy who had been in a summer stock production of *Hello, Dolly!* He thought Rory might find his Gabrielle in her.

Teresa called Rory at his hotel at noon; he was going to be on a plane by five. Could she meet him by two? She rushed over. Rory handed her two scenes and said, "Learn these." He headed over to Fat Burger for lunch. The lobby was too noisy, so she studied on the stairwell. She auditioned under an umbrella at the pool! Rory knew by one page that she had nailed it. She had been babysitting for an agency, had only $50 in the bank and had to borrow from her family to fly to New York to meet with the rest of us at Phil's office. Phil was not as thrilled. He still had the black girl in mind, and this might ace her out. He also felt that Teresa's voice might grate on people. He was right on that point; many people did make that comment, but it didn't faze me when she auditioned. I didn't think it was that big a deal. Allan was rather pleased as well.

On August 5, at the last audition at Equity, nine girls were called back for the role of Gabrielle. One was a friend of Larry Hochman's named Mana Allen. She turned out to be quite good. Debra Cole showed up. Although it wasn't public knowledge at the time, she was LuPone's girl-friend. Eartha Kitt's beautiful daughter, Kitt MacDonald, was there. It was very late notice for her, and she was going to be getting married any day. Veanne Cox was back, as was Phil's' favorite black girl.

Phil also requested Kim Freshwater to come back as a possibility for Gabrielle. He would not take no for an answer from us. A girl named Susan Scott arrived. The shock of the day was the return of Dee Dee Kelly. Inside of three weeks she had lost so much weight it was incredible. She looked much better. It also made me feel even more guilty that she didn't get the part. She still wasn't right for it, but I think her physical improvements were worth it all. She went on to be the co-host of *Attitudes* on the Lifetime Network and shortened her name to Dee Kelly.

Teresa, of course, was there as well. There was no doubt; Teresa was Gabrielle. I wrote "YES YES" on my comment sheet. She was given the role on the spot. I asked her if she'd like to celebrate and have dinner with me. She accepted. Later on she called to cancel. She said she was just too busy. I understood, but it turned out to be the beginning of my lack of any close contact with any of the leads. I was soon to find out why.

Chapter 9
The Rehearsals

On August 6 Allan delivered the new script to be used for the rehearsals. This 14th version (the three in between all had additional dialogue changes, but no more song alterations) was printed up professionally. It was thrilling to hold a script in my hand that had a deep red cover with a gold embossed title, *Late Nite Comic*. Now the first page included more than just book and score credits; it had Philip Rose: Director and Rory Rosegarten: Producer! The second and third pages had the scene breakdowns. The character of Mike was now completely eliminated. This was the last script that Allan ever rewrote completely. All changes that took place thereafter were made as we rehearsed…and believe me, there were changes!

Rory, in the meantime, was already getting his own publicity; he was written up in his community in magazines such as the *Great Neck Record* and *Spotlight* (which, for the only time in print, called the show *Stand Up*).

On August 9 a New London-area paper, *The Day*, printed the first ad for the show. Since we didn't know who the stars were in time for press, the ad stated that it was "a new American musical" by Allan and me. The highest priced ticket was $20.

During August, I was asked to write another song for Act One that would have David singing about the unusual places Gabby would get up and dance. I thought there was an overabundance of songs for David, but I was still glad to write a new one. I came up with "She Dances Anywhere She Can." Except for a slight note alteration, the crew accepted the new song and put it aside for Larry to orchestrate. Larry was pretty much finished by this time, but the song was put on the back burner until it was absolutely necessary to utilize. I think everybody realized it was overkill, and the song was dropped before it was ever performed. I do remember playing it for Bob LuPone in the beginning of our New London run and getting a favorable response. The lyric went:

> She'll dance on a park bench
> She'll dance on a table
> She dances anywhere she can.
> In alleys and hallways
> Wherever she's able
> She dances anywhere she can.
> It's really so funny
> We sometimes make money,
> And I've become her biggest fan.
> She loves the attention
> She dances anywhere she can.
> You'll see her on subways
> And even on buses
> She dances anywhere she can.
> The people surround her
> And ask what the fuss is.
> She dances anywhere she can.
> They love what she's doin',
> This hullabalooin'.
> They ask me how it all began.
> I give 'em my answer
> She dances anywhere she can.
> David, come join me
> Give it half a chance.
> Not bad for starters
> I think the boy can dance.
> She'll dance in the bowery
> And wake all the bums up
> She dances anywhere she can.
> In less than a minute
> They give her the thumbs up
> She dances anywhere she can.
> There's no way to top her
> And no way to stop her
> They'll have to introduce a ban!

But she'll just continue
Dancin' anywhere she can!

I was also asked to expand "Relax with Me Baby." The song had only one bridge, and since we were going back to the bridge again, I wrote an additional one and a closing verse. I loved writing for what was now a scene, as opposed to just a song.

"Think Big" was also too short; additional verses were needed, so I began to expand that song. It was particularly difficult, because, once again, the rhyme scheme limited me terribly. It was, however, a challenge, and I worked diligently until I had written a lyric that satisfied all.

On August 7 Harry Haun wrote in *The Daily News* that after going through 700 unknowns, Philip and Rory had finally settled on Robert LuPone and unknown Teresa Tracy.

On the 10th of August the first rehearsals began at 890 Broadway. This was ironic to me, because whose offices should be right in the same building but Jimmy Webb's. It was sad that not once during our two weeks there did he come by even to say hello. I'm sure he had his own situation to contend with. He had been working on two shows with Michael Bennett, both of which got shelved indefinitely due to Michael's illness (and subsequent death).

Phil asked Allan and me not to show up for the first three days of rehearsal, which involved mostly the dance staff and LuPone. Phil said he needed that time alone. We were a little annoyed, but decided to give him the space he requested. This was highly unusual, since most directors introduce the creators to the cast on the very first day.

I made myself useful during this time and played piano for Anthony Newley on Alan Colmes's WNBC radio show. It was an absolutely wonderful experience. Newley didn't play an instrument, so my services were necessary if he was to perform. I learned not only his standards, but a great song he wrote by himself, "Lunch with a Friend." He was thrilled to discover that I knew the song; it happened to be one of his favorites. He wished me luck on my show and told me to send his love to Teresa, who had been in a recent production of *Stop the World* with him.

I drove down to 890 Broadway on my bicycle; it was a beautiful summer day, so I decided a bike ride would be a relaxing way to get there. I had my Walkman playing my favorite Beach Boys and obscure Jimmy Webb songs. I felt great! I arrived at 10:30 that Thursday morning. I said hello to the cast and crew and made my way to introduce myself to the rehearsal

With Anthony Newley on the Alan Colmes radio show.

accompanist, Tim Stella. Tim was one of the most likable guys on the staff. He was so eager to please and made corrections in a most pleasant manner. He was a joy to work with, and he played my music impeccably. He later served as our assistant conductor and keyboard player in the pit, helping with the synthesizer programming also.

Rehearsals would last from 10:30 until 6:30 every day with an hour break for lunch. On this, my first day, I felt I deserved to take myself out to lunch. After all, I wrote all the songs these people were singing. My idea of a great lunch was a Blimpie sandwich and a Yoo Hoo. (My tastes are modest!) When I returned to rehearsals, one of our chorus people, Judine Hawkins, came over to say hello. She was particularly curious. What did I do on the show…write the words? I realized she had no idea what the hell I was doing there. I told her I wrote a little something extra…like the music. She laughed while I went over to Allan. He was there with his seltzer, looking a little frazzled. I mentioned Judine's remark to him, and he said he was pissed, too. It seemed that Phil had not bothered telling anyone who we were. It was not an oversight. He didn't want us to socialize with the cast. He wanted control—and for them to know who was in control. Allan complained to Phil about this, and he apologized immediately and introduced us to the cast. He then told us in no uncertain terms that any comments were to go through him. No actors were to have direct contact with us. Suddenly the reasons for Teresa's declining my dinner invitation and Bob's never even having coffee with me were becoming very apparent.

In the Friday edition of *The New York Times*, *Late Nite Comic* got its first official mention. It was a small spot in Enid Nemy's column, but it was a mention nevertheless.

On Monday, August 17, there was a read-through of the show. It was the first time the real cast was doing the actual lines and songs, and it was a thrill and a half. It was also the first time the Broadway piano parts were being utilized. Larry had done a great job on making real arrangements out of my songs. There was a thunder of applause at the end. It was just the beginning of extensive hard work.

The dance steps were still being devised, and sections were coming in every day. Phil had Bob in one room, while the chorus would be working on the dance routines in another. The cast learned their dances in a fair amount of time, but what they really needed was direction. Phil would tell the crew to hang on; he needed to develop things with Bob. His disdain for Teresa was becoming obvious. She was not his choice, and he was not hiding that fact. LuPone was a method actor and felt a need to overanalyze each word and think about things for long, drawn-out periods of time. Teresa would finally just go to lunch or practice her dance steps by herself or with Danielle. Days would go by without the rest of the cast being used. Everything was Phil and Bob. They chuckled and patted each other. It began to cause real anger amongst the chorus. They wanted direction. They were often left to fend for themselves. They read books. They ate. They were truly being wasted.

Rory invited Bob to the Comic Strip to see actual stand-ups in action. At first Bob was going to go, but instead he compromised by watching some tapes Rory had given him of Robert Klein. Bob felt that was enough.

At one point Bob sang a wrong melody. I went to point it out and was given a glare by Bob and Phil. Phil said, "You must go through Greg to correct Bob." From that point on I rarely had any contact with Bob.

One day Phil said to me that Bob didn't like the last line in the song "Late Nite Comic" that said "never yawn." I asked why. All I was told was that he couldn't sing it; couldn't he just repeat the words "carry on?" I explained that I worked very hard to have "gone" rhyme with "on" and "dawn" with "yawn." "Never yawn" had real meaning; when comics get on late at night, they have to keep that energy up. Yawning would be an indication of failure. He didn't care. He didn't want the line. This was my first confrontation, and I gave in. I didn't want to be petty; yet I wanted to have integrity. I knew they wouldn't treat anyone but a newcomer this way. He repeated the words. The original was never heard again. All this occurred without any direct remarks from LuPone himself.

Meanwhile, Teresa was always with Bob. They arrived together and they left together. She was married, but it was no secret that when she came to New York, her marriage was failing. Her husband remained in California. She had married young and was not happy. Bob was much older, and the role of David was very romantic. Bob also had a girlfriend, who would arrive with nice little lunches for him all the time. She was not very happy with all the attention Teresa was paying him.

I wandered from room to room watching the progress of my "baby." One of the most exciting moments was hearing and watching "Dance" for the first time. It was more than I imagined; I was so moved. This is one time when the reality hit me that this was MY relationship dramatized. There was a section toward the end when Gabby jumps into David's arms with sheer love and gratitude for her opportunity to dance at the Met. I actually had tears welling up in my eyes. No one could comprehend my deep connection to this scene. It's not that the scene really happened to me in my life, but the old feelings were there again. I wanted to videotape these rehearsals, but I was warned not to attempt this, as even the rehearsals are under union rules. I explained that this was to document the musical for my own memories, but I was shot down. It is truly a shame that those wonderful moments weren't preserved.

Late Nite Comic wasn't the only musical to be rehearsing at 890. I had fun hanging out with the casts of other shows. *Teddy and Alice* was one that was on its way (and met a similar fate). They were a nice bunch of people. I often saw girls who had auditioned for us, and I was genuinely happy for them. It's amazing how small the clique of actors really is in New York City.

I remember a pretty blonde girl doing splits in the reception area. She looked very familiar, but I couldn't attach a name to the face. Finally I asked the inevitable question: "Are you on a soap or something?" She seemed really annoyed and answered, "You may be thinking of *Dallas*." I said, "No, I don't think it's that…how about singing?" Now she seemed to be warming up. (No, not just from the exercise.)

"As a matter of fact, I do sing."

"A talk show…Regis!" I blurted out.

"Yes, that's right…I'm Charlene Tilton." She stopped doing her splits and started stretching in her light blue leotard. "What are you doing here?"

"I wrote all the songs for this upcoming Broadway musical," I replied. Suddenly I wasn't such a nerd. She mentioned her husband, and I mentioned that I had to go back to rehearsal.

While a run-through of "It's Such a Different World" was taking place, Phil asked me for a couple of lines for the girls to sing as an introduction. It had to fit the arrangement perfectly. I went into the lounge area with a pencil and yellow legal pad and spent the next four hours there for three lines! They were never performed loudly enough; consequently no one ever heard them. They were:

> Brilliant and new now
> He's long overdue now
> It's David's debut now tonight!

Astonishing that those three lines could take so long to write.

The club owners' song, "The Best in the Business," also needed some stretching out. The guys were so likable that Phil asked for some tag lines. They had to have a pompous attitude that was consistent with the rest of the song. Once again, they weren't easy to write, but they were fun.

> We knew 'em when they was startin'
> I even made Steve Martin
> No club has what mine does
> I wrote the jokes that Klein does.
> No one here corrects us
> Dangerfield respects us
> I'm such a brilliant fellow
> Gave Abbott to Costello
> I made a pretty penny
> On "takes" I gave Jack Benny
> Don't listen to the others
> Gave Groucho Marx his brothers
> We're the best; we don't need you!

Rory wouldn't have forgiven me if I hadn't included his client, Robert Klein. I was promised that these lines would be added, but no one got around to it, even though the actors loved them and rehearsed them on their own.

On Wednesday, August 19, *Variety* made the announcement that *Late Nite Comic* would have its tryout in New London. The cast and I were overjoyed at seeing all our names in print for the first time—all except Michael McAssey, whose name was spelled "McAwwey"!

On Thursday Michael was a bit happier; both he, the other club owners and our leads were featured in a photo used in *The New York Post.* The headline was, "Raising Cash for 'Comic.'" Rory was quoted as saying that he was committed to keeping ticket prices down to $37.50, as opposed to the new $47.50.

We had two full run-throughs; one was on Saturday, the 22nd, without an audience, and the other was on the 29th with invited friends. To the latter, Phil had invited his wife and Imogene Coca. I invited my family, as well as my publisher, Ray Fox, and Jimmy Webb and his assistant, Laura. Jimmy never made it, but Laura showed. I also invited a young actress named Nancy, whom I had met at 890. She was going to be leaving town the next day, so this would be our one opportunity to spend time together.

The show came to life that day. Everyone was at the top of their form. There was only a piano and the actors, but it was marvelous. The musical really showed signs of succeeding. Ray Fox whispered to my mother, "I think they very well may pull this off!" Allan, who sat in the back with his

Only photo that includes the "club owners."

seltzer, was quite pleased as well. Nancy never said a word. She smiled, thanked me, and I never heard from her again.

The following week I was told that the L.A. song would be axed. They said it wasn't working. Actually, the song showed great promise if it had been staged correctly. I finally got the full story; Imogene Coca had been sitting with Phil's wife and told her the song was stale...old joke—could never work. This was relayed to Phil, and the next day the song was out. I kept telling him that when I performed it as a solo, it went over great; making it a duet was killing the punchlines. He didn't care.

On August 26 *The Daily News* ran a photo of Bob with the chorus girls. The headline read: "Robert LuPone amidst lovelies at rehearsals." It was the first time the girls were seen, and they weren't pleased with the photo. Some of them were caught in unflattering poses.

Rory was thrilled; he made the cover of *Show Business*. I couldn't find a copy, so I took Michael Bennett's! There was Rory's picture and a publicity shot of Bob and Teresa inside. It was the first time a picture of our two leads was seen. Martha Swope was asked to do some publicity photos. The one that was utilized most was that of Teresa hanging on Bob's back with her feet in the air. These were not rehearsal shots, but rather studio photos for the press.

Allan Knee and I were interviewed by a *New York Times* reporter by the name of Alvin Klein. There was going to be an article on the show in the Connecticut edition on August 30. It was at this time that Allan made it quite clear that he did not want me to mention my conception of the show. He wanted me to project the image of two guys creating the musical from scratch. I thought that was ridiculous, and I had no intention of telling the

First photo shoots for the leads.

reporter that version. The autobiographical point of view was what was printed. In the same issue, in the Magazine Section, Mel Gussow (who was later to review the show) listed *Late Nite Comic* in his Selective Guide: Theater column. The listing looked so innocent of what was to come.

Teresa was getting publicity of her own. *The Palm Beach Post* quoted her as saying, "I'm practically playing myself. She's a nut." She went on to say, "I love this show. It's lighthearted with some real dramatic moments." On dancing, she said she had never had any formal dance training. "I've learned dance mostly from doing shows that involved it." On Philip Rose: "He's incredibly knowledgeable. He has those characters down, and if you have one question, he has the answer immediately." On LuPone: "He's the most incredible person I've ever met. He's so committed to this. I could have been incredibly intimidated or I could have said, 'Wow, I can really learn from this person.' I took it the last way."

Before we left 890, a fabulous surprise was delivered to the studios— *Late Nite Comic* posters. These were the lobby cards with everyone's names and credits under the logo. I grabbed up as many as I could. I knew my friends and family would want them, and I wanted a few for the archives. At the bottom of the poster was the name of the theater—The Ritz! I remembered the Ritz from my childhood; I used to cut school to see them tape *The Price Is Right* and *Girl Talk* at that theater. It was leased to ABC television. I still have some of the original tickets.

Another irony is that this theater was owned by the Jujamcyn Company, who, if you remember, turned down the show a few months earlier. I drove down to 48th Street only to find the entire block under construction. They were blasting every five minutes. I thought to myself, "Great choice…even if you do get some laughs, they'll be drowned out by a demolition crew."

Reality was setting in; this show was really happening. Schedules were handed out by Morty, our stage manager, and updates were posted on the bulletin boards.

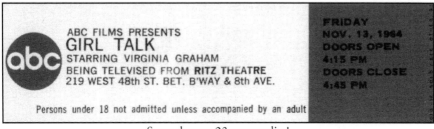

Same theater, 23 years earlier!

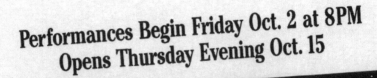

The official poster for the show.

That last weekend before New London I played piano for Alan Colmes at a comedy club on Long Island called Governor's. The show was a disaster. No one was paying any attention to Alan, and he was getting really fed up. About the best that came out of that experience (besides the pay) was a tee shirt they gave us that said, "Comedians Do It Standing Up."

On Monday, September 1, a run-through of Act One was scheduled in the afternoon. Tuesday would be dedicated to Act Two. On that day I met my father at Macy's to choose opening night gifts to take up to New London with me. I had been talking to my friend, *Drood* composer/lyricist/librettist Rupert Holmes, and picking his brain about all the amenities concerning opening night in both New London and New York. He was so unbelievably helpful, both in this case and even more later on. He even volunteered to come up to New London to offer his advice! My father and I decided Godiva chocolates would be nice for New London. I also got champagne for some of the principal people involved. Rupert said that although it wasn't a set rule, it certainly would be a nice gesture.

Wednesday was a run-through of both acts, but I chose to travel to New London to get there in time for orchestra rehearsals. This would be the first time I heard my score orchestrated!

Chapter 10
New London

On Wednesday, September 2, I set my Betamax to tape a week's worth of *Ryan's Hope*, left food instructions for my parents concerning my cat, Beta, and set off for my journey to New London. This time I brought my Beta movie camera with me, just in case I could get something on video.

I arrived at Penn Station, armed with camera, luggage and my bag full of presents for the cast. Allan and I were asked to come to New London a little earlier in order to do an interview with Michael Burlingame at *The Day*. It was no problem for me, since I was arriving early anyway. I urged a reluctant Allan to get there as soon as he could. He had other things to do before he made the trip. I emphasized to him that it was important for us both to be interviewed. He agreed, but only if it was done separately.

It was just a few hours on the train to New London, and they passed rather quickly, primarily due to my daydreaming about my exciting future. I dreamt past the show and into TV appearances, record deals and movie scoring. I thought of that obligatory Carson shot where I speak of how I wrote the songs while answering the phones at Catch a Rising Star. I'd perform a song on the show. Perhaps it would be "Gabrielle" or most probably "Late Nite Comic." I thought about what my next musical would be. Could I do it again? Maybe I had only one show inside me. I thought of all the shmucks who wouldn't give me a break, the ones who gave me the hardest time. I thought of my idols, like Jimmy Webb, and how surprised they'd be when the show hit. I remembered Charles Hunt and how he dropped the show. Before I knew it, the conductor was calling, "New London!"

The train station was not far from the theater. I was staying at the Radisson, which was right across the street from the theater. New London is an old fishing town with a wonderful history. All the stores and streets were from the 1700s and had a fabulous background. They even kept an old empty schoolhouse that had an extra room for the teacher to live there.

I walked up toward the theater and stopped to marvel at what I saw; there, on the marquee, were the words:

AMT'S WORLD PREMIERE
LATE NITE COMIC
SEPT 9—20

I couldn't believe my eyes. It generated a feeling I had never known before. This wasn't another record being released; it was a full-blown musical headed for Broadway!

I wandered into the theater and introduced myself to the ladies at the ticket booth. Mary Ellen, Carol and Carole were all very gracious and welcomed me to New London. I heard strains of my music, but in a whole new light. They were running down the songs in Act One. The first person I ran into was the drummer. He looked awfully familiar, and he said the same of me. It turned out that his name was Ron Tierno, and he played on my demo sessions with Lee Shapiro eight years earlier! He was a fantastic drummer, and it made me feel so comfortable that my music was in his hands.

I worked my way up to the office and met the directors of the theater. Charlie Peckham greeted me with a cigarette dangling from his mouth, looking like an old sailor—perfect for the town! He was warm and friendly and appeared to be excited about the show. It was their first production in some time. In fact, the posters were altered with a yellow sticker that read "The American Musical Theater and Rory Rosegarten present" where Rory's name had been by itself. Charlie introduced me to his partner, Daniel Morse. He seemed very together and ready for this production. A very

nice lady named Justine was their secretary. She even made up her own bumper sticker out of the leftover publicity Xeroxes.

Another man standing nearby was Arthur Pignataro. He was a very nervous guy who did just about everything at the theater. He was also involved in productions outside of the Garde, which was the actual name of the theater itself.

The first thing I saw on the wall of the office was a Xerox of their ad for ticket sales. My credit read: "Music by John Gari." Well, they got the spelling of my last name right, but I am not the old RCA recording artist by the same surname. They said they would correct it.

I rushed over to the Radisson to check in and zipped up to my room. It was a brand new hotel and extremely comfortable. I love hotels, especially when someone else's budget pays for them. I turned on the radio, and who should be on but me! I rushed over, turned up the volume and found it was a promo for the show. They had gotten a hold of my demos and used them in their commercial. I certainly didn't care that they didn't get permission (ASCAP even paid me nine months later), but it was hysterical that they were using recordings made at home, including "They Live in L.A.," which wasn't even in the show anymore!

I ate dinner with a few of the people from the theater, and the bill was covered by the newspaper that was to interview me. It was fantastic. I went to sleep that night feeling like one lucky human being.

The next day I made my way to a small coffee shop on Captain's Walk to have some breakfast before my interview. What a thrill to see shop window after shop window with the "LATE NITE COMIC" poster propped up on full display! I had my small orange juice and toast and rushed over to the theater for my interview. Michael Burlingame seemed like a nice guy and enjoyed my side of the making of this musical. He found it amusing that Allan and I asked to be interviewed separately, but he respected the wish. A photographer was brought along, and he took pictures of Allan and me sitting in the theater while the set was being built.

Rory arrived at the Radisson, and I met him later in the afternoon. I told him I was going to film the orchestra rehearsals, so he thought it would be a great idea if I also filmed him going to the theater for the first time.

Unshaven, dressed in a University of Massachusetts sweatshirt, Rory strolled along Captain's Walk and proceeded to give a running (or walking) commentary on the show's progress. "A year ago Brian Gari came to me with a script of *Late Nite Comic*. Now, whether I was an idiot or a genius, I decided that I wanted to produce it. So now, a year later almost to the day, we're here in New London, Connecticut, 1987, American Musical Theater (The Garde Theater), great old theater, 1500-seat house, where *Late Nite Comic*, in just a few short days, is going to make its world premiere. Are we nervous? Shitting a brick is a lot easier than what we're about to go through. But we're here...we did it. Allan Knee wrote the book; Philip Rose is gonna direct; Brian wrote the music and lyrics, and I'm the shmuck who's producing. So we're either right or we're wrong, but in just about six weeks from now, on October 15, six o'clock P.M., Thursday evening at the Ritz Theater..."

"I thought it was seven o'clock."

"Six o'clock.

"Two hours earlier than usual?"

"We'll be there early."

"Okay."

"... at the Ritz Theater, we're gonna find out if we're all gonna be millionaires, or I will be working at Florsheim Shoes. Now over here [pointing to the theater window display], this is the first display...*Late Nite Comic* [points to dangling ballet slippers]. Ballet slippers? I never wanted them in the ad. They've been haunting me for eight months."

"They should be [in the ad]."

"They shouldn't. You see this? [pointing to the man in the half moon logo] I think I know him. [looking at the *Late Nite Comic* tee shirts display] Even without asking us, they made up tee shirts. They're makin' a profit off MY play. See this? [pointing to their design] And they're ugly tee shirts. I wouldn't wear them to sleep...unless I got it for free. We're now entering the theater, cause in about ten minutes...it's ten to seven, we're gonna have a little band rehearsal to hear the second act of *Late Nite Comic*. Brian says it's great, but he also writes the kind of songs that Helen Keller thought were bad."

Philip Rose was already inside the theater, as was the music staff: Greg Dlugos was conducting; Larry Hochman was checking his arrangements, and at his side were his notating assistants, Emily Grishman and Deborah Eastman. I quickly went up to the balcony area and filmed the entire day's rehearsal from there. The rehearsals were taking place in the lobby because of the set construction continuing on the stage. Most of the musicians were local, including Tim Stella.

This day was even more thrilling for me than the day before. The songs and Larry's orchestrations were sounding phenomenal. "Dance" completely knocked me off my feet. If I loved it at 890 Broadway, hearing it in New London with an orchestra was beyond belief. When I heard "When I Am Movin'" for the first time, I felt that the orchestration was making it sound a bit like "Promises Promises." In no time Larry altered the arrangement. His hair would fall across his forehead in strands as he labored over a part. When he finished, he would always rotate his head to relieve the muscle tension. As I filmed the events, people arrived in the lobby to observe. Danielle was there to hear what she would be working with in the dance department. Frank Scardino, straight from the gym and dressed in sweats, checked things out with Danielle. Dennis Dennehy came in to listen and figure out a few more dance sequences.

Suddenly the company started bopping by in dribs and drabs. Aja waved to the camera, as Mason and Barry strolled in behind her. Michael and Sharon started slow dancing to "Late Nite Comic." Philip Rose, wearing his yellow turtleneck, came running up to me with orchestration in hand asking about a word change. He then started singing "Late Nite Comic" in his operatic style. Lauren Goler dropped in to listen and find the others.

There was a bit of a commotion when the cast discovered where they were staying. The motel in their budget was on the seedy side. They stayed the first night, but wanted to move as soon as possible. Pam Blasetti found another motel, so they switched. Ironically, it was at this new motel that Barry Finkel was robbed. It seemed that he had left his door open late one night for just a minute to stop by Sharon's room. He went back to his room to find that he was robbed of several items, including his first week's pay.

On Friday a press conference was held at noon. All local radio, television and newspaper reporters gathered in the lobby. *The Day* already had a picture of Bob and Teresa in their weekend entertainment section. Seated at a makeshift conference table was Rory in the middle, Bob on his right and Teresa on his left. A representative from The United Way started things

THE AMERICAN MUSICAL THEATER

```
CONTACT:    Evelyn Warner Casey
            Daniel Morse
TITLE:      Public Relations
            Associate Producer
SUBJECT:    LATE NITE COMIC
PHONE:      563-6548; 444-6766
```

THE AMERICAN MUSICAL THEATER

INVITES YOU

to

A PRESS CONFERENCE

for
THE WORLD PREMIERE OF

LATE NITE COMIC

Interview the successful 25-year old

Rory Rosegarten, co-producer of the show and co-stars

ROBERT LuPONE & TERESA TRACY

on

FRIDAY, SEPTEMBER 4th

at 12:00 Noon

AT The Garde Theater
325 Captain's Walk
New London, Connecticut

off with welcoming the show to New London and announcing that 50 cents of every ticket would be contributed to The United Way. Then Evelyn Warner, AMT's publicist, introduced Rory as the "remarkable 25-year-old producer." The first question from the press was "How does it feel to be a 25-year-old producer of a forthcoming Broadway show?" Rory answered that he was "living a dream." He added that "there was no dissension [amongst the company] anywhere!" He said that cast members were happily rooming together. When Bob LuPone was commenting about the hiring of Teresa, he said that "there was a chemical connection [he had] with Teresa." Rory jumped in with "they were not the cast members he had referred to earlier as rooming together!"

Rory was asked about the backers and if they were choosing to be anonymous. He answered "Yes...I can't show everyone all my tricks!" When Teresa was asked about what made the show so enjoyable for her, her reply was "the storyline." Bob and Rory added that "the music was really good."

They were all asked if they could pick a future hit from the score. Bob said he "wouldn't touch that with a ten-foot pole; there's a lot of stuff there that's really good." Rory interjected, "You'll be whistling the songs."

Another question asked was about the very short time span until Broadway. Rory claimed we were four weeks ahead of schedule. "It's in good shape, GREAT shape!" He also announced the low ticket price he chose for Broadway: $37.50. Bob pointed to the "tremendous foresight" that made the show work.

A very pretty, but businesslike reporter by the name of Kathy Calnen from Channel 26, a cable station in New London, interviewed Allan and me. This was Allan's first interview for television. None of his footage was used.

"How do you feel now that the play is in production—as a writer?

"Ah, nervous, excited…confused at times watching all the elements try to come together as one whole…and, ah, just trying to keep calm."

"What's your assessment of the musical?"

"Of our musical?"

"Yes."

"It's [laughing nervously] exciting. It's very new to me. There are moments of great highs and moments of great doubts. Mainly highs."

"Is it what you envisioned when you were writing this book... and then seeing it onstage...is it what you envisioned or is it different?"

"Um...at times [stuttering] at times it's what I envisioned, at times it's more than what I envisioned. Ah...I see most things through my own eyes, and everything is like me dancing, me singing; I'm all the characters. So first it's an adjustment that other people are doing this...and then I realize that it's more than I would have done...and that's when I'm very happy...when it's more than I would've done. Cause for two years it's me and Brian on it, doing everything, and now it's suddenly other people. It's almost a psychological adjustment, but it's a terrific adjustment. I mean I'm really happy about that. I think the most exciting thing is watching something that you wrote, that you repeat for two years, give it to someone else who really comes to life with it and makes it their own. I think that's what the theatre is about...the transformation. I'm afraid it's never gonna happen, but it does happen."

Channel 26 decided to use my portion, where I talked about seeing my relationship portrayed on the stage. I guess it had more of a personal touch. I called Kathy Calnen to see if she'd have dinner with me; the answer was yes. We decided to meet on Monday night.

Later in the day someone tipped me off that there was a free buffet at the Radisson in the late afternoons. My breaks were now spent there. I mean, how could I turn down free food? Seated at the piano in the lounge was a man named Ed. We spoke for a while, and it came up that I wrote the score to the show across the street. He was well aware of the show and asked me to bring in some of the music so that he could play it. Imagine Rory's surprise when he came downstairs one day and heard "Gabrielle" in the Radisson lounge. He loved the built-in publicity!

On Saturday, *The Day* newspaper was free to all the guests of the hotel. I picked one up and, lo and behold, there was a big photo of Rory with Bob and Teresa. I grabbed up all the remaining copies! The publicity was really coming. I walked over a little bridge into another part of town and treated myself to a sandwich and a shake at Friendly's.

The set was still not ready; it seemed the turntables were never measured, so the rest of the set had to be shaved down three inches to fit correctly. It was a disaster. (This happened again at the Ritz.) The cast and crew were whisked

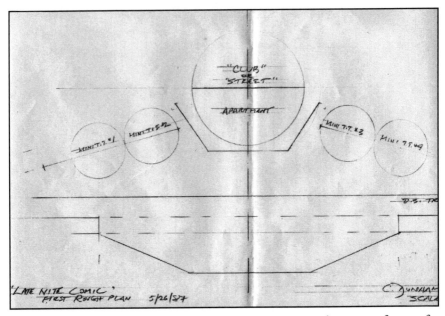

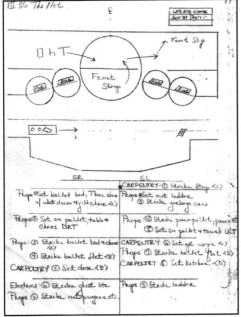

over to another part of town for rehearsals in a social center. It was kind of a mess, but some things did get accomplished. Later in the day we finally got a chance to utilize the theater. All scene changes depended upon the turntables; the tech crew ran them when given each cue. It was not as smooth as on paper.

Dinnertime, unfortunately, was not usually a fun time for me. I was sort of an outcast. Rory hung out with Frank, and perhaps Phil, in the more expensive dining room of the hotel. They usually didn't ask me to join them. Dennis and Danielle were together, while Allan found a friend in our stage manager, Brian. The cast had their own clique or a car to get them to an Italian pub called Mr. G's. I don't think any of it was personal, it was just that I wasn't around when they would make their plans, and by the time I found out, everyone was gone.

Sunday brought more publicity. This time it was finally something on Allan and me. It was the article written for *The Day* from our interviews earlier that week. *The New Haven Register* printed a huge photo of Bob the same day. The article was culled from the press conference.

Once again rehearsals were slow, so Arthur Pignataro asked me if I wanted to come with him to the Colonial Theater in nearby Westerly, Rhode Island, to see a production of *Company*. He was the production stage manager, so there was a reason for this pilgrimage. Actually, it was a lot of fun and a much needed diversion for me. It was a small production with two keyboards! The cast stayed there in a kind of rooming house adjoining the theater. (What some actors have to do to work!)

When we arrived back that night, the cast was sitting on the stage to hear the fully orchestrated songs for the first time. As the orchestra ran through each song, the cast applauded like mad. It really sounded like a hit score. When it

Brian,

I think you deserve another payment. This is just a little something extra to reward you for all these extra hours you put into life. While everybody else is sleeping, or just plain out having a good time, you are working late hours, burning the candle at both ends, as they say, trying to make this a better world for people like Phil Rose and Darla Hill to live in.

As for me, I am giving it my best shot and it doesn't seem quite good enough. I don't think I'll ever feel what I do is good enough. I just spoke to my older brother and he said I'm entitled to be a crazy man - that I'm not hurting anyone else with my craziness - and just go with it. I felt that was very comforting. But, of course, I did not believe him.

I wish I were back in school. I hated school. But I'd like to start again - and this time I'd do it right - or better. I'd sell my soul to the devil for a little genuine joy. But I made that deal a long time ago and it didn't work.

A.

Words of support from Allan.

was all over, Bob and the cast gave Larry Hochman a wild ovation. I'm sure Larry appreciated it. He deserved it. What hurt was that not one word of praise was said to me about my score. While it is true that one has to have one's own sense of worth, a songwriter, like everyone else, lives for the one pat on the back and the words "nice work." I never got that. I wish I had.

Monday was Labor Day, and the streets were pretty empty. I think there were some Equity rules limiting the rehearsal hours, so a rough dress rehearsal was set up for that night. It was to be an audience of invited friends of the theater. It was also a chance for other theater companies to see our show on their dark night. Daytime was slow, so I decided to take a walk around the beautiful town. As I wandered down Captain's Walk, I made a right turn past a Salvation Army shop. It was open. I rummaged through some scratched record albums and came up with nothing of any real value. I continued down the street past a curious looking shop with no windows. I thought I should check it out. To my surprise, I had wandered into the local porno store. Not a bad way to spend Labor Day! The only embarrassing part was looking up from a magazine and finding myself eye-to-eye with someone from our crew! We exchanged some mutterings that sounded somewhat like hellos and got the hell out of there.

Kathy and I had dinner at a rather expensive fish restaurant that night. We got along really well, and it was a pleasure being in the company of a female again. Although I was at the theater every night, we decided to try to see each other again after the opening.

The show that night was fair. Lines were being blown, sets were not working right, and we were going to have our New London premiere two days later. Rory was still very much concerned about the book and the direction. There were still very few laughs and no real direction. Phil kept reassuring Rory, but Rory was not becoming more assured. Phil was also quite angry with him for allowing the press to review the show so soon. He made Rory aware of *The New Haven Register's* critic being a "stringer" for *Variety*. This meant that if he hated it in New London, word would reach New York by way of his same review in *Variety*. This could prejudice a lot of critics, who read about all the new shows coming into New York. Rory basically ignored this warning, and unfortunately, Phil was right.

Wednesday, September 7, was our opening. Ready or not, we were proceeding. I gave the cast and all the musicians in the orchestra their gifts and wished them luck. My parents sent cards to the cast. They were put up on the backstage board. My parents and in-laws sent me congratulatory telegrams. My sister sent a card. My father sent one with Fred Flintstone on the cover that read, "You've come a long way since the Flintstones. I'm very proud. If God has a sense of humor, he might like the show. Love, Dad" ASCAP sent me a telegram saying they were waiting in NYC for a smash hit. My friend Tim Blixt said, "Break a leg...or go into traction with multiple fractures, if that's what it takes to make a hit." Even Darla sent a telegram, "My thoughts and love are with you tonight. Good luck. I love you."

New London Playbill.

The playbills were handed out. I read through one and found it quite interesting. Bob's bio was almost an entire page! The man has credits, but geez! Among others, Teresa thanked her husband for all his love and support. Allan's name was spelled wrong, which was just what he needed to see. Philip was listed as director, producer and AUTHOR, which is just what Allan needed to see. The rest of the cast was disappointed with their credits as dancer/singer ensemble; it gave them no distinction. "They Live in L.A.," which was never formally in the final show, was listed among the musical numbers. Rory and Phil laughed at my bio. I dedicated the show to three "late nite comics" who, I had heard, had committed suicide. Larry Cobb was among them. Rory started listing others I could include. He thought it was morbid and funny. I felt it was the least I could do for the memories of these young comedians.

Again, the show itself was not perfect. Mistakes were made, but the bottom line was that it was a comedy with no jokes. It was very painful for Allan. He was constantly rewriting and battling with Phil. He hated what was happening. He disliked how Bob was toying with his dialogue. He felt he was never saying it as written. He knew Teresa was being ignored in terms of direction. Despite all this, the cast was insisting that she was going to win a Tony. No matter what I said to Allan, he didn't want to hear it. What we were both in agreement on, however, was that Phil was a disaster.

The reviews were horrendous. I looked for the smallest compliment on my music; it wasn't anywhere to be found. I was getting trashed along with everything else. No one was separating the tunes from the lack of comedy. *The Compass* said, "'Late Nite Comic' likened to bedtime story." *The Hartford Courant* said it was a bomb, while the much needed *New Haven Register* headline read, "Jokes and singing fall flat." Markland Taylor called the book and the score "unoriginal." Because I wrote about Gabby's early days in ballet, "Clara's Dancing School" was interpreted as a rip-off of "At the Ballet" from *A Chorus Line*. I guess no one can write wistfully about ballet anymore. "Obsessed" was compared to a Danny Kaye number and the title tune to one of Frank Sinatra's. So what's wrong with that? "Relax with Me Baby" was "Hey, Big Spender." Well, considering the fact that it took place in a hooker's bar with provocative choreography, I guess I can see how that conclusion was drawn. It wasn't, however, the song's original intent. And yes, this horrifying review was reprinted in *Variety*. I tried calling Kathy; she never took my calls or returned them after the opening. I felt like a leper.

I had to relay these reviews to my family; it wasn't easy. I could tell we were starting to die. There were moments when the show looked as if it might come together—those were only moments. One day it was good; the next day it was embarrassing. One night, in my hotel, I got a call from my mother and Darla. They asked how things were going. I admitted that I was probably going to have a big flop. Those words are hard to say even to this day…especially to my mother and estranged wife. It was humiliating. I felt I had been doing a really good professional job, yet I was immersed in mediocrity and amateurishness. That call was one of the most difficult ones I've ever had to endure.

I spoke to Rupert Holmes, who very kindly volunteered to come up and offer his help. My parents were going to arrive that next weekend, along with my friends Tim and Lori Blixt and Allan and Cathy Greenfield. I only hoped that the show would be better by then. Realistically, I knew not much could change…or could it?

Rory asked to see me. I met him at the theater and we left for a walk around the block. He revealed to me that he was thinking of firing Phil. I looked at him and checked to see if I heard right.

"It's about time."

"I know." I asked if he had a new director ready. The look in his eyes told me who.

"You?"

"What do ya think?"

"I know you can do it. You've done everything else; you know the material; you'll be great!" He wasn't quite sure, but the all-knowing image seemed to please him a great deal. He said he would leave Phil's name on the credits, but he would take over. He had already mentioned it to Bob, and it seemed okay with him. On the other hand, Frank was on the lookout for a seasoned director to save this very ill musical.

I called my parents that night to relay the news. They were thrilled. My mother mentioned that Tony Tanner should be considered. She would investigate.

I showed up at the theater at around noon the next day and found Greg and Phil changing one of my songs. "Changing" is mild for what was going on. Phil was cutting lines and having Greg rewrite. I asked what they were doing. Phil muttered something about needing something done quickly. I screamed, "I'm across the fuckin' street; I could be here in minutes. Don't rewrite a fuckin' note without checking with me!" I was livid.

Greg did whatever Phil wanted. I was not being taken seriously. This was my first show. I had no big credits, so I was fair game. I realized where I stood with both of them from that moment on. I relayed the story to Rory, who just dismissed it with "He'll be gone soon enough."

The poor reviews threw the staff into a frenzy. They dropped "Obsessed" and decided to move "Stand Up" to a later spot in Act One. The opening would now be "Gabrielle." I thought that was grasping at straws. You don't change what works. "Stand Up" was written with the energy of an opening number. "Gabrielle" was too slow for an opener. They claimed it would work. "The Best in the Business," which was getting a great reception (taking into account the fine performance by the club owners), was moved up earlier in the first act. That was fine. Act Two was now to start with "Relax with Me Baby" instead of "Obsessed," and the title song, "Late Nite Comic," was put into the first act. Mason Roberts's ballet costume had to be changed; it was getting laughs, and that's not where we needed them. Susan Santoro was coming out as an old ballet teacher during "Clara's Dancing School." That, too, was getting laughs. She was obviously young, and the disguise made her look more like a witch on Halloween than an old teacher. Dennis tried to change it, but it usually came off comically.

At one point Rory asked me if he should bother continuing with the show. He said he could save the investors thousands if he didn't go through with the subway advertising and publicity in New York. I said that if we've gone this far, we should bring it to fruition. He said, "You're right; I'm not a quitter." Impending disaster or not, I couldn't see not making the last step after all this.

On Friday, September 11, *The New York Post* said the second quarter of the new Broadway season looks "equally promising." *Roza* was opening on October 1, *Mort Sahl* on the 11th, *Burn This* on the 14th, *Late Nite Comic* on the 15th, *Anything Goes* (starring LuPone's sister) on the 19th, *Cabaret* on the 22nd and *Into the Woods* on the 29th.

My family and friends arrived in time for the Saturday matinée. It was great to see them. I had been in the ups and downs of this musical for over a week now, and I welcomed some familiar and friendly faces. They were going to stay through Sunday and take me back with them for the next two days that we had off.

My parents, knowing the hell I was going through, arrived with an hysterical gift. There was a store in Times Square that made up newspapers with whatever headline you wanted. This one said, "Director slain by com-

With my parents.

poser of 'Late Nite Comic.' Crime declared justifiable." I couldn't stop laughing as I hid it in the bottom of my suitcase.

The matinée was pretty decent. Also, I met an attractive blonde usherette hired (for no pay) by the theater from a local trade school. We had some laughs, and I asked her out to dinner with us. She was flattered and

EXTRA

THE DAILY TRIBUNE

Vol. LWF   *"A Newspaper Dedicated to World-wide Unity and Interest"*   Latest News — Photos

DIRECTOR SLAIN BY COMPOSER OF "LATE NITE COMIC CRIME DECLARED JUSTIFIABLE

Dietetic Foods
Use Farm Products

Panic In New York;
Menagerie Breaks Loose

agreed to come along. Before we left for dinner, Rory asked my parents what they thought. They were very honest and said it needed laughs. My mother said she thought it was a mistake to have a natural opening number like "Stand Up" in the middle of the first act. Rory listened and said, "Don't worry…things will be changing very shortly."

My father contributed a line. When Gabby is talking about the nuns who taught her, she mentions one in particular that she loved, who got pregnant and married. My father said Bob should say, "Well, I guess she kicked the habit." Rory and Bob loved it. It went in the next day and got huge laughs.

We all chatted over an Italian dinner at the Gondolier up the block from the theater. My family and friends didn't hate the show; they thought it still needed a lot of work, but could possibly be saved.

The evening performance was better, in more ways than one. The girl and I couldn't keep our eyes off each other. I found myself incredibly drawn to her. (I probably would have been drawn to Roseanne Barr, given all the time since Darla.) My parents shared my room that night, and I agreed to sleep on the floor. Who knew this would be the BIG night for possibly…

The girl and I went back to her place, where we made out for hours, but her roommate came home, and it kind of cut things short, so to speak. Also, she didn't want to move THAT fast, so we agreed to meet again when I returned on Wednesday. I would trade up my two single beds for a king. When she dropped me off at the hotel at five in the morning, I felt as if I were 15 years old, sneaking back into the house. Of course my parents heard me come in and knew SOMETHING happened. Of all the goddam nights to get some action!

The next day at breakfast in the hotel Rory joined our table and whispered to my parents that all would be well—he was going to replace Phil in the next few days.

My friends, Tim and Lori, arrived for the Sunday matinée. It went pretty well, and Tim offered his comments. He said that although he didn't see many shows, he felt it was entertaining. He could tell it wasn't profound, but that didn't matter to him. Everyone grabbed up some tee shirts and posters and made their way home.

When I got back to New York, I called the usherette and got her roommate. I asked her to tell her that I called to say hello. (I didn't want my newfound friend to think I was just using her.) When I arrived back in New London on Wednesday, my king-sized bed was ready. The girl wasn't.

She was reluctant to come over and was acting completely different. She had never gotten the message from her roommate that I had called. We met in the hotel lobby, and she told me she had given it some thought, and she didn't want to be "that kind of girl anymore." Why is it they always want to turn over a new leaf with me?

While I was in the city, I arranged for a ride back to New London with one of the carpenters. I had my video camera with me, and I casually mentioned that I wanted to video tape the show for my own archives. In a snide, cocky manner he told me he'd report me to the union. Rory would get a huge fine, and I'd be in big trouble. I explained that it was to preserve something that was very special to me. He didn't give a shit. He would report me. Imagine continuing to ride with this obstinate jerk. He knew nothing of historical value. He was a union member, and he would uphold its rules. Screw history!

When I checked in with the staff back in New London, I was told to come up with a song to replace "Nothing's Changin' This Love." They could never stage it right, so it was going to be deleted. That was a real disappointment. The song had value and was a favorite of many people in the cast. The suggestion from Phil and Dennis was another song for the club owners about what it's like for them to be in love. I immediately came up with "Having Someone" and played it for Phil. He called in Dennis and then Bob and the club owners. It was thrilling; everyone loved it and started learning it on the spot. Michael, Don and Patrick now had a song written specifically with their characters and attitudes in mind. It was tailor-made. It would go into the show immediately with just a piano arrangement until Larry could get a more complete one done for Broadway. Greg notated the song for me outside the theater while everyone was on a lunch break. As we worked, he asked me to think about expanding "When I Am Movin.'" Any suggestion from him annoyed me after what had transpired earlier with changing my song. I did, however, want to please everyone, so I went upstairs to the costume department, where they had an old upright and played "When I Am Movin'" over and over until a bridge came to me. I went back to Greg first and had him hear it. It worked for him. He was encouraged by the change and thought it would make the song much stronger. He was right.

Another change was the chopping down of "Dance." It was too long for the audience. (I actually thought it was fine.) They weren't really cutting my song, but rather the expanded orchestration. It was still moving.

Original work sheet for "Having Someone."

Don Stitt was very good at improvising. One of his roles was that of a busboy whom David asks to cover for him onstage. He exclaimed, "But I'm the busboy" and muttered what seemed to be Mexican obscenities as he went off stage. It got great laughs.

At one performance Danielle spied the light of a tape recorder. She reported it, and the machine was confiscated. I went out to see who had been taping. I was flattered. My songs being bootlegged? What fun! It turned out that the guy was Robert Sher, who produced albums of unsuccessful musicals. He also collected every show in all its incarnations. He said he would get in touch with me about the album of my show. Oh, yes, he got back his machine *sans* cassette.

Meanwhile, "Having Someone" was added during our last couple of days in New London. I was horrified to find that they took the club owners' identities away and replaced them with ethnic interpretations. The whole point was to bring back these funny CLUB OWNERS—not new characters to digest. Phil was missing the point, but the song was working despite its misdirection.

Also, during our last week, Rory sent for his client, Joe Bolster, to help bolster the unfunny dialogue. Coincidentally, it was at a fund raiser for Senator Bill Bradley that Joe appeared and where Rory met his angels.

I would hoist myself up on the back of the seats with Joe and watch him cringe at some of the lines. He had had no previous experience in writing for the theater, but he was (and still is) a great comedian. He came up with alternate lines. Phil was annoyed. Allan was sometimes annoyed, sometimes just plain indifferent. They even got desperate enough to steal lines directly out of my lyrics! While David is sitting at the piano taking requests, one patron yells out "Unforgettable." He responds with "I forgot it." The song "Stand Up" included that line, which I got from comedian Larry Miller. I was furious. I told them it watered down my lyric by presenting that line ahead of my song. No one cared.

I thought Joe was doing the best he could with what he had to deal with. I asked him about how he would be compensated. He told me he didn't know, but that "Rory would probably be fair" with him. I thought it was the kind of thing that should be in writing, since this was actually being brought to Broadway. Joe eventually got a credit in the New York program as "comedy consultant."

Martha Swope came up to get some photos of the show on a stage. These were the actual photos used outside the Ritz. Strangely enough, the club owners, who were getting such a big response, were not in any publicity shots. Photos must have been taken, but there were none outside the theater or in the possession of the press agent.

Sunday was to be our last day in New London. Ray Fox was coming up to check things out and give some advice. He arrived in time for the Saturday evening performance. He could tell things were not going well. He could also see that I was being alienated from the rest of the staff. The

Robert LuPone as David Ackerman.   Robert and Teresa as David and Gabby.

(left to right) Susan Santoro, Sharon Moore, Pamela Blasetti, Lauren Goler, Judine Hawkins, Aja Major, Kim Freshwater, Robert LuPone.

Teresa as Gabby.

(standing left to right) Kim Freshwater, Mason Roberts, Pamela Blasetti, Aja Major, Judine Hawkins, Sharon Moore (front) Susan Santoro, Robert LuPone, Lauren Goler.

(standing left to right) Brian Gari, Rory Rosegarten, Teresa Tracy, Robert LuPone, Philip Rose (seated) Morty Halpern, Allan Knee.

show was in trouble, and I was the only one they couldn't find fault with. This is a problem in itself, since it makes you look as if you think you're perfect. It seems to be human nature not to like someone who doesn't have to alter much of his work. First, music is subjective—you either like it or you don't. They wouldn't have done the musical if they hated the tunes, so that could remain. The only thing they could rip apart would be the lyrics. I changed whatever they needed. Ray suggested that I fix "The Best in the Business" just to show that I was still willing to work with them. He showed me where he thought it could be improved, and I felt he was right. I worked for hours and tidied up some lines. Ray is a good lyricist, so I respected his suggestions, particularly in this case. The change went as follows:

Cause you know we're the best in the business
We know how to tell a joke you bet your life
Yes, you know we're the best in the business
Johnny Carson comes in free, but not his wife

This was much better than rhyming "paying at the gate" with "Johnny and his date." Carson was married again, and this was more accurate. The changes went in right away, but it was like replacing one brick in an already collapsing building.

That night, after the show, we all went to a closing night party at a bar in town. Pamela Blasetti and her boyfriend offered me a shot of Tequila and proceeded to get me plastered. Lauren Goler was as sweet as ever and tried to keep me encouraged. Ray came along and partied with us. He also found Lauren to be absolutely charming. I'll tell you, if Lauren hadn't been engaged, I would have been the first one at her door. There was something so warm and compassionate about that girl. The party went on for hours, which was not the best idea, considering that there was a matinée to do the next day.

I arrived at the theater early. In my frustration at not being able to tape the show, I approached one of the theater staff one more time. He told me to go up to the balcony when the lights go down and tape from there VERY secretly. I thanked him profusely and scurried upstairs. I checked where the outlet was, because I knew that due to the length of the show, it would be better to plug in rather than depend upon batteries. Everything was perfectly planned—or so I thought.

The lights went down, and I fumbled in the darkness for the outlet. I plugged in as I heard the first few bars of music. The camera wouldn't start. I pushed and knocked and did everything I could. There was no electricity

Ray Fox chatting with Jeff Olmsted.

up there. My last shot at taping in New London was lost. What a disappointment! Maybe it was for the best, because the cast was rather wasted after the night before.

Ray advised Rory a bit, but he didn't have too many encouraging words. Rory, on the other hand, told Ray that Philip was being replaced momentarily. He had a handle on this fiasco.

We headed back to New York with Joe Bolster and his girlfriend, Patty. She was another very encouraging female in my life up there. Our ride back was pleasant, considering all we had been through. Joe was in my corner, so we could laugh and joke about everything.

I arrived home to find the ad for the show in *The New York Sunday Times* entertainment section. The countdown was beginning for Broadway.

Chapter 11
White Out Then Blackout

It was Monday, September 21, and Darla was opening in a dinner theater version of *Biloxi Blues*. She asked me not to attend the opening, as her new boyfriend would be there that night. I sent a telegram anyway and said I would come to the next week's performance.

Meanwhile, Allan and I were still not getting any checks from the *Late Nite Comic* company. I did, however, get reimbursed for my New London expenses when I showed up at Frank Scardino's office. Then I rushed over to Alan Colmes at NBC and did a "live" version of "Stand Up" on the radio as a preview of the score. Interestingly enough, some time later in the week a man who called himself the "official singer" for the Alan Colmes show called and wanted to sing "Stand Up." Alan was a little taken aback. (He probably thought I put the guy up to it.) It turned out that the man had taped me and learned the entire song from the tape! He did a nice job at that.

On Tuesday Frank Scardino and Rory asked Allan, Joe Bolster and me to meet with them and a new addition to the staff; we were to meet the new director. His name was Tony Stevens. First we met at Frank's office to get acquainted. I thought we might still have a chance. His background, I later found out, was mainly as a choreographer. I figured this would not thrill Dennis Dennehy, but at least we were getting some fresh blood. Stevens had been an original contributor to *A Chorus Line*, but left to work on *Chicago* with Bob Fosse. He was well known for his work in industrials. I had no feelings, good or bad, other than being relieved that Phil would be leaving, and perhaps we would have a shot. We left Frank's office to head over to Nola's rehearsal studios on West 54th Street to get into a more creative meeting. We talked there for a while and just hoped for the best. Allan and I explained the core of the show and what we thought needed to be accomplished. Tony seemed to take it all in and was on to his next appointment. I told him he had my complete cooperation.

By 4:30 I was at NBC, as Alan Colmes had asked me to play piano for oldies artists Danny and the Juniors and the Dovells. I enjoyed my "other" life as a rock 'n' roll musician on the radio.

I called everyone I knew about the change of staff on *Late Nite Comic*. My parents were the first to breathe a sigh of relief. I think we all still had a realistic perspective that we had very little chance despite a new director.

On Wednesday, the New London review appeared in *Variety*. It was bad enough to experience it in New London; the reprint for New York eyes (and everyone else's) was devastating. I prayed no one saw it.

For the next three days we went back to 890 Broadway to work for the short amount of time we had left until opening. A decision was made that there would now be an overture. Larry orchestrated one from Greg's arrangement. I was thrilled. I had always believed in overtures and was finally getting one on my own score. I felt it was an exciting way to start the show. The guys did great work on putting it together.

Sunday was the sole publicity stint that I got through Henry Luhrman; it was a Columbia University's college radio station WKCR. A very nice, knowledgeable gentleman by the name of Ezio Petersen interviewed me. I performed several songs from the show "live" at a piano. It went fine, but where were TV shows like Regis and Kathie Lee? Some people mentioned (after the fact) that I should have hired my own publicist.

Things got even busier on Monday. I called the Lincoln Center Archives about videotaping the show; the response was that if we didn't come up with thousands of dollars, it wouldn't happen. Rory was not about to fork up that much, nor was it in the budget. The show would have to be lost forever.

At 4:00 Bob, Teresa, Allan, Rory and I all went on the Alan Colmes show to promote our Broadway debut. This was the one time I got to accompany the stars of the show. I was finding that Greg was being assigned that job without anyone ever asking me. An Arlene Francis radio show was booked with Greg on piano. Here I was, the composer and lyricist, losing every shot of having people know who I was. There would be a twofold reason for me to play; I could play it the way it was written AND get my name known. It was frustrating to say the least.

Tickets were being given away during the show. When Rory was asked what a producer does, he said, "He settles disputes, arguments and fights...which I'm certainly connected with now." New London was still fresh in his mind.

A NEW AMERICAN MUSICAL

A love story...
with a punch line.

Take DAVID ACKERMAN, a young man whose only dream is to stand on a stage and make people laugh. Mix him with GABRIELLE, a beautiful, yet slightly eccentric young woman who'll do anything to dance professionally. Throw in an on-again, off-again romance between these two kindred spirits, add some clever music, and the result is LATE NITE COMIC, a new American comedy-musical. Follow David, Gabrielle and the entire cast of LATE NITE COMIC up the shaky ladder of success. From the seedy piano bars to the great concert halls; from the romantic duets to the lavish production numbers, their pursuit of fame and love sets off an avalanche of laughs.

LATE NITE COMIC has music and lyrics by Brian Gari and a book by Allan Knee. Tony Award-winner Philip Rose will direct, with choreography by Dennis Dennehy, sets by Clarke Dunham, lighting by Ken Billington, costumes by Gail Cooper-Hecht and sound by Abe Jacob. It is produced by Rory Rosegarten.

Robert Lupone stars as David Ackerman. He is well known to Broadway audiences as Zach in "A Chorus Line" (for which he received a Tony nomination), "The Magic Show," "Jesus Christ Superstar" (both on Broadway and the film), and Off-Broadway as the title role in "Lennon." Teresa Tracy makes her Broadway debut as Gabrielle. She was seen in the National Tour of "Stop the World, I Want To Get Off" with Anthony Newley. The cast includes Pamela Blasetti, Danielle Connell, Barry Finkel, Kim Freshwater, Lauren Goler, Patrick Hamilton, Judine Hawkins, Aja Major, Michael McAssey, Sharon Moore, Mason Roberts, Susan Santoro and Don Stitt.

One of the flyers given out throughout Manhattan with half-price offer.

Bob said, "I kept telling Phil when he hired me that he made a mistake, cause I didn't think I was funny. I'm known as a serious actor." (He sang "Late Nite Comic"—very well, I might add—while I played piano for him.)

Teresa performed "When I Am Movin'," complete with the added bridge. She did a great job and was totally professional. I was amazed that I made it through in HER key!

About a dozen of Alan Colmes's listeners got free tickets for previews: I wish I knew what they thought.

Tuesday morning I was at Carroll's Musical Instruments on West 41st Street to watch the Broadway orchestra rehearse. I was absolutely elated. Part of our New London gang were there, including Tim Stella and Ron Tierno. With their permission, I videotaped all the songs. Greg led the orchestra, while Larry sat with the original orchestrations, checking each note and giving all changes to his assistant, Emily. There were rush trips back and forth from Associated Copyists with newly printed additions to the orchestrations. Every second of the rehearsal was cherished by everyone.

At 3:00 P.M. Darla and I went to the Michael Bennett tribute at the Shubert. It was a memorable time for me. I was so moved by the entire event. His loss was tragic for everyone, and I felt it from Darla's association with *A Chorus Line*. Jimmy Webb sang his "Only One Life" from the incomplete *A Children's Crusade*, which he had worked on with Bennett right before his death. Although the song had been written for that show, the lyric had a very strong meaning in the context of a Michael Bennett tribute. Stephen Sondheim's performance of "Move On" was also very touching. When he rushed away from the piano, I was crying. Donna McKechnie's speech really put me away. Being with my estranged wife, and watching McKechnie, made the connection that much stronger for me. I had met Michael only briefly one day when I was visiting Jimmy Webb at 890. His loyalty to the casts of *A Chorus Line*, and particularly to Darla, made me appreciate him as a human being as well as a great talent. The tribute distracted me from my own troubles.

Darla and I rushed away from the Shubert, as she had a performance in *Biloxi Blues* and had to make a train to Elmsford. I had to get uptown to meet my parents, who were driving there. Darla's performance as Rowena was just as wonderful as I had expected. It was great to see her on stage again.

Wednesday was jacket day. Yes, there were going to be *Late Nite Comic* jackets for us to purchase. Orders had to be in that day or you missed out.

They were available in two designs; one was the more expensive leather and wool, while the other was a canvas material. I decided to order one of each for myself. I also thought my parents should have jackets for Christmas. We were told we would get them in plenty of time for Christmas. I had "Mom" and "Dad" inscribed on their jackets. I figured I might never have a chance like this again, so I'd go ahead and get a great momento. Allan ordered his with the stage manager and got special blue canvas—but it arrived with his name spelled "Alan."

I also thought I should call the record labels before it was too late. Who knows how long we'd stay open? I had just done that WKCR radio show and met Stephen Sondheim's longtime record producer, Tom Shepard. He was very nice and asked me to call him. I did, but never reached him in time for him to see the show. I also called Atlantic, CBS and any other labels that might want to do a cast album, but I found myself giving away tickets to every secretary who wanted a free night out. No one of any power showed up.

I called the staff at Regis Philbin's TV show, but no one was interested in the composer of a forthcoming Broadway musical. I knew it was because I was representing myself, but there was little else I could do.

Stopping by the Ritz to see how things were going, I found a big banner with the name and logo of the show now hung on the side of the theater from the roof facing Broadway. There was so much construction going on around the theater that this was the only way anyone could see there was a show playing there! Both sides of the street were being blasted and torn down; dust was everywhere. I likened it to the ruins of Pompeii! It was hardly conducive for ticket purchases.

When I walked in, I saw Rory, who asked Allan and me to come up to the balcony to talk. "Guys, I just want you to know that the critics are probably going to carve you new assholes." I laughed and hoped he would be wrong.

Later I ran into Judine on the lunch break, and we discussed another song of mine that she liked. I had given her a copy to listen to, and she said she had learned it. I went into the pit and played piano for her while she tried it out. We were in the middle of it when Greg and Phil walked back in. The look on their faces was obvious. They did not like what we were doing. The next thing I knew, the musician's union representative came over to me and asked me to stop. I asked why. He said, "You are not allowed to play in the pit." I immediately knew that Phil and Greg had said something. I informed him that I was a member of the union as well. He repeated that I was to stop. I went after Phil. I screamed that his jealousy of my relationship with a cast member (and a black one at that!) was obvious, and he could go to hell. He was shocked. Later a staff member revealed that there were more people involved in keeping me away from Judine and the pit. I felt that Phil had it coming either way.

I called Rupert Holmes that night, and he said he often played in the pit during rehearsals for *Drood*, and there was no rule to keep composers away. He also said he would come to a Broadway preview the following week to see if he could help with suggestions. I was very grateful for his support.

During the rehearsals I found new lines and new pieces of business being inserted into the show. LuPone had a line about getting his education from an Italian University—Whatsa Matter U. I'm sure he thought this contribution would help. It got the usual groans every night. Joe Bolster, on the other hand, had some clever lines like, "You wanna hear my impression of Michael Jackson? Nice guy, good singer, face is always changing. That's just my impression." It was certainly a better joke, but good jokes alone were not going to save this show.

One of the worst changes was Phil Rose's inclusion of a conga. It was supposed to happen when David and Gabrielle are walking around the city, and she suddenly breaks into dance. Well, no ballet dancer I ever knew would have broken into a conga! This was so dated, and even though I voiced my opinion, it remained in—and an embarrassment—til the day we closed.

Friday arrived with a *New York Post* item proclaiming "'Late Nite Comic' with Robert LuPone." It was the announcement that previews would begin that night. All day I was busy putting together my list of people who needed tickets for opening night. I was entitled to two free ones, but the rest had to be paid for.

The first preview started with the addition of the overture. To hear it in rehearsals was great, but in a Broadway theater it was indescribable. We had the legendary Abe Jacob in charge of sound. His work was well respected in the theatre world, and I was proud that he was involved in our show.

The set looked somewhat different. On the wall of the comedy club was a blackboard that had comedians' names on it. Obviously Rory was in on this, as the names were very familiar. They were actual comics I had worked with at the Comic Strip! To see names like D.F. Sweedler and even Joe Bolster was a real kick. The show was basically the same as in New London, except that "Having Someone" was now orchestrated. Once again

Larry Hochman did a superb job—and on such short notice. My parents were both there and were apprehensive, yet proud.

On Saturday I decided to make the inevitable call. I was going to tell the inspiration of the show, Janet, that the musical was opening on Broadway. This would be my first contact with her in twelve years, other than a brief meeting on a street corner a few years before. I was very nervous dialing her number. I knew she was married and had a child, but I was hoping she would answer. She did. I asked her, "Guess who this is?" She gave me a half-dozen male names other than mine. I finally revealed my identity.

"Janet, believe it or not, I wrote a musical inspired by our relationship. I would like to give you and your husband opening night tickets."

"That's very flattering. Should I speak to a lawyer?"

I laughed nervously. "It's really a tribute to you in many ways." She said she was very busy in publishing and with her child. She didn't think she could squeeze it in, but thank you just the same. I was devastated. Here was the woman who inspired it all, the girl I loved, the girl who broke my heart, and she was doing it again! The call ended with "Good luck." I couldn't believe it. I swore I would never contact her again. How could anyone not want to see a musical based on herself? It really depressed me.

I immediately went back to business and called Joe Franklin to see if he would book me on his TV show. I was getting no publicity, so I thought perhaps he might give me some exposure. He booked me for the 12th to air on the 13th. He also slated me for his radio show that night at midnight.

I then got ready for the theater. We had our first matinée that day. Previews were becoming a constant worry; new dialogue was being inserted constantly, and because of the turntable design of the sets, things were not turning and/or breaking daily.

Larry Hochman had invited our French horn player, Kathy Morse, and her friend Lisa to the evening performance. We all decided to meet at Tony Roma's afterwards to get a quick bite and then head over to Joe Franklin together. Rory seemed interested in appearing with me, so I brought him on the show as well. Joe's radio show was rather informal, so I thought he wouldn't mind. It was raining when we left Tony Roma's, so there we were, Larry, Kathy, Lisa and I, jumping over puddles to make it to the studio by midnight. It seems that Larry and I both liked Lisa, and I found out later that they went out for quite some time after that night. Lucky guy!

Rory and I plugged the show like crazy on the broadcast. Rory mentioned that "Philip Rose directed." Joe commented, "Marvelous director."

Rory answered, "Yes, great director."

On Sunday, Philip Rose got the news; his services were no longer needed. Tony Stevens had arrived. An insert was included in all future playbills that read, "Philip Rose voluntarily withdrew as director of 'Late Nite Comic' as of October 4, 1987." He immediately requested that his name be whited out of all the playbills! This was going to be an unbelievable task, and one that the critics were going to have a ball with. It leaked into the paper on Friday when *The New York Post* called it "Comic Changes— There has been a parting of the ways between 'Late Nite Comic' producer Rory Rosegarten and the show's director, Philip Rose. According to a spokesperson for the show, 'Tony Stevens has been brought in as a consultant to help in certain problem areas.' The spokesperson insisted the parting is 'friendly' and says Rosegarten still considers Rose 'a member of the 'Late Nite Comic' family.'" The interesting thing was that Tony Stevens didn't want his name on it either. It was becoming the show with the invisible director.

The new playbill finally gave the ensemble players individual role names as opposed to the New London generic "ensemble" credit. I think the cast was pleased. The playbill also sported an interesting change; Teresa had eliminated her husband's name from her bio.

I called Janet's old roommate and dancer friend, Garielle, to invite her to the show. The reception from her was a far cry from the one I got from Janet. All she kept saying during the show was, "Janet should be seeing this." She was really enjoying it, and seeing a situation she had originally been a part of portrayed on a stage was an amazing experience for her. It was a small consolation for me, but one I cherished.

On Monday I spoke to Rupert Holmes again and set a time for him to come see the show. He saw it a few days later and commented that it had some problems. He wondered why I hadn't gone ahead with my original idea of writing the book as well. He felt I was capable and shouldn't have let it get so far out of my hands. He said the ballet was way too long, and

---

RITZ THEATRE

PHILIP ROSE VOLUNTARILY WITHDREW AS DIRECTOR OF **LATE NITE COMIC** AS OF OCTOBER 4, 1987.

We had our fill.

the direction was not helping. I basically knew everything he was saying, but it was pretty much out of my control at that point.

On Tuesday I was feverishly racing around town to find a present for my mother, whose birthday was two days later. I decided on a framed poster of the show with the inscription, "Because of your encouragement…Love, Brian."

There were no obvious changes with the first Tony Stevens preview. The inserts were falling out of the playbills throughout the theater, but no one was falling out of their seats with laughter. The audiences were considerate and seemed to be enjoying it despite the problems we were encountering.

There was not going to be a matinée on Wednesday; since Columbus Day was coming up, there was to be an exchange. Equity rules specify only eight performances a week, and since we needed the extra time for repairs, it was decided that this matinée be dropped in exchange for a Columbus Day matinée, when we would ordinarily have been dark.

It was fine with me, since I had the usual million things to get done. After spending most of the day catching up on odds and ends, I thought I'd drop in at the theater. Rory came running over to me very excited. "Where were you? We've been trying to reach you all day!" he exclaimed. I answered that I checked in with my phone machine and never got a message from him. "Well, anyway," he continued, "Tony has a great idea, which we need your approval on. We would like to take 'Late Nite Comic' out of the first act to speed things along." My first reaction was that they were kidding. My second reaction, when I saw they weren't, was to be flexible.

"They will still hear the song in the second act," Rory quickly explained.

"Yeah, but that's a reprise."

"It'll be great; just try it." It sounded sort of like the first time your pal tries to get you to smoke a joint. "I'll try it, but I reserve the right to have it put back if it doesn't work for me." Rory was ecstatic. I was skeptical.

My mother had tickets to see the show again that night; I prepared her for what was going to occur. I watched the show carefully. In the spot where LuPone was to sing the song, the piano lightly hinted the "Late Nite Comic" melody as though the audience would understand. Of course, they had never heard the tune before, so the melody was just any melody. I waited until Thursday afternoon to mention anything. I went over to Tony Stevens and said the change didn't work for me and that I wanted the song back in. He shrugged and seemed slightly annoyed, but agreed to do as I wished.

I went over to the Russian Tea Room to meet Ray Fox and a reporter. It was my first time in the posh hangout, so I just soaked in all the notables surrounding me. Most were just there to be seen and didn't faze me. I did see Paul Shaffer at a corner table and went over to say hello. He was really excited for me about the show and said he had just read something about it in the cab ride over. His enthusiasm was so overwhelming that I offered him tickets. He gladly accepted. When I saw him after the show the next night, he was so encouraging and complimentary that I was very happy that I had invited him.

It was my mother's birthday, and she was seeing the show for the third time on Broadway that night. She was horrified that "Late Nite Comic" had been removed, but I assured her that it was back in that night. I was also sneaking in my video camera, since it was never going to be taped legally. I sat down with the camera between my legs, so that I could direct it with my thighs. It had to remain hidden, and this was the only way to do it. Unfortunately, just as the overture began, the man next to me decided he wanted to move. This meant disrupting my set up. We almost came to blows, as I wouldn't budge from my secure position with the camera. My mother finally explained to him what I was doing, and things calmed down. The worst part came in the middle of Act One; "Late Nite Comic" was once again missing from the show! During intermission I ran down to the lobby and found Rory. "What the fuck do you think you're doing?" I screamed. Rory told me to calm down and speak to Tony. I said, "You're the producer—YOU tell him." I was livid.

"Bob doesn't want to put it back in."

"What? You tell him that's not his decision. He was hired to do what is written."

I then went back up to my seat with the camera between my thighs. When I returned home and stuck the tape in my VCR, it was a total blur.

On Friday I was advised to make the Dramatists Guild aware of my song's exclusion. I spoke with Ron Sandberg, who alerted the executive director, David LeVine. They informed me that it was going against my contract and that it was in the producer's best interest to restore my song before legal action was instigated. Ron told me to see what happened that night; he gave me his home phone number to inform him of the progress. It was amazing to find such compassionate people who truly worked for you.

That night, still trying to video tape, I watched in horror as the song was still deleted. At intermission I called Ron, who was totally shocked by

With Ron Sandberg at Dramatists Guild reception.

their bold defiance of my contract. He said he would contact David LeVine, but it was unfortunate that they were pulling this kind of a stunt on a long weekend. Monday would be Columbus Day, and the Dramatists Guild would be closed. The show would have a matinée, however. I confronted Rory again during intermission, and he looked at me in disbelief and said, "Didn't you hear? Bob had a breakdown today. I guess Phil just got to him. He was crying and saying Phil's name."

Somehow this pathetic image did not impress me. "Well, he's performing anyway, isn't he? I want that song back in, Rory."

"You better talk to Tony."

I went right over to Tony and demanded that my song be restored. I reminded him that it was a blatant violation of my contract.

"Didn't you hear? Bob had a nervous break—"

"Yes, I heard. Put the song back in or there'll be a lot of trouble."

I arrived home and slipped the tape into the VCR. This time it was an excellent picture of the ceiling.

On Saturday I called a friend of mine with an auto focus video camera. He was reluctant to lend it to me, but I promised its safe return. Besides, he knew how much a tape of the show would mean to me. I also called

Larry Hochman. I wanted to know his feelings about what was going on with the song. I could tell that he didn't really want to get involved, but he did blurt out that he didn't think the song's deletion was the key to fixing the show. I suppose he was a little disappointed that the title song with his wonderful orchestration was not being heard anymore. I asked him what some of the other members of the company thought, particularly Dennis Dennehy. It seemed that Dennis was still in constant touch with Phil. Even Phil was appalled by the song's removal.

Once again I tried to tape the show that night, but I just couldn't get the right angle without a monitor. Although there were sporadic clear shots, most of the show was not in view. My friend wouldn't allow me to borrow the camera again for another try.

In the Long Island edition of *The Sunday New York Times*, a huge picture of Rory with the chorus girls appeared. The headline read: "A Comic's Dreams Play on Broadway." The article, by Alvin Klein, started with "Now that he's an established entrepreneur in the world of comedy..."

Sunday's matinée was the sixth performance not to include the title song—and the sixth time I did not get a usable tape. The Dramatists Guild told me to come in for an emergency meeting at 12:30 on Tuesday. I would meet with

A note addressed to me/David from Allan.

David LeVine. I spoke to Allan Knee, who reluctantly agreed to attend. I use the word reluctant, because he mentioned that they screwed around with his dialogue, and no one came to HIS defense. I wondered why HE hadn't gone to the Dramatists Guild. I put it to him plainly: "The song being out is not helping things. You always wanted this song in the show. From the very beginning it was part of your vision. Please don't let them get away with this."

On Monday Joe Franklin had his limo take me to his new studios in Secaucus, New Jersey. I chatted with the driver about the show. I asked him for his card, since I thought I could use his services on opening night. I had made the decision that I was going to arrive in style for the first time in my life. A moped wouldn't do.

I decided to let the Joe Franklin audience know what was happening; I performed "Late Nite Comic" at the piano and revealed its current status. The strain was showing on my face. I didn't look rested. You could see it in my eyes. Joe tried to console me with examples of Kern or Porter having songs cut, but ending up hits a few years later.

One of the panelists was Ricky Ritzel, who was a friend of Michael McAssey's. He mentioned to Michael that I had been on with him talking about the situation. Michael told the other "club owners," and when I bumped into them outside the theater the following day, they all related their resentment toward me for standing up for my rights and thereby jeopardizing their jobs. I said if their contracts were violated, I'm sure they would do the same. I was hurt and angry by their accusations.

All of these conflicts were picked up by an energetic reporter by the name of Lisa Kaplan of *The Gannett Westchester News*. "There's no dispute," Rory retorted. "He wrote two versions of the song. We feel the most powerful version is in the second act. He's a little upset about it." Two versions? The second one was a reprise of the first. A reprise, by its very definition, is "a return to the first theme." Without that first version, a reprise makes no sense!

Before I left for the theater that night, I found a messengered letter from Rory on my door. It read:

> "Dear Brian:
>   In light of your continued attempts to obstruct essential adjustments required in connection with the play, which has been approved by your co-author, Allan Knee, and the consultant, Tony Stevens, who was engaged at your request and the request of your co-author to replace Philip Rose and make such adjustments, and your most objectionable and prejudicial statements to the cast and the press, which have already caused and will continue to cause substantial, irreparable damage to the production of the play, producers right therein and the morale of the company, you are most emphatically requested immediately to cease and desist from such improper actions on your part."

The letter brought me more disappointment than fear. I didn't want to dislike Rory. He had started off as a hero in my life; now he was my enemy.

At Monday night's performance a distressing sign was posted backstage; the closing notice went up. Rory reassured the cast that this was just to protect himself; if the show happens to get great reviews, the notice comes down. This way he wouldn't have to secure any more paychecks if it didn't do well. According to the notice, signed by Frank Scardino, the show would have its last performance on Saturday.

Rory called me on Tuesday morning and asked if he could attend the meeting at the Dramatists Guild. I gave a wholehearted thumbs up. The Guild called me to ask if that was okay. I told them I had agreed to it. They also asked if we had been paid our next royalty yet—it was due upon first preview. I said we received nothing. They indicated that this was also a violation of our contracts, and they would look into it as well. Allan called

FRANK SCARDINO ASSOCIATES, INC.
1650 BROADWAY SUITE 900 NEW YORK NY 10019 212 333 5252

October 12, 1987

TO: ALL COMPANY MEMBERS employed by
        LATE NITE COMIC COMPANY LIMITED PARTNERSHIP

FROM: FRANK P. SCARDINO
        General Manager

RE: CLOSING NOTICE

In accordance with the rules and regulations of your respective governing unions, this will serve as the official closing notice for the musical play entitled LATE NITE COMIC and your individual termination.

As this is posted prior to half-hour of the evening performance on this Monday, October 12, 1987, the above mentioned "closing and termination" will be effective at the conclusion of the scheduled performance, Saturday evening, October 17, 1987.

FRANK P. SCARDINO
General Manager
LATE NITE COMIC COMPANY
LIMITED PARTNERSHIP

FPS/wv
cc: Actors' Equity Assoc.
       ATPAM
       AFM Local 802
       TWAU
       Makeup & Hair Local 798
       IATSE / International

The dreaded closing notice.

and backed out of the meeting. I was furious and disappointed. He didn't want to make waves. I told him our royalties were at stake as well. He wouldn't show up. I slammed the phone down. That was the last time I spoke to him during the run of the show.

Rory arrived impeccably dressed and exchanged quips with David LeVine about their mutual stomping ground, Great Neck. I was not fond of Rory at that moment, so no cute jokes were going to amuse me. A copy of the Gannett article was on LeVine's desk. He asked Rory if this was the kind of press he enjoyed. Rory, of course, said he didn't. LeVine went on to ask him a few questions.

"How long is the song, Rory?"

"Isn't it about two or three minutes, Brian?" Rory asked. I responded affirmatively. LeVine went on.

"How do you feel about the song itself, Rory?"

"It's a fabulous song."

"When are the critics coming?"

"Well, they start with tonight's performance," Rory revealed.

"Okay, let me get this straight. It's a fabulous song that doesn't take too much time, and the critics are coming tonight. Don't you think it would be worth it to you to restore the song and avoid any kind of legal repercussions you will have to incur if you don't?"

I couldn't have said it better myself. Rory stood up sheepishly and said he'd try. He turned around and walked out. It wasn't a battle of principles; it was now his ego versus the absurdity of removing the title song from a Broadway show. I thanked LeVine, and he asked me to keep him abreast. He thought the song would be restored that night.

I went up to the 50th Street subway station to meet my father at Lincoln Center; we were going to look around the gift shop to see if we could find appropriate opening night gifts for the cast and crew. As I reached the bottom of the subway steps, a huge poster of the show was staring me in the face. Not even these tough times with Rory could take away the proud feeling I had seeing my baby plastered on the subway wall. I found my father already browsing through the gift shop. We selected little ballerinas on chains for the chorus and silver music stands onto which I placed tiny personally inscribed music paper for the orchestra. I found a beautiful piano key chain for Larry Hochman. Bob LuPone got a silver comedy/tragedy theatre pin, and I located a silver ballerina pin for Teresa. Dennis Dennehy and Danielle were given male and female dancer pins respectively. I also found special pins for the club owners. I decided at that point to skip Greg, Allan, Tony and Rory. I just didn't feel I could ignore all the crap I had been going through with them. I did, however, want to make sure that Lynda Watson got a gift. I knew she had gone through hell on this show, and I wanted her to know she wasn't forgotten. Maybe she was somewhat forgotten by some, as I saw her at one of the performances seated in one of the worst seats in the balcony. Surely this woman should not have been made to feel responsible for what Philip had done.

After I left Lincoln Center, I rushed home with the gifts and found I had only minutes before I was to meet Alan Colmes's "traffic and weather" girl, Jane Gennero, at NBC. She was to be my date that night. I grabbed my bike and rode downtown, locking it up near the theater. Then I went to pick her up. I spoke briefly with Alan, who was trying not to get involved with the Rory situation, as Rory was also his manager. He knew Rory was violating his friend's contract, but all he could do was to ask us to try to work things out. He agreed that the song belonged in the show, but it was a very delicate situation for him.

Jane and I strolled up to the area under the marquee. We were met by the manager of the Ritz, Jim O'Neill. I had always had a good relationship with Jim, and I smiled and reached for his hand as we were about to enter. He was not his usual self, however. With Jane at my side, Jim sternly told me I wasn't allowed in. The adrenaline zipped through my body like a prizefighter receiving an unexpected blow.

"What are you talking about?"

"I have instructions not to let you in," Jim explained uneasily. Jane looked at him in disbelief. She knew Rory from his being Alan's manager, but was amazed at this highly vindictive behavior. I grabbed Jane by the hand and pushed us into the theater. Jim didn't follow. We scrambled up to the balcony, where we stood for a moment to rest. Rory came along and looked shocked. He saw me with Jane and had to acknowledge us.

"Looks like your scheme didn't work, Rory," I commented. He looked at Jane quickly and then back at me.

"What do you mean?" he asked innocently.

"You're never going to keep me out of my own show," I calmly told him.

"Who did that?"

"Jim O'Neill told me I couldn't come in."

"The only thing I said was not to let you backstage." I had put up a note to the cast which obviously needled him. It read:

> "Dear Cast,
>   I feel compelled to write you all this note after feeling from some of you that I tried to do you wrong. It has never been my intention to do that, and I'm sure that somewhere in your hearts you do understand how much I feel

and have felt for each of you during what could be interpreted as 'difficult' times. This has been my baby for many, many years, and I have always hoped that it would shine through. Please understand that the exclusion of the original lyric of the song that got us all this far greatly distressed me. I asked that it be restored immediately, but unfortunately, I was ignored and it went on too long. This was not an ego-based decision, but rather a heartfelt one. I am sure that if your Equity contracts were violated, you would have been as incensed. The show has never been any worse with the song included. As we all know, we have been plagued by much larger problems. I love you all very much and hope you can understand that the exclusion of the song without my consent was a violation of my contract. You are all very talented and wonderful people, and I feel very honored to be working with you. Love, Brian."

Rory walked away from us. I pointed to a seat for Jane, while I stood in the back. (Of course there weren't any tickets left for us that night, so no seats.) Celebrities were popping by every now and then. I saw Elayne Boosler that night in particular.

While I waited to find a seat, I took off my jacket and placed it on my shoulder bag, which I left next to the concession stand. The song "Late Nite Comic" was still not restored, which was evidently the reason Rory didn't want me there that night. After intermission, I watched as the concession man broke down the stand, and I finally found a seat in the back row. When the show was over, I went back to get my stuff. The bag was there, but the jacket was gone. I knew nobody had been walking around except the concession guy. I frantically raced down to Jim and asked what happened to the guy. He asked why. I told him my jacket was stolen and he was the only guy around it. He said he didn't think he would do such a thing, and I should keep looking. I was a wreck; my keys to my house AND my bike were in the pocket! Jane couldn't believe the whole evening. She left. My friend Paul O'Keefe, who played the kid brother, Ross, on *The Patty Duke Show*, came over to congratulate me. "My jacket's been stolen—I can't talk!" was all he heard from me as I raced around the theater. I called my roommate at another number and begged him to open the door for me. He said he would meet me immediately. I froze going home

without my jacket. Not only was it a warm leather one, but it had senti-
mental value for me, as it was given to me by another songwriter by the
name of P.F. Sloan as a thank you for putting together his show for him.
Of course, my bike had to remain outside the theater all night.

Wednesday morning's *Daily News* had an article by Pat O'Haire called
"In a Family Way." There was a huge picture of Patti LuPone and a small
inset of brother Robert. It traced their backgrounds and commented on
the coincidence of Bob's opening the next day and Patti's opening in *Anything Goes* the following Monday.

I called my lawyer, Jay Harris, about my song situation. He asked me
to come by as soon as possible. Finding a duplicate key at home, I took a
cab to my bike, which was still outside the Ritz. I jumped on and headed
for Jay's office on 3rd Avenue. He contacted Rory's lawyers and firmly told
them that if the song wasn't restored immediately, there would indeed be
litigation. He was great. He said if it was not in time for the matinée, it
would have to be in that night's performance. I thanked him profusely and
went off to the matinée. A hand-delivered letter from Rory's lawyer stated
that the song would be "reinstated in the first act of the Play, beginning
with tonight's performance. Such decision on our client's part is not to be
deemed an acknowledgment of any wrongful act as our client asserts that
the omission of said song from the first act, and other changes, were authorized by the authors." AUTHORIZED! What a crock!

When I checked in for messages, I found that the Dramatists Guild
had called. I learned from Ron Sandberg that their pressure finally brought
about a check that was due since the first preview. That made my day even
better, but there was a topper still to come.

I arrived just in time for the matinée. Stewart Klein, the critic for Channel 5, was there, as were many television cameras. During the first act,
disaster struck. As LuPone was supposed to enter his apartment, the turntable didn't turn properly, and the sound of cracking wood blared through
the theater. It crushed the door to his apartment, so he entered laughingly
through the set itself. It would have been really funny had the critics not
been seeing the show for the first time. I watched Stewart Klein take out
his pencil. As the first act was ending (still *sans* the title song), light from
the lobby doors shone through as the concession guy was carrying in beer.
I couldn't believe my eyes—he was wearing my jacket! He must have thought
he had stolen it from a person who wasn't ever going to return to the
theater. Not so, my dear friend. I said, "Give me the fuckin' jacket! The

police are waiting downstairs for you." He threw the jacket at me and ran. I ran to the lobby—all this during "Think Big." Jim O'Neill was shocked when I told him. They went looking for him. Meanwhile, I found his cigarettes and paycheck in the pocket. When I saw him, I yelled, "Where are my goddam keys?" He claimed he knew nothing. He left the theater.

Rory stumbled upon this whole thing and didn't know what was happening. A film crew was there to do a documentary about American versus British theatre. They interviewed Rory; then they looked at me and asked if I was involved in the show. I ended up being filmed as well. The piece aired over New York University television stations months later. Imagine looking at yourself on film after going through all those events; I was not a pretty sight.

As I turned to go back in for the second act, I saw Stewart Klein leave the theater. He never returned.

Wednesday night was my proudest; "Late Nite Comic" was finally restored. It was a huge triumph for me. It still worked. More critics showed up. It seems there is a rule that reviewers can start checking out the show up to two days before an opening. This is a pity, since some shows need every last second to fix things. We needed a year.

I awoke Thursday morning to a phone call asking me if I'd seen *The New York Post* yet. It seemed they picked up on the story that I might sue Rory over the song's deletion. The headline was: "Late Nite faces suit over song." It said that I was actually suing Rory over "the deletion of one of my songs—a song very similar to another in the show." When would they ever understand that there was only one song of which there was a reprise? "I have nothing in particular to say about the suit," said Rosegarten. "Brian and I have been friends for some time, and I am saddened that the excitement of a Broadway opening has to be dampened by this. However, I have enough confidence in our friendship that it will be resolved." Incidentally, a few pages earlier in this same edition, *Late Nite Comic* received a "Best Bet."

I had hired the same limousine people as Joe Franklin had utilized. My date for opening night was none other than Darla. She really wanted to come, and there wasn't another person who could have felt the excitement of this opening more than she. Despite our struggles concerning the show, I felt in my heart that she wished me well. I sent the limo to her apartment to pick her up first. I set my video machines to tape every news broadcast. Then I donned the same black suit I was married in and headed downstairs to wait for the limousine's arrival at 5:30. When it came, there was Darla, opening up a bottle of champagne provided by the limo service. "Let's get the full treatment," she cheered. She looked beautiful in a red sequined dress. I was very pleased to have her as my date. As I got into the car, she handed me an opening night present. I opened it to find a black-and-white watch uniquely sporting Cyndi Lauper's lyric to "True Colors." I had never seen a watch like this before; I have not stopped wearing it since. Everyone comments on it every time I wear it.

Next we picked up my father, who lives only a few blocks away from me, and my mother, who lives only a few blocks from the Ritz. (Aw, what the hell…we had a limo…might as well make good use of it!) We also picked up another West Sider, composer Arthur Siegel. I jammed as many people as I could fit into that car. It was a hoot! My parents also got me an opening night gift. It was a gold piano on a chain, which I also cherish. The accompanying card said, "Keep writing… this one is only for practice. We love you, Mom and Dad."

We arrived at the theater half an hour before curtain. Huddling under the marquee I saw my sister, Amanda Abel, my brother-in-law, Bert, and their daughter, Allison. My best friends, Don Ciccone, Tim Blixt and Nick Shaffran and their respective wives all greeted me. Alan Colmes, who usually didn't get off the air until seven, actually put together an hour of prerecorded material so that he could be there in time for the 6:30 curtain. Chuck Irwin, who engineered the *Fame* soundtrack, as well as some of my early demos, arrived with a singer named Saundra Messinger, who had just recorded a couple of my songs on her new album. It was an amazing night; just having that much love and support was worth it all. I looked at the poster in the glass. Philip's name was now whited out of the posters as well. Upon entering the theater, I saw ushers feverishly struggling to make sure his name was whited out of all new programs. I also noted that someone had altered my bio into the third person, so my thanks became impersonal. Somehow it just didn't work to say "with love to the original Gabrielle…or should HE say Janet." I had had "should I say Janet." I have no idea who took it upon himself to change that.

I made my way to the dressing rooms to give the cast their gifts. They had already received *Late Nite Comic* bathrobes from Rory, as did Allan Knee. Bob LuPone gave me some very fine Tiffany stationery. Lauren Goler surprised me by handing me a gift; it turned out to be a mini-stress punching bag. I think she had things down very well. Her note said: "Dear Brian…This might make getting through tonite a little easier. Thanks for your beautiful music and have a wonderful opening! Love, Lauren."

Opening night ticket.

Next, I traveled down to the pit and gave the musicians their gifts. I got a great bottle of melon liqueur from Larry Hochman. (It didn't last too long, I love the stuff!) His note was touching: "Dear Brian, It was a great experience orchestrating your score—I hope we continue to work together on many other projects—I wish you much success on your Broadway debut!"

There were telegrams waiting for me backstage; the Shubert Organization sent one, as well as ASCAP. David Cassidy and his mother, Evelyn Ward, sent one. They are old family friends. Doc Pomus, the lyricist of mega hits like "Save the Last Dance for Me," said he "hopes it runs for years." I saw one from Philip Rose; it said: "Best of luck to the best of companies of actors, singers and dancers. You are wonderful and professional and I would be happy to work with any and all of you again." I saved that one as a souvenir.

I came back out in time to see the people seated around me. I went over to say hello to Robert Klein. I put out my hand; he didn't shake it. He said sourly, "How could you do that to Rory after all he's done for you?" I could tell that responding to that would take time, and this wasn't the time or place...and besides, he already had his mind made up that I had screwed Rory.

I saw Joe Franklin and his director, Bob Diamond, seated across the aisle. Charlie Peckham and Dan Morse came in from New London. Near them was the WNBC critic, Pia Lindstrom. In back of me was Jeffrey Lyons, the critic for WPIX-TV. That is a grueling experience, having a critic directly in back of you. The hell with it all; I was going to enjoy my opening night no matter what. The lights came down and the overture began. I knew this was the greatest experience of my life up til then.

Act One ran smoothly; laughs were coming. Yes, opening night audiences are usually polite, but this time it seemed as if the show were actually going to make it. During intermission, I tried to second guess Jeffrey Lyons and Pia Lindstrom. Did they realize my career depended on their words? They didn't even know who I was. I couldn't catch Jeffrey Lyons's eye; Pia looked and smiled at me. Could I take that to mean she was having a good time? I wouldn't know these answers until the 11:00 news.

As Act Two came to a close, the ovations were enormous. It really felt as if everything was going to work out after all. The cast, in the customary fashion, pointed to the orchestra and conductor for their bows, and out to the audience as well. Rory came running down the aisle and up to the front of the stage. It appeared as though he thought the cast was going to bring him up onstage with them. They did not. As he came back up the aisle, I went over to him and hugged him, extending my thanks and congratulations. He was not responsive. His parents totally ignored me. I found out later from his secretary that if there hadn't been people around, he would have slugged me.

My friends were all supportive, thrilled and genuinely impressed. They actually liked the show. My family went back to my mother's to watch the reviews, while Darla and I went to Sardi's to meet the cast.

The 10:00 news was on in the bar. Darla and I went upstairs and sat at a table with some of the chorus. Not much was said about the performance. People were buying each other drinks and simply enjoying the festivities. Alan Colmes and his girlfriend, Natalie, had drinks with Darla and me. As I looked up on the TV screen, I saw a preview of *Late Nite Comic*. I knew I wouldn't be able to hear there, so I ran downstairs and bumped into Teresa. She and I decided to pop into Michael McAssey's limo, because it had a TV. Stewart Klein began to speak as we entered the car. "You usually know in minutes if a show is a bomb..." That is how he started. He then referred to an old rock musical entitled *Marlowe* having an opening number that went "They didn't have toilets back in 1593." He continued, "...As for *Late Nite Comic*. I'd say about twelve seconds after the curtain rose, death set in. A stand-up comic is telling jokes, and he says, 'I went to a pet show to buy a pet peeve.' That tells you about the show's humor." I never saw that line in any of Allan's scripts. It must have been one of the many "jokes" added in later to try to save the show. Klein continued, "...a moment later a young woman tells the comic, 'Say, you're very funny.' That tells you about the intelligence of the characters. The two of them then start a shaky romance singing many numbers that are not quite up to the level of 'They didn't have toilets in 1593.'" Next they showed a video tape of "Dance," as he commented further. I was appalled. He hadn't even been there for "Dance!" "You may not care for her singing," he went on, "but she plays an aspiring ballet dancer, and doing her first plié, she tripped and fell." I looked at Teresa, who was turning increasingly paler. "When the tacky set revolved, part of the scenery got caught in the turntable amid great noise of ripping plasterboard. I looked at the program to see who staged this crime and discovered that the show was directed by white out; the director had painted his name out of the program, and I don't blame him." Isn't it incredible? Philip was not being held responsible at all! "For the record, the leads are Robert LuPone, who has charm, and Teresa Tracy, who has a problem." Teresa was now anxious to leave. Who could blame her? The kicker was Klein's last remark. "*Late Nite Comic* was produced by Rory Rosegarten, who, according to the program, is 25. Rotten kid!" Klein and his cronies laughed. I found out later that Rory was fuming. He even went as far as confronting Klein, who couldn't have cared less.

Teresa and I left the car. She stayed on the main floor, while I went back to Darla, Alan and Natalie. They had seen some of it up there and were sympathetic. We all went downstairs for the 11:00 news. As we gathered in front of the TV, a drunk kept yelling loudly at the set. I finally had to go over to him to get him to quiet down; I probably should have let him ramble through all that I was about to hear. CBS was on, which meant that Dennis Cunningham was next. "*Late Nite Comic* is a record low. *Late Nite Comic* is so bad that when I went outside for intermission, I stood under the marquee of another theater." I can vouch for that; I saw him there. "…and I went back in for Act II to make sure that *Late Nite Comic* was indeed, in more than nine years of reviewing Broadway, the worst thing I've ever set horrified eyes on. It certainly was. And that's 'was' as in please, God, the past tense. Please. By tomorrow they should all be changing their names and you certainly aren't going to hear their real names from me. The occasion calls for full-scale mercy. Let's just say that these two play a pair of nonentities we're supposed to care about, but it's hard to care while squirming in your seat with your eyes shut and your ears blocked out to keep out the god awful sights and sounds of this ghastly enterprise. *Late Nite Comic* doesn't even meet the minimum standards for a Broadway flop. It lies somewhere in the netherworld far beneath flop. If I tell you this is about a dancer who can't dance and a comic who isn't remotely funny, you get some idea of what a grueling thing is *Late Nite Comic*, and you can thank God that some idea is the most you'll ever get."

Darla held onto me; Teresa turned away. Alan suggested that we leave. There was the opening night party to attend. The only thing was—I wasn't invited. Yes, it is true; Rory's secretary, Ronna, was vehemently instructed not to mail me my pass. I didn't even know I was supposed to have one until I got to the Tunnel, where it was being held. The person at the door asked for my invitation; Alan came to my rescue, obviously figuring that Rory never sent me one. The party was horrible; it was supposedly catered by Rory's friend at the Carnegie Deli. There was no food that we ever found. We were allowed one drink; any more had to be paid for. Funny thing about this party—some people got invitations with a wrong address. The *New York Post* reported it this way on the day we closed: "Party Prank— The opening night party for 'Late Nite Comic' lived up to the musical's name. Two batches of invitations to the event at the Tunnel were printed up—one with the correct address (12th Avenue and 27th Street) and the other directing the chic, black-tie audience to 12th and 20th. We're told those ladies and their escorts who dutifully limoed to the Spike, one of the city's more notorious leather bars, were unamused. 'The Tunnel had nothing to do with the typo,' a spokesman said.'"

Darla and I took a cab up to my place; the limo had long gone. When we got in at 1:30 in the morning, I called my mother to find out if there were any reviews I could look forward to before I played back the video tapes. She

Party prank.

delicately answered no. Darla and I got into bed. That in itself was sad. We were almost divorced by now. She held onto me as I played back Pia Lindstrom on WNBC, who began with "I didn't laugh at all during *Late Nite Comic* except when the ballerinas came out. I've never seen such big ballerinas…big breasts and 40 yards of tulle en pointe doing the most excruciating choreography. But I had a premonition when I arrived at the theater and saw that silver tinsel curtain. Halfway through the overture I'd had enough, and then the curtain went up." At that point WNBC ran a videotape of "Gabrielle." Perhaps the most pleasant thing about this review is that nine months later I got paid for the use of the song. She continued, "…Robert LuPone, Patti LuPone's brother, is self-satisfied as the lousy comic who falls in love with the shrill Teresa Tracy, who uses at least three notes whining through this inane music." I grabbed Darla tighter. She watched my face intensely. "Her dancing is too inept to speak of. The lyrics, like 'Late Nite Comic, your audience is gone, you grab the microphone and carry on' are pretty pitiful." I was stunned. What was pitiful about that lyric? I racked my brain to see her point. The song had always moved audiences when I performed it as part of my nightclub act. She went on "…The jokes, like 'I went to a pet show looking for a pet peeve, they didn't have one, that ticks me off,' are uninspired. And the actors are overly concerned with being cute, doing asides to the audience. But in an amusing detail, the director, Phil Rose, had his name inked out of the playbill. I can just imagine him one night going to the theater and crossing his name off every single program and running out screaming, 'I can't stand this.'" Oh, if only she had known the truth. She concluded with "…*Late Nite Comic* is not ready for Broadway or Podunk. Get the hook."

I played back Joel Siegel's review on WABC. I was more or less in a daze by this time. I couldn't, however, stick my head in the sand. I continued to watch. "This production, choreography, set, script, songs are not good enough for a college musical. It's probably unfair to criticize the cast given the material, but suffice to say stars Teresa Tracy and Robert LuPone were not capable to rising above it. The songs, by the way, were written by Eddie Cantor's grandson, who got his musical talents from the OTHER side of the family." This obviously meant that my father and his side of the family had no talent. It was a remark that sticks with me to this day. The audacity of this man to put down my family in this manner.

One last review that night was by the man who had been sitting in back of me. He might as well have had a knife. Once again attention was drawn to

Philip's disappearance. "When a note is slipped into your program announcing that the director has voluntarily withdrawn from the show two weeks ago, that should tell you something." It seemed to him that Philip knew it was shit and wanted to leave! "Allan Knee's book is empty and Brian Gari's songs are routine at best." It was almost masochistic to listen to all this. It was also my career...or what was left of it. Darla stared into my eyes and asked if I was all right. I said I was. I was as all right as anyone could be after being kicked in the stomach for the last few hours. All I could think about was all the work, all the energy, all the arguing...and for what? This kind of response? We made love for what was probably going to be the last time together. Sleep finally brought an exhausting night to a close.

Friday morning I answered the phone with "Brian Gari's suicide hotline!" I couldn't resist. I had my choice to survive or collapse. I figured I'd make it easy for the callers. A humorous attitude would put people at ease...or perhaps make them think I flipped. The newspapers were out. It was back to some masochism. *New York Times* critic Frank Rich wasn't available; Mel Gussow took over for this one. He actually said some interesting things. In describing Phil's departure, he said, "This could be compared to the captain of the Titanic having his name removed from the ship's log after the ship hit the iceberg." Finally someone realized what had been going on. He criticized LuPone for "not having the soul of a stand-up comic." He went on to say, "If Mr. Gari's music and lyrics are pedestrian, Mr. Knee's book is a jaywalker, moving every which way to no apparent purpose." Much later Allan told me he did not hear or read any reviews except for Gussow's. He wrote him a complimentary letter.

Clive Barnes, in reviewing for *The New York Post*, started by saying, "I find it curiously difficult to have any respect for people who spell 'night' in that vulgar phoneticism 'nite.'" If I had thought, back in 1977, that I would be offending this almighty critic a decade later for how I chose to spell "nite"...He continued, "The music is pitched somewhere between a jingle and a trickle. Gari's lyrics are pitched somewhere between banality and stupidity, and the book (Allan Knee—as in 'I Left My Heart at Wounded Knee') is just pitched." He called the scenery cheap and referred to a preview where "a proper refrigerator fell apart on a revolve." Isn't it wonderful that all these critics had to see that same preview?

Howard Kissel of *The Daily News* wrote only two sentences, concluding with the suggestion that "it be put out of its misery at once." When confronted by a caller on a radio talk show about the score, he couldn't remember why he didn't like it. He just didn't like the show, so the score got trashed with everything else.

I don't like the concept of having critics to begin with; I agreed with Jimmy Webb's philosophy in the lyric to a song he wrote as an opener for his Dorothy Chandler Pavilion show back in 1970. It went:

> How many songs of love have you written in your life, sir?
> How many have you destroyed?
> Who is the man who doesn't pay to see the play, sir,
> And angry with his wife
> Takes out his knife
> And puts the show away?

I believe people should be able to read what the show is about to see if it interests them. Judging from my experience now with critics, I would never feel comfortable not seeing a show just because some people with no credentials (and often not enough sleep) told me not to go.

I got a phone call that day from a "friend" in the music business. He was calling to tell me how sorry he was that my show was going to close. I thanked him for his concern and hung up. After mulling over his words for a few minutes, I realized that he had never called me when the show was hitting Broadway, only when it got hit. I resented his call very much.

A person who wanted to remain anonymous called me with an interesting piece of news. It seemed that he had a friend who was a critic. That critic, knowing his friend knew me, let him in on how my show was being handled in reference to the critics. Our publicist had contacted them indicating that they wouldn't be missing anything if they didn't show up. This was highly unusual; it was also something that made the critics aware that the show should be slaughtered.

On Alan Colmes's show that day a caller commented to Alan that he hoped he didn't lose too much money backing that *Late Nite Comic*. Alan's response was: "I had no money in it, but I'll tell you something. Those reviewers are really vicious, and here's what really galls me. These reviewers come in and six of them stay for only half the show...left after the first act. I thought that was extremely mean. I'm not a barker of the show, because that would be a conflict of interests. I have no financial interest in it. The show is not a great show, but it's a fairly good show, and it's better than [what] the reviewers are saying it is. I think they were just gratuitously mean. Stewart Klein didn't even stay for the whole show, and he has no right reviewing it unless you see the whole thing. If you get paid to review the whole thing, you see the whole thing. You don't leave before the show is over. I think it's unprofessional. You don't review art by looking at half the painting. The music is great, the acting is great, it could be tightened up a little bit, but it's not as bad as everybody is saying, and it just really bothers me that these critics can really determine the fate of people's careers." Alan really cared.

Rupert Holmes and I spoke. He said something that really stuck. "No one saw or heard ALL the reviews except you. Most people caught only one or two. Keep that in mind. In a little while it will all be forgotten and just be considered another show that came and went." I appreciated that a lot.

When I walked down the street, I wondered who knew…who saw the reviews? I likened it to being insane for one night, stripping off all your clothes and marching down Broadway. You constantly wonder who saw you. It is absolutely humiliating.

I didn't know what to expect that night at the theater. Allan Knee refused to attend any more performances. Maybe he was right. The show that night was an embarrassment. I didn't realize it right away, but when a show receives such bad notices, the following night's performance is usually a fiasco. The audience is pissed that they bought tickets for a show that is now considered crap. They make loud comments to the performers and snicker at everything not intended to be snickered at. When David and Gabby kissed in one scene, someone made a smooching sound. It actually broke up Robert and Teresa. The audience even booed at the end when Gabby asked to come back—again! They had had it with her. Right before "Late Nite Comic" was going to be sung, the audience was particularly rowdy. I watched in horror as Robert stood patiently onstage until he had their attention. I was proud of him, and I rushed backstage afterwards to tell him so. His girlfriend, Debbie, was there as I relayed my congratulations on the way he handled things. He responded with "Well, I'm sorry you put the song back in." A wave of anger blasted my entire body. I just looked at him and said, "Well, I'm not, and I guess you'll just have to live with that, won't you?" His girlfriend apologized and said he had been under strain. I was sick and tired of all these excuses for his behavior.

I returned for the matinée on Saturday. The audience was filled with everybody's friends and families, and whoever else wanted a free ticket to a doomed show. This time the actors were going to have fun. The actual dialogue from the script was being thrown out right and left. When Patrick Hamilton was doubling as a club patron, Robert, in his role as inquisitive comedian, asked him what he did for a living. He answered, "I'm a critic." I must say I laughed myself. Later, in the Las Vegas scene, as Robert pushed his way through the god-awful tinsel curtain that everyone got tangled in, he talked about losing in Vegas. A woman in the audience yelled up that she was a big loser. Robert asked, "How are ya doin' tonight?" With that the lady responded, "Not in your category!" Everyone laughed. Robert quipped back, "Did ya read the reviews?" The audience went wild. It was becoming a free-for-all at the cost of what was left of the show's dignity. "This is funnier than the material, believe me," Robert added. He asked how the audience liked his red sequined jacket. When he stumbled on his next line about how cars would react to the jacket, Don Stitt came running out and gave the punchline, "They keep waiting for it to turn green." Again the response was hysterical. Don was great at improvising, especially in tough situations. Later, during "It's Such a Different World," the club owners are supposed to come back with the lines like "I always knew you'd make it, Dave." Well, this performance Michael McAssey added, "He's always been my kind of guy; despite what Stewart Klein said, I could listen to him forever!" I thought this was another great ad lib. The chorus girls had their fun as well. During "Relax with Me Baby," the hookers are supposed to pull David over the bar and attack him. Well, during this performance someone got the idea to pull his pants off behind the bar. I was tipped off that they were going to do this, so it was particularly funny for me as I watched Robert frantically trying to get away from these maniacs!

I arrived at the last performance, armed with my hidden camera, to try to get one decent tape of my dying child. I was stopped at the stairs by Jim Brandeberry, Frank Scardino's associate. He asked if I had a camera. I answered in the negative. He then asked if he could search my bag. I repeated my answer. I liked Jim, but I also knew my rights and that he had been put up to this. I said he could, however, watch me during the entire show. At that point Jim O'Neill came up to me and said it had been rumored that I intended to tape that night. He wanted me to know that the union would break my legs if I did. My response was, "If I were going to video tape, do you really think I'd wait til the last performance?" Rory came running up the aisle to take a quick look at the phantom videotaper. There was nothing to see, but he kept watching me. I stood in the balcony while Jim Brandeberry watched me. He got tired and asked an usher not to take her eyes off me. Such attention! Then I found out why; in the scene where Don Stitt is supposed to tell David he's on, Rory came running out awkwardly and did the line. This, of course, was breaking union rules, and I'm sure he didn't want THAT on tape.

In the conga dance all actors and now understudies were onstage together for the first and last time. It was a bittersweet feeling. When it came to the Las Vegas scene where Michael McAssey is supposed to say, "Now, for the first time in Las Vegas," he changed it to the "last time." It was all over. The curtain came down, and it was finished. My Broadway days were no more. I had no success. My show failed.

As I left the Ritz for the last time, I saw the carpenter who told me he would report me if I taped. I couldn't resist. "Hey, Bill...guess what? I taped five shows. Have a nice life." I made my way to Charlie's, where the cast and crew were having a final goodbye. Everyone was there, even Allan Knee. Rory and his parents were there. They didn't say a word to me. Greg came over and put out his hand. "I know you think I hate you, but I really don't," he said. I cordially said goodbye. Robert's girlfriend brought me over to Robert. She reiterated that he didn't mean the nasty things he said. I faked a smile and said goodbye. I hugged my friends in the cast and left. We didn't even have our jackets in time for closing.

Chapter 12
Aftermath

It was the day after we closed that I went to the piano. I thought I might not be able to write anymore, but even with all the negativity about my work, it couldn't stop my compulsion to compose. I sat down and wrote the music and lyric that began: "It started off without a soul that had a doubt for us."

I continued writing what was seeming to be a mini-epic about the show. I couldn't stop. By the time I was through, I had written what I thought to be a bittersweet tribute to my failed musical. It was not only a song for my show, but it actually encompassed other musicals that either closed early or just ended. I decided to call it "Late Nite Saga." I played it for a number of people; most cried. My mother was tearful, yet apprehensive. "What do you intend to do with it?" she queried. "I intend to play this song wherever I can," I answered. She did not agree. She felt my pain should not be shared in such a public fashion. I didn't care; I had written about lost love so often and shared that—why not a lost show? Since I wasn't performing anywhere, I did put it aside…but only for a short time.

I decided to write a letter to Rory to try to repair our friendship. I was quite disturbed by the break and thought I could mend things with a heartfelt letter. It went:

"Dear Rory,

For a person who makes his living working with words (or at this point, possibly used to), I find it very hard to put this together. The pain of losing a show is obviously not the easiest thing to deal with. Yes, we all must go on…certainly you have a million projects and clients that will keep you busy. For me, I have only my songs. The worst pain, however, is this situation with us. We were all living under desperate circumstances and perhaps a bit crazed. You had over a million at stake and I, my reputation. I don't know if I can get across to you how painful it was for me to have to sit at the Guild fighting the person who meant so much to me. That whole week was a nightmare. I know you felt let down, but just try to understand this for a moment. That song was not just another song to me; it was a part of my heart. Songs came and went with this show, but this was different. I realize that for you it was certainly a business venture…but for me, it was my guts in that song. Otherwise, I would've let it go like the others. What's losing a song about L.A. or the streets of New York or an obsession? 'Late Nite Comic' was the whole basis for the energies we all exerted. I'm putting my heart on the line, Rory, because I really do care. However you want it to be, I will always be eternally grateful to you for your belief in my music and the good times we experienced.

Love, Brian."

I sent a copy to Alan Colmes as well. He had encouraged me to write the letter. Rory never responded.

On Monday, two days after the show closed, I stopped by the Ritz to see if there were any momentos I could pick up. Jim O'Neill told me that Frank Scardino gathered up everything for Rory. He had taken the banner, and even some of the costumes, such as the red sequined jacket that Robert had worn during the Vegas scene. The only things I could have were Playbills.

Michael McAssey was playing a local cabaret that night called Don't Tell Mama. I went down to support him; the encore was poignant—it was "Late Nite Comic."

Alan Colmes called to ask me to accompany some of his guests again. Don McLean, of "American Pie" fame, was booked the next day, while Mary Wilson, formerly of the Supremes, was scheduled the day after McLean. I busily refreshed my memory of their songs and showed up on Tuesday for McLean. It so happened he accompanied himself, so my services weren't needed. The next day, however, proved to be well worth the refresher. Mary Wilson and I performed many of the hits she had with the Supremes. It was a ball.

I got a call from Judine Hawkins. She wanted to know if I would accompany her on the Joe Franklin show. I, of course, said I'd be happy to. Judine was the person singing with me in the pit at the Ritz when we were so rudely interrupted. Now she wanted to do that song of mine and, coincidentally, a song from *Purlie*. It turned out she was allowed only one song, so she opted for the standard from *Purlie*.

Meanwhile, I heard from Alan Colmes again—this time with a conflict. It seemed that Rory was putting pressure on Alan not to use me as the bandleader on the upcoming "live" show Alan was doing from the comedy club, Caroline's. I told him the band should not lose work because of Rory's problem. (Our checks came from Rory's office, and this didn't sit well with Rory.) Alan finally decided to allow us to continue despite Rory's protests.

My main concern was figuring out how to preserve my music. I got a call from Robert Sher; he was the one illegally taping in New London. He was also a smooth talker. "I'll produce the whole album; my fee will be $15,000." I told him he should call Rory. I didn't need a producer to pay. I could do it myself. I'd had quite a bit of studio experience by that time. Rory thought about it, but finally said no. Sher came back to me, but I said I could not raise the money.

I happened to stop by a record store called Footlight, whose owners included my old math teacher, Gene Dingenary. He had produced several musicals, such as *The Streets of New York* and *The Ambassador*. He opened the record store that specialized in theatre and movie soundtracks. He was quite sympathetic and told me about a man named Bruce Yeko, who had originally been part-

Bruce Yeko.

ners with Sher, but was now on his own. The label was called Original Cast. Gene gave me Bruce's number. I called him on October 26. To my surprise, Bruce remarked, "I'd be very interested in putting out your album; I saw the show three times and loved the score." I was amazed and flattered—someone actually complimented me. This was definitely a rarity during the last few weeks! We agreed to meet the following Saturday.

Kim Cermak, a young actress and singer, now married to Art Garfunkel, asked if she could sing "Clara's Dancing School" at an audition. I was very pleased that anyone would do the song after what the critics had said. She didn't care; she loved the song and could relate to it. She also asked me to play for her. We went down to Nola's and did the song. The people listening were so moved by the song they asked Kim where it came from. She pointed to me and said it was from the recent Broadway musical, *Late Nite Comic*. The look on their faces was comical; it was as if they were thinking, "Hmmm...that wasn't so bad...I wonder if I'm remembering the right show."

I called the Dramatists Guild to say thank you. Ron Sandberg asked me if I had gotten my orchestrations. It seemed that because the show ran such a short time, the orchestrations were now legally mine. I said that I never got them. He told me I should contact Frank Scardino. I did so immediately. He said he would ask Rory. Meanwhile, the Dramatists Guild said there was more money due from the show for me, but they were having a bit of a hassle getting it. Finally, after days of phone calls, I was told I could go to Frank Scardino's office and pick up a check. While I was there, I saw the orchestrations sitting on a table. I had the urge to grab them; however, I wanted to do it the right way. In retrospect, I wish I'd grabbed them. What should have been a smooth return of my property became a battle that was to last for months.

Bruce Yeko arrived from his home in Connecticut on Saturday. He frequented New York almost every weekend unless there was a show previewing in Connecticut or Pennsylvania. Bruce has seen and sees everything. He had seen my show in New London as well as in New York. He knew every cut song, every change in the show. He kept all programs and read every daily paper (especially the theatre section), evidence of which was all over the floor of his small car. His hair was gray, but it was still hard to tell his age. He was not as young as I, but he was not a contemporary of Grandma Moses either. I invited him in. He fumbled through his pockets for some scraps of paper. It turned out to be my contract. He told me what he wanted, I told him what I wanted. We basically agreed, and to this day I haven't signed the contract! What impressed me most was his honesty. It didn't matter that I wasn't signing with Columbia; I could tell this man cared. My idea was to get my music out there. The only inexpensive way seemed to be a piano/voice album. I told him I would investigate studios, etc., and let him know the cost. We shook hands, and a deal was set. (And who says a handshake deal isn't worth the paper it's written on?)

Bruce really wanted to do an album with the original cast—or as close to that. He contacted Robert LuPone, who asked for the full orchestra plus his leading lady to be flown in from California. Bruce told him he didn't have that kind of money. Robert declined. What I didn't know until recently was that Robert also insisted that I not be at the session. "You cannot

not have the writer of the score at his own recording session!" Bruce said in disbelief. "Well, then, he can be there, but he can't say anything," was Robert's response. Bruce couldn't accept this.

As I was driving down Broadway one day, at about 72nd Street, I saw Laurie Beechman on the corner. I called out to her, and she looked surprised and interested in my pulling over. I did so immediately. She gave her opinion of the show, but spoke highly of my music. I was thrilled. I had no idea she would be so responsive. My instincts were telling me to ask for her number. She gave me her private number, and I told her I would call. What began was simply amazing. She gave me the boost I needed so badly. She was doing *Cats* at the time, so she returned my call when she got home after the show. Our first phone call lasted four hours. She would tell me over and over to stop being a victim; I should follow my own instincts and stop allowing other people to direct my career. "Those people didn't know what they were doing," she would say. "It was your baby…next time you'll have a smash!" She was like magic; she had come back into my life at just the right time—and seemed really together this time. I asked her out.

We met at the backstage door of the Winter Garden Theater and de-cided to head over to a Mexican restaurant on Eighth Avenue called Caramba's. Her eyes were piercing. She listened, truly listened when I spoke. I was enthralled with her. Her eyes seemed to pick up on everything. It was an intensity that I had known before only from her. We went back to her place, and I mentioned the album project to her. "Not only will I do it, but I'll get all my friends from other Broadway shows like *Starlight Express* to do all the songs I don't do." I couldn't believe her generosity. All I could think about was how negative things can turn into such positive things. We kissed for the first time in ten years. It was like having a second chance. I went home and wrote a song called "We Meet Again." I never played it for her; it was not only written about her, but it was also written with her voice in mind. I called Bruce the next day and told him about Laurie's offer. He was thrilled. The next step would be the studio.

I called Rupert Holmes and told him about Laurie and the offer. He thought it was great and said he would be happy to do the liner notes. He would be producing Barbra Streisand, but would always be accessible to me. I thought how lucky I was to have such wonderful friends in the business.

It was November, and I still didn't have the orchestrations or my correct royalties. The Dramatists Guild had discovered what they believed to be incorrect calculations. Letters went back and forth between Frank Scardino and Ron Sandberg. It was a battle I was getting used to.

I called Larry Hochman about playing on the album. He was very nice, but said he really didn't feel right about not using all the original musicians on the date. I told him I didn't have the budget; this was a labor of love. He thanked me for thinking of him, but it was impossible.

Next I went to my buddy Don Ciccone. He immediately felt that Lee Shapiro, another Four Seasons member and the guy who did my early demos, would be a better choice. I met with him on November 3 and explained what I wanted to do. "No problem, pal…consider it done." I was amazed. I told him my budget was nil, so he gave me a price for a piano/voice recording. I agreed, and he said, "When would you like to start? And how's this—I'll throw on a few extra instruments for you; it'll be my pleasure." I couldn't believe it. My luck was changing.

By November 10 another Alan Colmes show came up. This time I was to play for Lou Christie and Ben E. King. It was fun playing for them, but there was something going on between Alan and me. It was not hard to guess where it was coming from.

On the same day, cabaret songwriter/performer John Wallowitch and I ran into each other, and he consoled me about the show. He asked me for a copy of the music to the song "Late Nite Comic." In one of the nicest gestures a songwriter could ask for, he performed the song that night on his cable TV show.

One of the pleasures of making money is spending money. I thought it was time I did that. I decided I could buy myself a few presents; I had earned it! The first thing was to get a new carpet for my living room. I had had one for twenty years, and it was way overdue to replace. What a relief when that carpet arrived, and knowing it was paid for by my own music! I also thought I earned a new 12-string guitar. I had been using my original Yamaha for about twenty years, and it had seen better days. I had bought it from Dick Weissman, one of the original Journeymen with John Phillips (later of Mamas & Papas fame.) John, in fact, offered to buy it back from me as a surprise to Dick, but I refused. Too many memories attached to those strings. Instead, I ran into a supreme guitarist and friend of Jimmy Webb's named Larry Coryell. He helped me get a brand-new beautiful Ovation. It was my first really expensive guitar, but worth every dime. I also thought it was finally time to get a good moped. I purchased a Honda Spree motor scooter, which I haven't regretted to this day!

On November 23 I received a letter from Rory's lawyer. It instructed me to pick up the orchestrations from him in Great Neck at 1:00 P.M. on December 2. No other time was allowed. I called the Dramatists Guild; they said I really couldn't be picky. I had to pick them up there. "But what if it's a trick? What if he doesn't show?" I exclaimed. I called my brother-in-law to see if he could go as my lawyer. He agreed. It was only a hop, skip and a jump from where he worked. No sweat.

In the meantime, two more checks came from Frank Scardino's office. The Dramatists Guild was right; they did owe us a lot more money. I had finally gotten all of it.

On December 1, Alan Colmes played a tape on the air made by one of his interns, Barbara. It was called "The Making of 'Late Nite Comic.'" It included the first public statement by Rory that Philip had been fired! "I fired my director...had to bring in a new director." One cast member said, when interviewed, "You know, I have a hunch that I won't have to do any time in purgatory, cause I've seen my hell on earth right here!" The whole interview was conducted over one song ... "Late Nite Comic."

December 2 arrived, and my brother-in-law picked up the box of orchestrations. I called Larry Hochman to see if it was all of them. I brought them to his house, where we spread them out on his dining room table. All the original "Deshons" (masters) were missing. The battle was to continue.

Right after *Late Nite Comic* closed, the American Theatre Wing and the City University of New York had some television tapings of seminars scheduled; one was called Performance, while the other was titled Playscript/Director. They were to include the major forces behind *Late Nite Comic*. Robert LuPone was asked to appear on Performance; Philip and Allan were to appear on the other. Since the shows were taped a few days after our closing, Philip declined to attend. There was an empty seat on the panel with Allan. These shows ate me up alive. There was no recourse to what was being said, and, to add insult to injury, they aired (and continued to air) over a New York cable station ad infinitum. Imagine turning on your television at any variety of times and having to see and hear this over and over. Hosting was Isabelle Stevenson, the president of ATW; Edwin Wilson, a critic from the City University of New York; and Jean Dalrymple. The poster of *Late Nite Comic* was hanging in the background. They misspelled "nite" on the screen.

Dalrymple (introducing LuPone): "You were splendid in *Late Nite*... (she stumbles)

LuPone (completing her sentence): "That bomb." (laughter)

Dalrymple (continuing): "... *Comic*. You really held the play together.

Robert gave his three important influences that made him become an actor and added: "...These were all decisive points in my life about acting as is the show I just closed in (laughter) a decisive point in my life about acting."

Wilson: "You were quite good [in *Late Nite Comic*]...marvelous. Every actor has to go through what you went through last week, because the actor's the most exposed person."

LuPone: "I'll say!" (laughter)

Wilson: "You were exposed in material, quite frankly, which wasn't nearly up to you, and that's true in terms of songs and lyrics and in terms of the book and everything...You acted as if you believed in it all the way, which is a tremendous tribute to you. I don't know where along the way you realized...I mean everybody believes in their material..."

LuPone (jumping in): "The first day of rehearsal! I asked the producer and the director both, first of all, why they want me; and second, why they want to do this play?...(laughter) They said I was funny. Their response to doing this play was that they raised the money and they believed in it. Well, out of town, you know, that awful reality hits that the professional judgments were completely off kilter. I mean, there was just no play, no book, across the boards! I mean, the reviews stated exactly what the problems were. So, I knew the first day going in that I was going to have trouble with this material...I suffered through weeks and weeks of rehearsal doing bad jokes that didn't get any laughs out of town and also in New York for that matter! (laughter) It was the best experience, really. Oh, it was wonderful!....My situation as of doing that play: going in I had to find much deeper resources than I've ever had to find, because I was overwhelmed with the material. Cause I was onstage for two hours! Literally! I was going from a scene that was quote unquote supposedly dramatic or funny into a number that made no sense into a dance that made no sense. (laughter) And yet the testimonial to the actor is as you just said I was able to pull it off...I'm grateful reviewers were very kind to me, but I'm telling you the way to learn about the theatre and the way to learn about yourself as an actor is to do things like I just did...Successful actors who have not experienced that are (sarcastically) missing something, let me tell ya. (laughter). The director trusted me, which was a blessing...Onstage I was able to ad lib every night and found in myself lines that were funnier than the text! (laughter)...I think it deservedly closed. (giggles) I'm not at all ashamed. I'm glad that it closed, because I think if you're gonna go with a standard of Broadway or American Theater, I think that it had a purpose. I think it was very educational for me. Why they ever went into it in the first place, I don't know."

Stevenson: "Would this have had more of a chance Off-Broadway?"

LuPone: "I think so...it was too small a story for a Broadway stage. The fact of the matter is we're beholden to the material. The material was not up to snuff, period ... I would do it again in a second."

Wilson: "It sounds like a modern version of 'Commedia Dell'Arte.'"

LuPone: "No, it sounds more like 'Moose Murders.' (big laughs) What I got from this, man, is a will. Boy, they did everything in their power to destroy it. They, meaning the creators, trying to find a way. John Guare came up to me at my sister's opening last night, which, of course, is a major hit, right? (laughs) 'I love you actors—how you could have put up with what you had to put up with...I mean in terms of all that sort of stuff.'"

Question from an audience member: "What is the best training for theatre?"

LuPone: "Failure" (laughter)

If that show wasn't enough, Allan Knee's appearance aired the following week. Out of the entire hour show, Allan spoke for about 11 minutes. It was a show involving playwrights and directors, but there was no counterpart for Allan. He was asked about Phil.

Knee: "I had met him when I got out of Yale in the early '70s, and he was very responsive then; he just said he liked my work and any time I finished anything, he'd like to see it. It was like 17 years later, I sent him something [*Late Nite Comic*]"

This baffled me. How could he say that? Did he really not remember his lack of aggression on doing something with this show after Charles Hunt turned it down? Did he really forget my setting up the appointment with Phil after Darla urged me on?

Knee: "...It was a very good beginning. We worked almost a year together in getting the script ready. It was the happiest time of the collaboration."

Stevenson: "You're here all alone; how far back does that collaboration [with Phil] go?"

Knee: "We met each other about a year ago; we did a showcase together at the AMAS Theater, but we knew we were going to do *Late Nite Comic*. And as I said previously, the preliminary work, the working on defining the script and focusing a script, particularly a musical—I mean I had not worked in musicals in the past, so it was a new experience for me and one I was excited about and looking forward to, and I didn't know what I was letting myself in for. I would say if playwriting is masochistic, writing a book for a musical is the height of masochism. (laughter) It's a sort of living suicide. There reached a point (we started in New London) where the producer asked me to stay in my room for a few days and not come around because I was depressing the director. And I was relieved. It was really rather nice. And I'd get reports like how it was going. It always went well when I wasn't around. I've discovered that, too. I seemed to have missed all the good performances. (laughter)...The book writer tends to drift more and more into the background. There were days I would be shocked when I'd come and there was a simple solo [that] was now a Las Vegas number with 14 people onstage, and I'd just say...'What does that mean?' (laughter) And no one ever told me." (laughter)

He was asked about his other theatre experiences and he answered that he had worked at the Manhattan Punch Line and the Chelsea Theater in Brooklyn.

Knee: "Those were different experiences and pretty much preferable to me."

Wilson: "The split [between Allan and Phil] became really visible to the audience in seeing that his name was no longer on this program. Did the two of you get pushed further and further apart?"

Knee: "He had actually warned me. This was like near the end right before production started. He said, 'I know we've been getting along terrifically now, and I just want to warn you this is almost like a parting of the ways. I'm not going to be around for you once we start.' (pause) But he said it so warmly (laughter) that you don't quite believe it. And it did. And it hurts. Maybe it's the nature of the beast in the musical. It does kinda hurt when you see you're rather unnecessary to the process. You do your writing; you say, 'Can we have a new scene here?' but after a while, you just give 'em the new scene. You don't even know what [the musical's] about anymore. And then you look up one day and you say, 'Okay, this is what I have to live with' and you live with it. Whatever it is, you live with it. The split with the director and me...I don't think it has to happen. I don't think it has to be that far apart. (pause) This situation was, but I don't feel that is necessary even in a musical...I was surprised that he wanted his name removed. I did call him after I heard that news, and I said, 'This really surprises me and bothers me since it's yours—whatever it is, it's yours.' (laughter) He said he dealt with his conscience and wanted his name removed. That was all."

Isabelle Stevenson lost all tact with her final comments.

Stevenson: "I think that musical comedy writing is quite different; the whole approach to it is different than a straight play, and I think that's the answer to it. And you found out the hard way, but I hope you'll go on—not necessarily musical comedy (the audience laughs nervously), but go back to the straight plays."

Christmas was coming up soon, and I wanted to send out cards; however, I couldn't ignore my insane year. I decided to design my own card. I took some horrible headlines from the reviews of the show, the picture of Rory being kissed by the chorus girls, Philip's "withdrawal" announcement and my divorce lawyer's confirmation letter and pasted them all over the front of a card. At the bottom I drew a tree with presents all around and printed "TIS THE SEASON TO BE JOLLY!"

Most people laughed and were amazed that I still had a sense of humor; Alan Colmes thought it was sick and distasteful. I loved it. I sent it to every close friend—but not to my ex in-laws.

Bruce Yeko was anxious to get the album done and asked me what was happening. Laurie told me she'd be very involved in a "special" audition she was preparing for a new show. I think it was *Chess*. She had gone home to Philadelphia, but said she'd be accessible as soon as the audition was over. She didn't get the show. That was the last I heard from her. We never had another date, nor would she return my calls. I was angry at myself for trusting her again on a dating level, but she also wasn't living up to her promise of doing the album. That was something professional, and I had to answer to other people. I finally wrote her a letter on Christmas Eve that basically told her off. The album had to be put on hold until Bruce and I could come up with another direction.

Christmas Eve was becoming a disaster for yet another reason; the *Late Nite Comic* jackets, including the presents for my parents, were still not delivered. I finally screamed at the company that I was sick and tired of the postponements. The jackets had already been paid for, and they were Christmas presents! A secretary told me she would get the jackets from the factory, and I would have to meet her at her house that night on the East Side. So, armed with my family's other Christmas presents, I trekked out into the cold night air to pick up these albatrosses. I must admit, though, I am still extremely proud to wear it.

The year closed with no solution to the orchestration problem with Rory and an album with no vocalists.

Chapter 13
The Album

January of 1988 opened with a phone call from my mother; she had just heard from a friend that there was a good review of my score in a current magazine. "Which one? Where can I get it?" I asked frantically. "I think it's called *Dance Magazine*," she replied. I raced out in sub-degree temperatures to buy a copy. (Imagine how desperate a songwriter's ego must be to be this urgent.) I walked forever before I finally found a newsstand that had a copy. I flipped through the pages as I walked home with my fingers frozen to the point where they had trouble turning those pages. The cover was ironic: a picture of Patti LuPone with the cast of *Anything Goes*.

Suddenly there it was. Kevin Grubb wrote, "Allan Knee's book was so heavy on one-liners and bad puns that we waited, unfulfilled, for a plot to take shape. Instead, Brian Gari's respectable score (his first Broadway effort) came to the rescue." I was thrilled. Finally someone was recognizing my work—and in print! In all fairness to Allan Knee, I believe most of the one-liners and bad puns Mr. Grubb referred to were inserted into the show later by "others." I decided I would thank Mr. Grubb publicly by writing to the Letters column in the magazine. They published it in April. It was printed under the heading "Bright Spots" and read:

"My heartfelt thanks to Kevin Grubb for being able to separate my work as the composer/lyricist of 'Late Nite Comic' from the rest of the show. It is not uncommon for a critic to dismiss everyone's contribution when disenchanted with a show. It is also quite ironic that I should be complimented in *Dance Magazine*, since the ballet references were inspired by my real-life relationship with a dancer from Eliot Feld's company back in the early seventies. There was never a time when I didn't see Dance Magazine all over her apartment. Grubb's insightful comments were the bright spot at the end of a very dark tunnel."

In retrospect, I think I should have spelled "bright" "brite!"

The "live" Alan Colmes shows from Caroline's were coming to an end, not because of me, but it just didn't seem feasible to Alan and Rory anymore. I also wasn't being called very much to play for his guests. Alan's producer was quite friendly with Rory, and the writing seemed to be on the wall. I confronted Alan about it, and he agreed that while there were some "hard feelings" about me among his associates, it would never affect his hiring me if a guest needed my services. He also mentioned that the theme song that I had provided for him gratis when he started on NBC might be dropped. "It was really a creative decision," he insisted. I did a few more jobs for him and then was simply not called anymore.

The Dramatists Guild and David LeVine were still working on Rory to get him to turn over the Deshon orchestrations to me. Rory's lawyer was now involved and called LeVine. LeVine told her that her client was completely out of line and did not have the right to ANY part of the orchestrations anymore. She responded with a reference to her client being defamed on a Christmas card of mine and that he was seriously thinking of pursuing litigation for that. When I heard that, I laughed for hours. Imagine starting a lawsuit over something that was harmless and had already appeared in newspapers previous to my collage Christmas card! LeVine retorted with "that has nothing whatsoever to do with Brian's orchestrations." Finally, on February 16, a letter (unsigned) from Rory was sent to me and the Dramatists Guild. It read:

"Mr. LeVine:
    Despite the fact that the Producer has the right to retain the enclosed material,
    I am delivering same to you for Brian Gari to put an end to his harassment."

I couldn't believe he still maintained he had the right to the material, when it had been proved legally that he didn't. The harassment line made me laugh as well. I won everything fair and square. My dealings with Rory Rosegarten were over. I felt as if a heavy weight had been taken off my shoulders. (Incidentally, it turns out the "pit" orchestration books were never returned to me and are missing to this day.)

The Guild asked me to write the story of my experiences with how they helped me. I wrote it, but it never appeared in their magazine. I think it was too complicated for many reasons.

I had been watching a local cable show (or should I say "a friend had been watching") called *Midnight Blue*. For those who don't know what it featured, let me just say it was a sexually-oriented show. On it, there was an announcement that they were going to have a segment on new comics. Well, in my never-ending search for exposure of my material, I called them up to volunteer my song "Late Nite Comic." I didn't realize they'd be so interested. They asked me if I could sing it on camera—with my clothes on. I gave it some thought and decided to accept the offer. After all, I'd have been a hypocrite to decline the invitation. I did watch the show. They treated me very nicely, and it aired some time later. I'll tell you…I think more people saw that version of the song than on Broadway!

Bruce Yeko and I discussed other possibilities for vocalists. I decided I would sing the male lead songs; Michael McAssey said he would make himself available to reprise his club owner songs, and Robin Kaiser would finally put her signature song, "Relax with Me Baby," on vinyl. We did, however, need a "name" female singer at least to do the female leads. We thought of Kaye Ballard, but not only was she unavailable, but she probably wasn't right for all the songs. I had gone to high school with Julie Budd. "Oh, she'd be a very good choice," Bruce responded. "I wonder if she'd be willing to do it," I pondered. I called her manager, Herb Bernstein, who thought it sounded like an interesting idea. He said that Julie was in California, but if I called her number here, she would get back to me.

I did, and she called back immediately. I described my plight. "Julie, it's the only way I can preserve my music," I said in a semi-pleading tone. "If it's okay with Herbie, it's okay with me," she answered. I was ecstatic! This superb singer, whom I wanted to have sing my songs for years, was going to do the album. I called Bruce Yeko and Lee Shapiro, booked the studio time, and the project was underway!

The sessions began on March 16 at 1:00 P.M. They actually took place in an office on the twelfth floor of 1697 Broadway in New York City. When I was fifteen, one of my earliest demo sessions took place in that same building. Now here I was actually recording my first album!

Lee asked me to bring along just the original lead sheets for the songs. He did not want to copy Larry Hochman's arrangements, but rather create his own in the style of a Pop/Broadway record. I chose to record all the songs that were ever performed on the stage, as opposed to all the songs that were ever considered. I thought that was a realistic approach and one the collector would appreciate. At first I thought I would play the piano parts myself, but Lee is such a great player that I changed my direction immediately and had Lee take over. He played on every song except "Relax with Me Baby;" that was because I knew Robin Kaiser's stops and starts better. It so happens my rhythm is not great, and I cringe every time I hear my playing on that track.

Almost immediately after recording the first song, Lee turned to me and said, "We can't do this as just piano tracks; your songs deserve definite orchestrations." "But Lee," I answered, "we don't have the money for that." "Forget about money…we're gonna do this right," Lee retorted with a grin. This was one helluva guy.

The tracks were all recorded on an extremely expensive keyboard called a synclavier. It wasn't just a keyboard with a few sounds—it truly sounded like an authentic orchestra. Lee added layer upon layer. The album was becoming everything I always dreamed of. I would describe to Lee what type of song it was and usually play a piano version for him. Within seconds Lee would come up with the whole arrangement, playing bass, piano, drums, horns, strings and even a guitar—all on a keyboard! It was astounding. We recorded everything on digital equipment that went from the synclavier to tape or even DAT, a new form of recording without tape. This eliminated all hiss. If anything bothered me about the arrangement, Lee would listen and change whatever I needed to make it sound exactly like what I heard in my head.

Only one disaster occurred; the entire track to "Having Someone" was erased. Luckily, I had a cassette copy of the track, and we actually utilized that without much loss in quality.

The vocals were also done in this office studio. I was singing in the office entrance, while Lee engineered about two feet away! I didn't mind; it was a real joy to record under such unpressured conditions. I did most of my vocals at the second session.

During my relaying the progress of the album to Bruce Yeko, he commented, "You are going to include an overture, aren't you?" "Gee, Bruce, I didn't know that was important," I answered. "Oh, yes, Brian," Bruce went on, "it is of major importance to the show music collector to have an overture. You definitely have to record one."

I went to the piano that night and wrote my own overture, I was never asked to write the one for the stage, so this was my chance to do it the way I saw fit. All the songs went through my head, and I prepared them with great care. In about an hour I was able to play the entire overture myself. At the next session, on the 22nd, I played it for Lee, who asked me to help play it on the recording. I was thrilled. It turned into a track of which I am extremely proud.

A vocal session with all the other performers was set up for March 26. The day before I met with Julie Budd to rehearse the songs. That took place at my mother's apartment because of her central location. I had given Julie a tape of her songs ahead of time. She was very cooperative and a quick study. We had the songs down in an hour. It was sheer ecstasy to hear that golden voice on my songs. They fit her so perfectly that I wished she would record all my songs.

The session started at noon; we had it paced so that all vocalists would do their parts one after another. I think they were all stunned that such a good sound could come from such a small space. Robin got hers done in a few takes, while Julie had more tunes, which took a little longer. Her manager and conductor, Herb Bernstein, was there and acted as co-producer on her vocals. Julie was just as cooperative as the day before; she would work until it was perfect for all concerned (including herself). When she finished her magnificent rendition of "When I Am Movin,'" Herb commented, "This would be a great audition song for you, Julie, even an opening number for the act." This was the reaction I had always hoped for.

Michael McAssey and I had a ball recreating the club owners' parts on "The Best in the Business" and "Having Someone." Michael would reprise his parts, while I tried a few of Don Stitt's or Patrick Hamilton's inflections. We sometimes doubled and tripled the parts.

The recording was mixed over the next two weeks in two or three sessions. Lee gave me the opportunity to finish recording to my satisfaction. He knew I wasn't wasting time; every minute that he afforded me was utilized to the fullest. I felt that Lee deserved credit as co-producer, so that's exactly what I had printed on the back of the album.

With Julie in town for a relatively short time, I thought a photo session would be a nice touch for the album. I asked Bruce if he would spring for one, and, surprisingly, he agreed. I inquired among some friends about an inexpensive photographer and located a wonderful lady named Anita Bartsch. We opted for a session in front of the Ritz Theater. The time was 2:00 P.M. on March 27, and it was a chilly Sunday afternoon. I had on a gold baseball jacket, while Julie had on a thin raincoat. We both froze to death that afternoon, but held onto each other for warmth. I climbed up on top of the marquee, but ended up too far away from the camera. Instead, we shot mostly

in front of the theater. The session was over in an hour. That was the last time I saw Julie. She approved the photos by mail.

I immediately sent the cassette of the album to Rupert for his liner notes. They were not to be very long, as I had plans for my own contribution. I called Rupert several times over the following weeks, but never heard from him. Finally, I had to give up; the album could not be delayed any longer. I have no idea to this day what happened; I imagine he just overextended himself.

My liner notes took a few days. I wanted them to explain why each song was on the album and also how the show ever happened in the first place. I did several drafts before I was satisfied. There was a fine line between writing accurately and writing bitterly (as is the case with this book). Some people thought it was bitter; I reread them many times and don't see it that way.

Next the album cover had to be designed. Bruce asked if there were any good quotes about the music that could be used. I laughed and confirmed his suspicions. "Can we use the Broadway logo?" asked Bruce. "No," I replied, "I'm sure that belongs to Rory. I do, however, have the original artwork that my father had done." I showed it to Bruce, and we decided on one of the several he had worked on. It was perfect; my father's work was not going to be for naught—and I didn't have to pay him royalties! (Incidentally, the comic silhouette, my father later revealed, was actually based on Steve Martin.)

The cover information was given over to a designer that Bruce knew named William Krasnoborski. He took my father's artwork and put the titles over it. Bruce requested that it look like a Broadway cast album with all appropriate credits—except director and producer (I wonder why). Even Allan Knee had his name in equal size to my credit. The back cover would include all photos, notes and album credits.

The tapes were sent to a pressing plant that Bruce used called Cook's. I was ecstatic when the test pressings finally arrived the following month. I put the needle on the record and heard what sounded like nails on a chalkboard. The pressings were disastrous. I called up Bruce and said, "You've got to be kidding! Even my cat's hair is standing on end." Bruce very calmly told me to check out some other places; most were unbelievably expensive. I finally came upon Europadisk on Varick Street in downtown Manhattan. Their prices were fair, and I knew their quality from some of my favorite albums. I asked them to press it on very good vinyl and use nice plastic inner sleeves, instead of paper. They would also do direct metal mastering to cut down on hiss. This is a little more expensive, but well worth it. After all, this was my first album, and I wanted it to sound the best possible!

Meanwhile, the labels and album cover were being printed out of town, and Europa would not start the presses until they had labels and jackets. This delayed the album further. Bruce was in charge of that, and he was not overly aggressive. I finally had to call the printers myself. They promised to send them directly to Europa.

I spoke to stores like Colony, Footlight and Tower and was told by all that they would stock the album as soon as I got them. My friend Ritchie Turk at Colony begged me to deliver to him first.

I finally got a call from Europa that the albums would be ready on July 19. The first pressing was 1,000, and Bruce couldn't come in with his car until the weekend. I had promised the stores they would be in that week, so I drove down to Europa and promptly loaded my moped with boxes of 50. It was a hot summer's day, and I could get only one box on the bike at a time, so I made several trips back and forth to Varick Street all day long to make sure the stores were accommodated.

First I went to Colony up on Broadway and 49th Street; then I went back down to Varick and grabbed another box for Footlight on East 12th Street. I then delivered another 50 to Tower's Lincoln Center store. The two theatre people there, Jordan Tinsley and Jan Sugarman, were of enormous support and help. Jordan made up little signs that informed customers of this new release. They couldn't have been nicer.

My last stop was to the downtown Tower store on Broadway and East 4th Street. By this time I was sweating and thoroughly exhausted. I rushed back to Europa just before they closed; I had to pick up a box for myself!

As I traveled back uptown, I ran into an entrepreneur named Sid Bernstein; Sid was the man who brought the Beatles to Carnegie Hall for the first time. I had known him through the years and yelled out to him from the bike. I handed him an album. "Hot off the press, Sid," I said, trying to catch my breath. "This is great," replied Sid. "How about doing my cable show on Monday to plug it?" I answered affirmatively, and suddenly I had my first bit of publicity set for the album!

I stopped by my mother's apartment and dropped off an album to her. She was impressed and thrilled. I told her I couldn't stay; I had to get back home and take a much needed shower. My back was also killing me from carrying all those boxes into the stores.

After I showered and ate some dinner, I lay back on my bed with an
album. All I did was stare at the cover. I read everything at least a dozen
times. I had done it. I finally had an album out.

Chapter 14
Do You Also Do Windows?

A few days later I decided to check in with Colony to see how the record was doing. The proprietor, Ritchie Turk, grabbed the phone. "Brian," he said excitedly, "this album is selling like crazy. We're almost sold out. Get me some more!" I was amazed…and thrilled. I bopped by Tower at Lincoln Center. Jordan Tinsley and Jan Sugarman said the same thing. "We could use another box, Brian." Jordan exclaimed. "It's really moving." Suddenly I had reorders from every store in town. I believe that what was first looked on as a novelty or cult item was suddenly becoming a respected release. Word of mouth was good. It was also the first recording by Julie Budd in quite some time. I sent a copy to her right away. To my surprise I never heard from her. Gene Dingenary of Footlight doubled his order and put it in the window. Other stores told me that they, too, would like to stock the album.

Ritchie Turk also gave me part of an entire side window display featuring a dozen *Late Nite Comic* album covers. I couldn't believe my eyes as I walked on Forty-ninth Street; there was *Late Nite Comic* splashed all over the window! Every time I spoke with friends they would say, "Saw your album in the window of Colony! Congratulations!" My biggest surprise was when I walked into the downtown Tower store and saw a life-size replica of my father's artwork from the album cover. The Styrofoam piece was gracing an entire beam in their show music department. Bigger albums than mine didn't even have that! It was basically unheard of that a small label would have such a prominent spot. I even had my picture taken in front of it. My thanks must go to Joe Facey, who, I believe, was responsible for that one. My next job was publicity.

I called Cindy Adams first. I never took into account her reputation as rather "tough," shall we say. I had forgotten that Raquel Welch had recently

Tower Records.

Colony Records.

walked out on an interview with her. I just called the number I had for Cindy Adams. She called me back, but I missed her call. I called her back, and she couldn't take my call.

She returned my call, but again I wasn't home. Finally I reached her. She seemed annoyed. I apologized for our missing each other's calls. "What's up?" she asked abruptly. "Oh, well, I wrote the score for the Broadway show *Late Nite Comic*, which lasted a very short time, but I just put out an album with my former classmate, Julie Budd. Everyone pitched in to help keep my music alive, including my father, who did the album cover. You might also be interested in knowing that my grandfather was Eddie Cantor." "Fine," she answered quickly. "I can't promise anything, but I'll see what I can do." I thanked her and that was the end...or so I thought.

On August 8, I dropped by Alan Colmes's office to pick up a check. His producer was laughing. "What's so funny?" I asked innocently. "Didn't you see Cindy Adams column today?" he responded, still with a big grin. "What did you do to get her so mad, Brian?" he continued with some sarcasm. I grabbed the paper. The piece read:

"BRIAN GARI is a composer
Also Eddie Cantor's grandson.

Also the writer of a Broadway floppola, from which comes the new album 'Late Nite Comic' on Original Cast Records. Brian's school chum Julie Budd is on it. Brian's father, Roberto, designed its cover. Brian himself is delivering it to stores. Also driving me insane until I mention it."

I couldn't believe that after what I went through on Broadway and the hell I went through to get an album out that she would treat me in this manner. Why "Broadway floppola?" Why "driving me insane?" Why this nasty attitude? I left Alan's office feeling thoroughly humiliated. I had hoped they would read a positive piece; instead, it was an embarrassment. I called a few associates and asked their opinion of my responding to Adams. It was unanimous that I should respond. I put together a letter and hand delivered it that night.

"Dear Ms. Adams:
If you thought it was easy for me to watch my show fail after working on it for ten years, it wasn't.
If you thought getting out an album on a show that failed was easy, it wasn't either.
When we missed each other's calls, I didn't think you would consider my returning your calls 'driving you insane.' Quite the contrary. I thought returning a call was GOOD manners.
I am working day and night to ensure this album's success. I had hoped you would admire that."

Two months later I got a letter from the office of the *New York Post* with my name and address handwritten on the envelope and my original letter inside with an additional piece of paper. It was pink and had no name on it. It didn't say "Dear Brian," nor was it signed by anyone. It read:

"Get it clear. I never phoned you so that you could do anything for me. YOU phoned ME because you wanted me to do something for you. Thus, the person who had good manners—which you ascribe to yourself—was me...because I was courteous enough to return your phone calls when I hadn't elicited them nor particularly even wanted them in the first place.

You wanted a plug. Your plug was not such that I was atwitter with excitement at the opportunity to print it. I was doing you a favor. However, in order to mention your album, your show, your father, you, etc. etc.—all of which were needful to make this plug work since you are not exactly a household name—I worked for over an hour just to craft that one paragraph.

To give it a little spin, to make it bright rather than boring. I amuse—I don't abuse. It's needful for people to still read me and find me interesting despite the encumbent difficulty when people like you just need to use people like me for your own ends.

Your response to my bothering to write your plug is such that you need not worry about how I handle you in [the] future because I won't. And since my staff opens my mail for me, it will be pointless for you to respond to this.

Fortunately for me others in their early stages of show business are not so ungracious. They're appreciative of a mention."

Gee, I was shaking in my boots. I had incurred the wrath of the great Cindy Adams. I must have read that letter to everyone I'd ever met in my life; it was hysterical. I read it to Jordan at Tower, who actually Xeroxed both my letter and hers and incorporated it into his nightclub act! The topper of the whole story is that I got a phone call from her husband, Joey Adams, who asked me to do his radio show that same week. I guess he either didn't read his wife's column or didn't care!

Things did, however, turn around for me. That one negative piece was not indicative of more to follow. Quite the contrary. It seemed that Jan and Jordan saw enough initial sales in my album to tell *Pulse Magazine* (Tower's giveaway mag) that *Late Nite Comic* was number 10 out of all the films and shows put out by an independent label. This appeared in an issue that was available in every Tower Record store all over the country. Suddenly I had orders from every store. It was an automatic stock item. Broadway shows have a life of their own once they're recorded. Now don't get me wrong. The stores don't call you. I called every one of the 50 stores myself and had to introduce myself to each manager. Bruce Yeko would not make any calls; he insisted I was the best one for the job. I got so inundated with numbers and orders that I had to start a computer disc to keep track of every store, the sales, and those who still owed (and believe me, it's not always easy to collect). Bruce would only mail out the records. It was my job to do sales, promotion, distribution, radio, TV, print—EVERYTHING!

With that *Pulse* piece in hand, I proceeded to contact every newspaper in town to tell them of the rise and fall and rise again of *Late Nite Comic*. I sent out hundreds of free albums, which obviously accounts for fewer profits. I kept track (and still do) of every album

INDEPENDENT LABEL FILMS & SHOWS TOP 10:
Compiled by Jan Sugarman and Jordan Tinsley, Tower Records Uptown (Manhattan), for the week ending July 18, 1988.
TITLE, Artist Label/List
1 SARAFINA, Original Cast Shanachie/9.98 List
2 MACK & MABEL, Original London Cast First Night/13.98 List
3 LES MISERABLES, Original London Cast Relativity/13.98 List
4 FOLLIES, Original London Cast First Night/19.98 List
5 AMADEUS, Soundtrack Fantasy/19.98 List
6 THE BIG EASY, Soundtrack Antilles/8.98 List
7 DIVA, Soundtrack DRG/10.98 List
8 THE SEA HAWK, Soundtrack Varèse Sarabande/10.98 List
9 WINGS OF DESIRE, Soundtrack SPI Milan (Sepam)/10.98 List
10 LATE NIGHT COMIC, Original Cast Original Cast Records/8.98 List

Pulse Magazine.

used for promotion purposes. I would not let ANY slip through the cracks. If an album was sent out to be reviewed, I stayed on top of the writer until I saw something in print—or until I was told to drop dead! I wasn't obnoxious, just tenacious.

One day I received a call from a writer named Joe Williams at *Cash Box Magazine*. He interviewed me over the phone; he had gotten the album and loved the inside story of the romance. Reading the September 17 issue, I couldn't believe my eyes. The review took up almost half the page.

"It's not unthinkable that a failed show can pack a steamer trunkful of talent, and such is the case with 'Late Nite Comic,' a musical by Brian Gari. The story of how the play came into existence is almost as good as the record itself…"

I was reading this in the middle Tower Records and almost had a heart attack. I went up to cashiers, bag checkers—anyone—to read them this review! He called Julie Budd's voice "the equal of Streisand's." (This was the first of many raves for her performance on this album.) He quoted me saying, "It's gotten much more attention as an album than it ever did as a musical." The review continued

"… "and with good reason. It's a bouncy, modern score. Tin Pan Alley by way of *Saturday Night Live*. Songs like 'Think Big' are in the great pull-yourself-up tradition, while the double-time 'Obsessed' has been rightly compared to Danny Kaye. And it's almost all funny, as befits the material, while skirting the edges of camp. Gari's got a wonderful knack for avoiding cliché, even as he's working in a form that's as threadbare and familiar as a hallway rug."

This is what I had been looking for. I immediately called to thank Joe profusely and Xeroxed 100 copies to send out to radio stations and newspapers.

My old friend Patricia O'Haire wrote in her column for *The Daily News* that I was "moving on up." Diana Maychick of the *New York Post* put it into her column. *Newsday's* Susan Mulcahy put it in under the headline, "Late Nite Revival." The Page Six column of the *New York Post* is one of the hardest to get on. I called them. They seemed interested, but then backed down. Suddenly they called back and said they would run it. They liked the human interest side of my delivering the albums to the stores on my moped. It appeared under the headline "Single-handed." I Xeroxed everything and built a press kit. People were actually calling me to see who was doing my publicity. I even had offers to do theirs! By the time Christmas came around, I came down with a cold that kept me in bed for two weeks. I was completely exhausted.

There was a newspaper item that dealt with obscure Broadway show album releases written by one of the critics who knocked the show. When I saw my album wasn't even listed, I called my friend who knew the critic. He said he would ask his friend about mentioning the album. The critic made us a deal; if he liked it, he'd write something. If he didn't, he wouldn't write anything at all. After many months I asked my friend what happened; the critic had never bothered to listen.

I happened to run into a music critic to whom I had sent the album a year earlier. I asked him point-blank why I never saw anything about it. He laughed and said the shrink wrap was still on the album.

One record store I called said they had my record in stock. This was strange, since I stocked every store myself, and I knew I had never stocked them. It turned out that the manager from a nearby store had asked me for some promo copies and was selling them to this other store!

As I was having dinner with a friend at Columbus Restaurant, I was introduced to David Letterman's producer. He chuckled when my show was mentioned. He thought I had ripped off my title from their *Late Night*. I explained that my song had been copyrighted many years before their show. I don't know if he ever believed me, but it was definitely the truth.

I began to receive some of the nicest letters about the album. The first came only a few weeks after it came out from none other than Allan Knee. It read:

> "Dear Brian,
> Congratulations on getting the album of 'Late Nite Comic' out. I bought it this week at Colony, and it brought back some pleasant memories of our early days with the project.
> Julie Budd sounds terrific.
> I hope you are well and not fretting too much in this heat.
> Best wishes in the future.
> Sincerely, Allan."

I called Allan, and we've been friendly ever since. I think he was surprised that his name was in just as prominent a spot as mine on the cover. I couldn't get over that people like Allan and Danielle, our assistant choreographer, had actually gone into a store and paid good money for the album, and I was pleased that they still had some fond memories of the show.

I thought maybe Steve Lawrence and Eydie Gorme might actually do a few of the songs, so I sent the album to them. They sent me back a note, which read:

> "Thanks for the copy of 'Late Nite Comic.' Everything about it was first rate, the writing, the performances and the orchestration."

Wonderful people.

David Brown, the producer of *Jaws* among other films, had worked with my grandfather in the early days. He wrote this letter:

"Thank you ever so much for your album 'Late Nite Comic.' It is terrific and I am glad to have it.

I would expect no less from a grandson of Eddie Cantor. I have great memories of him and it was wonderful to meet you and be reminded of one of Broadway's and Hollywood's brightest stars.

I wish you great success in your own career.

Warm regards, David"

This is a classy man.

The most incredible experience happened on Sixth Avenue. As I was leaving my friend Nick's office at CBS, I saw George Carlin coming down the street. I shouted to him and blurted out that I not only was a major fan, but also had a huge collection of his early records and TV appearances. He was extremely gracious, but in a rush to get to a David Letterman taping. I thanked him for all the wonderful laughs throughout the years and hopped on my moped, taking off down Fifty-third Street. As I was driving, I thought to myself, "Jerk! You should have given him an album!" I tore down Seventh Avenue to Fifty-second Street, ran the light and proceeded back up to Sixth Avenue, where I found George again amongst crowds of people getting out of work. "George," I yelled as I threw off my helmet. "I'd like you to have my album. I wrote the score to this Broadway show and thought you might enjoy it." Once again, he was so gracious. "Is this your address?" he asked, pointing to the back of the album. "Yes," I replied. "I'll definitely write you," he answered. He then headed toward the NBC studios and disappeared into the Sixth Avenue madness.

As I drove up Sixth Avenue on my way home, adrenaline shot through my body. "I have his name in the lyric to 'Stand Up,'" I said to myself. "Wait til he hears that!" I also looked at the reality of the situation. He was doing David Letterman. He'll have to go to makeup, he'll sit in the green room, he has to go back to his hotel, he has to pack the album. It's a pretty safe bet he's never going to bring it back to California, where he lives, let alone sit down and listen to it.

Within two weeks I got a huge package in the mail. It had George's return address on it. "Oh, he's sending me back my album," I thought. What was inside was beyond belief. First, I saw an autographed copy of HIS latest album. Next, there was a video tape of a concert of his that I was missing. In addition, there was an audio tape of a private show he did in 1964, and last, but certainly not least, there was a letter.

> "Brian,
>   I enjoyed the show album very much. I wish I could have seen the show.
>   Your music is great. It's my first "mention" in a lyric.
>   Thanks, George."

I have since heard from numerous people that their experiences with him have been similar. He's just an extremely decent person.

I got another brainstorm. Julie Budd must have a mailing list. Her fans would probably love to know that this album is available. I called her manager, Herb Bernstein, immediately. "Herb, how about this idea? If you'll let us use your mailing list of Julie's fans, we'll send a flyer out to each one that will have a code on it. For every sale that comes in, we'll give Julie a portion of the profits that would normally be made by the stores!" Herb said he would ask Julie. The answer came back a flat "no." "Why?" I asked in total disbelief. "Well," Herb responded in his casual manner, "Julie doesn't want to waste her shot with the mailing list people on an album that features her on only a few tunes. She'd rather wait until she has a whole album out." "Herb," I replied calmly, "that could take another year. There's room for both." "Brian, you're a nice sweet guy, but I kinda agree with her," Herb answered. That was it.

I was totally on my own. Not only that, but all the enthusiasm that Julie and Herb had about doing the songs in her act or elsewhere never happened. Every time she did a TV show or interview, she never mentioned the album or did a song from it. Despite all the rave notices I sent Herb and Julie, there was no further support. I saw her on Pat Sajak and later on Johnny Carson, and all she did was cover a Laura Branigan hit, which was currently in re-release by its composer, Michael Bolton. It made no sense. Of course, she did it exquisitely, but it wasn't hers. It was a waste of two important shots. I will always be grateful to her for participating on the album, but I seriously have to question her business sense.

Radio stations had to be serviced by me as well. On one rare occasion I heard the album was being played on a college station here in New York. I tracked it down and found that a young man named John Sanpietro at WNYU had gone into Tower on his own and bought the album. I called to thank him and ended up as a guest on his show. Ezio Petersen of WKCR had me back to promote the album. Joe Franklin had me on both his TV and radio shows. Jerry Alicea and Paul Cavalconte at WFUV were incredibly supportive and had me and Robin Kaiser on as guests. Arlene Francis interviewed me on her WOR radio show. Bob Sherman of WQXR did a most unique thing; he covered three generations of my family. He played my grandfather's records, followed by music written by my mother and then mine. My mother and I were interviewed together. It generated a great deal of listener response.

I got a list from Columbia Records of every station throughout the country that played show music, and I began to call and service each one. Of course it was not all hearts and flowers with the stations. WNEW-AM here in New York I believed to be important for this record. I sent a copy to Jonathan Schwartz, a radio personality and the son of composer Arthur Schwartz. I included a very nice cover letter, but I never heard anything from the album on the air. I called once, but he said he hadn't gotten around to listening to it.

My father, who was an avid listener to Ted Brown at the same station, recommended that I send one to him. As I was delivering the record to the station, I happened to run into Jonathan Schwartz. "Mr. Schwartz, I'm Brian Gari, and I wondered if you were able to find time to hear the album I did with Julie Budd of my..." Before I could finish, he looked back at me, and in a very cold manner (that even embarrassed the receptionist) said, "Look, don't bug me. I'll get to it when I can. Got that? And as far as Julie Budd is concerned, I never liked her. Thank you." With that the music librarian came out to accept the album for Ted Brown. He heard of my plight and my experience with Schwartz and said to get him five more albums; he would then get them to all the D.J.'s. I thanked him and returned with all the albums. The record was still never played. I called back and found out I should speak to the program director. He said I should get him more albums. I got him more albums. Still no play. I was disgusted. At least a dozen albums were supplied to this one station, and I was getting no airplay. Finally, when I ran into the librarian again at Tower, he assured me he would get it played. He actually did. It wasn't a lot, but he came through for me.

The album also generated more interest in the value of the songs. I saw the name of Mark-Leonard Simmons in the same column by Diana Maychick in which I had appeared. It said that he was producing a show that featured songs from short-lived musicals. I finally tracked him down and found out he had already planned to do a few of my songs from *Late Nite Comic* in his show. Needless to say, I was very flattered.

I got a call from another director named Ronald Russo, who was also doing a similar show. Again my songs were being included.

A man by the name of Ed Linderman created a musical revue called *Broadway Jukebox*, which allowed the audience to choose selections from lesser-known Broadway shows. He included "The Best in the Business."

The most ironic circumstance relating to a song from *Late Nite Comic* came when Marc Malamed was putting together a show with a critic from *Back Stage Magazine* named Marty Schaeffer. It was called *Damned If You Do*. They had decided to use "Clara's Dancing School" in their show. The irony was that Marty Schaeffer trashed my score when he wrote a review of *Late Nite Comic* for *Back Stage*.

> "Gari's music is just this side of banal and is only exceeded in triteness by lyrics which would make a grade school child blush with same…only Larry Hochman's orchestrations made this otherwise completely undistinguished score sound better than it really was."

This was too good to pass up. I called Diana Maychick at the *New York Post* and told her the story. She loved it. Two days later her column read like this:

> "Martin Schaeffer panned Brian Gari's 'Late Nite Comic' last season in Back Stage, expressing a particular dislike for the score. Now that Schaeffer's on the other side of the lights, however, his taste has changed dramatically. In the cabaret musical he created, 'Damned If You Do,' at Don't Tell Mama, Schaeffer has included the song 'Clara's Dancing School.' Gari wrote it. For the show Schaeffer hated."

It couldn't have been said better if I had written it myself!

The girl who performed the song was named Robin Shipley. She and I were just coming back to Don't Tell Mama after doing the song on a TV show when we were approached by Schaeffer.

"Did you see the *Post* today?" he asked in a very perplexed manner.

"No, why?" I responded innocently in an equally perplexed manner.

"Well, it seems I said some terrible things about your score to *Late Nite Comic*. Did I?"

"Yes," I answered.

"Gee, I'm really sorry. I don't remember at all," Schaeffer replied. Oh, the wonderful world of critics.

One of the funniest novelties sent to me was a bootleg tape of the actual Broadway musical. There was no dialogue—just the songs. The cover was a miniature reproduction of the Playbill. Congratulations to whoever did it!

At about this time the record industry was changing. The compact disc was becoming the new configuration, and *Late Nite Comic* was available only in the ever-declining LP form. We had to get a CD out there. Bruce Yeko agreed and decided this would be his label's first venture into that format. I thought we should include a bonus track to entice people who had already bought the album in LP form and possible new consumers. Bruce and I agreed I should record "Late Nite Saga." I made my last investment in a home recording studio. I knew I couldn't handle the entire thing myself, so I called my buddy, Jeff Olmsted. He had been doing some wonderful things with his four-track cassette studio, but I knew he wasn't realizing half his potential on that equipment. "Jeff," I said on the phone, "would you be interested in combining your equipment with some of today's newest recording equipment?" "Sure," he answered, "but how?" "I'll put up the money for a real studio if you'll run it. You're a great orchestrator, but not enough people know that. How about our setting up a real studio with you in charge?" He was floored, but totally for it. We went down to see my friend Jim Godwin at the Sam Ash Music store and bought tons of equipment. Jeff set it all up.

"Okay," I said. "The first thing I want to record is 'Late Nite Saga.' Here are my ideas." I gave him the basic format, while Jeff really made it come alive. He truly captured every feeling I ever wrote. I did the vocal with ease. One reason—I was recording at home. Secondly, Jeff has the ability to make the singer feel comfortable; he has a great deal of patience.

When I finished the vocal, I knew I wanted the production to be bigger. I decided to include a quote from a review of the show within this recording. I leafed through the reviews and found a quote from Dennis Cunningham: "'Late Nite Comic' is so bad that when I went outside at intermission, I stood under the marquee of another theater." Yeah, that would do it.

Next I had to decide who would play the role of a reviewer. I thought Alan Colmes would be an ideal choice. He declined. He was still being managed by Rory, so he felt he couldn't. I was very disappointed. I called New York's legendary D.J., Cousin Bruce Morrow. I sent him a copy of the song, but he declined as well. Because I mentioned local WABC critic Joel Siegel, Bruce thought he might be offending him. I even approached my uncle, who was very big in commercials. He told me no because he found a great deal of the song offensive.

I racked my brain and finally came up with a name—Joe Franklin. He always came through for me before, but this was a different situation. I called him up.

"Joe," I started, "this is Brian Gari."

"You are THE best, my friend," he immediately answered. "How is my boy?"

"Well, Joe, I'd like you to make a guest appearance on a record I'm doing."

"Anything, my friend. Call me Tuesday at 10—don't fail me."

That's Joe. After many return calls, he finally set a time.

"Come to my radio show," he said.

"What time?"

"I go on the air at midnight on Saturday, come by at 1:00 A.M."

It was a little late, but could I be picky? I set out on my moped after midnight, knowing full well that I was insane, but the irony of Joe being on this recording would be wonderful. When I got down to his studio, his engineer, John Sanders, took us into another room on a break and recorded Joe in about four takes. I added the words "my friends" to the quote to make it distinctly Joe. The next day Jeff and I fed it into the master recording.

I also ventured to call my ex-wife Darla to say the line "Are you all right?" I thought that would be yet another irony to have the real person who said those words to me say them on the recording. She agreed and hence, the sound of the "compassionate voice" on the "Saga."

Even though the recording was finished, it was not so easy to go from LP to CD. Lee Shapiro had originally put my whole album on DAT tape, so I was almost all set for the great quality on compact disc. I did, however, have to find someone to make the back of the LP into a CD booklet. I found a man named Lee Lebowitz at *Billboard*, who did a great job of cramming all the album's info into a tiny booklet, all in his spare time. Next I had to get a printer. Someone recommended a man named Joe Lipton at New York Printing, who helped me get a label for the CD and get the booklets printed.

I had to carry all the huge original artwork to all these people on my moped and then take the finished product over to JVC, which pressed up the discs! I almost had three accidents trying to keep this stuff from getting crushed on my tiny bike.

I wanted it in the stores for the Thanksgiving rush. JVC promised me they would be ready. When I didn't receive them by the date promised, I raised hell, and they finally sent them by Federal Express. I grabbed the boxes of CDs and got them all into the stores the day before Thanksgiving. They sold out in no time.

More reviews continued to come. Roy Hemming said in *Stereo Review*:

> "Less than a year after 'Late Nite Comic' got clobbered
> by the New York critics in the fall of 1987, Brian Gari went
> into the recording studio with a few colleagues to give his
> words and music another chance—a deserving one.

...As recorded here, the songs are genuinely likable...A
line in one song declares 'I'm through playing Harold Arlen/
I'll be the next George Carlin.'
I hope Gari doesn't mean that literally, for he shows
promise of becoming a major new songwriter."

That review took months before it ever hit the stands, but it was well
worth the wait. Again Colony asked me for a blow-up and put it in the
window with the CD booklet. There are some kind folk in this world.

With all this action I decided to make a live appearance in the cabaret
scene. Jan Wallman's seemed to be a comfortable place to start. I called the
show *Is There Life after 'Late Nite Comic'?* Robin Kaiser repeated her performance from the album, and I did a few other songs and, for the first
time, the "Saga." The shows were sold out.

"Saga" captured the ear, once again, of Marc Malamed. He put it into
a revue called *Buried Treasures* at the Gene Frankel Theater. A wonderful
pianist/arranger named Stephanie Gaumer had put in some work on the
vocal arrangement of my song, but she got another job offer and had to
leave. When I saw a rehearsal, I offered Marc my services as pianist on the
one song, and he accepted. It was a most joyous time teaching a talented
and warm-hearted cast their parts. I gave them all solos and played piano
for every performance. It was a totally different experience from my Broadway one. I even remember telling them on the last night, "I just want you
all to know that if I had to choose between working on Broadway again
and working with all of you, I'd choose you all without a moment's hesita-
tion." They said they felt the same about me. They were a lovely group.

Late Nite Comic is prominently featured in three books that I know of.
There is a full page in the 1987-88 *Theater World,* as well as a page in *Best
Plays 1987-88.* Some songs from the show have write-ups in the 1988 edition of *Popular Music* edited by Bruce Pollock. The Playbill showed up in
the strangest places; Pizza Hut had several miniature ones imbedded in their
table tops. I guess I should have eaten there more often. Capezio Shoes,
where most dancers get their ballet slippers, had a poster on the wall.

In June of 1990 I received a letter from Jay Brownfield out of Chicago. He was putting together a show on June 11 that would feature seven-
teen of Chicago's most important cabaret performers to raise money to
help AIDS patients in emergency financial situations. He told me that
someone named Becky Menzie was singing "Relax with Me Baby," and he

wanted my permission to utilize the song on a cassette release of the show. I waived all royalties and hope it did well.

On August 15 Rupert Holmes was doing a rare solo performance at Michael's Pub here in Manhattan. Although it's a rather expensive club, I decided to splurge and lend some support to this talented gentleman. The show was everything I hoped it would be—and more. Before his last song Rupert announced that he would like to introduce two people who had come to the show that night. The second one was Jason Alexander. "…The first is a gentleman who I admired as a songwriter for many, many years; I would feel very bad if I didn't acknowledge him. He wrote a musical with a very fine score called *Late Nite Comic* and it didn't…last. It kinda sunk. There are many components to a musical and it isn't always the score that's the reason that…I mean, when the Titanic sank, no one asked how the band was. And the band probably was really good on the Titanic, and the music was really good in this musical, as is all his music, and his name is Brian Gari, and I'd appreciate your giving him a round of applause."

I can't begin to describe what those words meant to me…and in public. This kind of magnanimous attitude is what separates the real people from the phony people not just in showbiz, but in life.

Two months later I opened a musical revue at a cabaret called Don't Tell Mama in New York City. The show contained various songs of mine about relationships. I decided to call it *A Hard Time to Be Single*. I even included "Obsessed" and "It Had to Happen Sometime." For this show the reviews were quite good. I produced an album of it (again for Original Cast Records) which also did very well.

At the same time I continued to try to get sheet music published on the songs from *Late Nite Comic*. Finally, after all this activity, a company decided to take a chance. Margaret Whiting had recorded a song of mine called "The Coffee Shoppe" and was performing it in her act. The song caught the attention of a large publishing company. They liked my work and were intrigued that *Late Nite Comic* was available for sheet music. A deal was struck. However, a few months later Frank Military from Warner Brothers Publications was at Margaret's show and also heard the response "The Coffee Shoppe" was getting. He and his two associates, Jay Morgenstern and Sy Feldman, said they would publish sheet music on "The Coffee Shoppe." When I told Jay that I had a deal with the other company on *Late Nite Comic*, he thought I should keep my songs under one roof and try to see if the other company would allow me to bring *Late*

Nite Comic over to Warners. The other company was kind enough to allow that to happen. The greatest news was that Warners had decided not to publish single sheet music, but would release an entire folio! Once again, it was incredibly ironic, because this was the same company that sent me a rejection letter exactly one year before. My tenacity had paid off again.

Warners was allowing me complete artistic freedom with the design of the folio. I decided that the artwork should be in line with the original album cover, so I sent Warners my father's original artwork for the folio cover. However, this time the word BROADWAY musical would be very prominently featured!

I also had the idea to include testimonials from some of my biggest supporters. My first idea was to use the George Carlin and Steve and Eydie letters. Both declined. George called me and was quite nice about it; he never allows his name to endorse anything. It was a bit of a disappointment, but how can you fault such a great human being? Steve and Eydie

WARNER BROS.
PUBLICATIONS

Sy Feldman
Vice President
& General Manager

Warner Bros. Publications Inc.
265 Secaucus Road
Secaucus, N.J. 07096-2037
201-348-0700 Ext. 904/05

April 23, 1990

Mr. Brian Gari
Tenacity Productions
650 West End Avenue - Suite 7B
New York, NY   10025

Dear Brian:

I enjoyed the "Late Nite Comic" album.

After consultation between my Sales, Editorial and Marketing departments we
have decided to pass on the print rights.

This is very special material that must be marketed to a particular target
audience. Warner Bros. handles the broader print market catering to rock and
heavy metal buffs.

I appreciate the opportunity you gave us to consider your material and wish
you the best of luck in all your endeavors.

Sincerely yours,

Sy Feldman

Rejection from 1990.

Published by same company 1991.

wouldn't even answer me. Finally, after many phone calls, their secretary told me to forget it; Steve and Eydie wouldn't even endorse a Sammy Cahn folio. I asked Jimmy Webb and never got a response. At the last minute his assistant said he'd pass. I was blessed with some beautiful letters from Neil Sedaka, Lesley Gore, Margaret Whiting and Rupert Holmes.

I had just begun an association with Jana Robbins, who was in the revival of the Broadway musical *Gypsy*. We were working on her nightclub act, which featured some songs from *Gypsy*. One day, while I was looking through the *Gypsy* song folio, my eye caught some very small print that said, "applications for performance of this work, whether legitimate, stock, amateur or foreign, should be addressed to TAMS-WITMARK." This was the licensing organization for this show. It hit me: now that I have a folio about to be released by a big company, shouldn't I take a shot and contact these companies again? I rushed into my office and looked through all my rejection letters. The one that seemed the most encouraging was from Tom Briggs at the Rodgers and Hammerstein Theatre Library. I called him immediately.

"Tom? It's Brian Gari. Listen, I have a song folio coming out on *Late Nite Comic* with Warner Chappell Music, and I noticed that all folios have info on stock and amateur rights. Since you were always so gracious to me, I thought I would ask you if you might reconsider *Late Nite Comic?*"

"I think you called at a perfect time," Briggs answered. "I'm going to bring it up at the next meeting." The result was that *Late Nite Comic* was represented by the prestigious Rodgers and Hammerstein Theatre Library. Four years after Broadway it was finally available for new productions. This is a source of great relief to me. It may not be on Broadway, but just to see it mounted again would be very satisfying. It has since been acquired by the highly respected Samuel French organization.

The folio was stocked in every major sheet music store from coast-to-coast. Colony continued its support of my endeavors, while Rick Starr was a major morale booster at Hollywood Sheet Music. He even sends over cute gifts every time I play the Gardenia in LA.

Warners showed their ongoing faith in *Late Nite Comic* by including the title song in their *Best of Broadway Today* and *A Decade of Broadway & Cabaret* folios, and "Gabrielle" in their *Broadway Classics*.

Probably one of the highlights of this whole rollercoaster experience was in 1992 when I received a check from ASCAP for a performance of "Gabrielle."

I looked closely to see where it had been performed. *Late Night With David Letterman?* Must be a mistake. If I call ASCAP and it is a mistake, then they'll take back the money. I better shut up. My curiosity got the best of me. I called NBC and asked who the guests were on November 20, 1991. Robert Wuhl? I knew that comedian personally. Talented guy. Sang "Gabrielle?" Didn't think so. Crosby Stills & Nash? Oh yeah, right after

"Woodstock." Hardly. Tennis player Gabriella Sabatini? Could it be? How?? Turns out Paul Shaffer remembered the song from over four years earlier and played Sabatini on from memory. This guy is one in a million.

I continue to write, perform and produce, including eight solo albums of my own. I did one album with Jana Robbins singing my songs, which featured three from *Late Nite Comic*. In fact, after Jana performed "When I Am Movin'" during her nightclub act, a popular singer named Denise Tomasello from Chicago came over to me and said she did the same song in her act. My friend Eddie Rabin, a top notch Broadway audition & rehearsal pianist that I knew from my Catch days, will often tell me of auditioners coming in with songs from *Late Nite Comic*. I've heard this same scenario from pianists in Chicago and Los Angeles. Even my sister, a successful performer herself on the west coast, was doing "Relax With Me Baby" one night in a cabaret when a girl came up to her and said that was her song! My sister said "not so…I got it first. My brother wrote it!" I am still grateful to both my sister and the other singer, the gorgeous Pixie Warren, for keeping the score alive.

Sidney Myer, the talented performer and proprietor of the New York City cabaret, Don't Tell Mama, often tells me that "Relax With Me Baby" is sung quite frequently in their piano bar area by such wonderful performers as Heidi Weyhmueller, and in years before at the cabaret Eighty-Eights by Ginny McMath. One of the funniest versions of the song was by the female impersonator, Beverly Hills (Bobby Pearce). He actually did a great job!

One day in 1996 I got a call from Roger Schmelzer and Ellen Kingston of Indianapolis. They were putting together a musical revue called *Lifesongs* and wanted to include my songs. No less than ten of my songs were going to be performed including "When I am Movin'," "Having Someone" and "Relax With Me Baby." Well, not only did I fly to Indiana, but they asked me to be the opening performer. It was a wonderful time. The songs were finally having a life of their own.

I've written a few more songs for some new show ideas. Who knows? Maybe someone will even turn this book into a musical. I only hope the director doesn't have access to WITE-OUT!

Updates

ALAN COLMES went over to WMCA radio in New York after WNBC went all-sports. When WMCA changed formats, he did morning drive for a station in Boston, but moved back to New York to become partners in a radio network. His big break came when he became the co-host of the successful Fox political talk show *Hannity & Colmes*. He also hosts his own radio show and continues to be managed by Rory Rosegarten.

PATRICK HAMILTON died of AIDS on November 8, 1991. He was 45 years old.

MORTY HALPERN died on January 3, 2006, at the ripe old age of 96, with more than 40 Broadway shows to his credit.

DARLA HILL continues to act in plays, television and films, including the hit *One Fine Day*. She has never remarried.

CHARLES HUNT left the Fifi Oscard Agency and moved to California. He died of AIDS on April 23, 1989. He was 45 years old.

STEWART KLEIN continued at Channel 5 until his death from colon cancer in 1999 at age 66.

ROBIN KAISER switched careers and became a make-up artist, garnering two Emmys for her work on *All My Children*.

ALLAN KNEE continued writing plays with productions at Harvard and The Jewish Repertory Theater. The film *Finding Neverland* was based on his play *The Man Who Was Peter Pan*. He also adapted *Little Women* for Broadway.

HENRY LUHRMAN died of pneumonia and heart failure on April 11, 1989 at the age of 47.

ROBERT LUPONE went back into his role of Zach in *A Chorus Line* and made some films and commercials. He opened his own theatre company, and in 2004, he was one of the producers of *Frozen*, which was nominated for a Tony.

CHARLES PECKHAM continued with The American Musical Theater until his sudden death in April of 1989 at age 55.

JAMES RAITT was the musical director of *Damn Yankees* on Broadway and *Forever Plaid* Off Broadway when he succumbed to AIDS on April 25, 1994 at the age of 41.

PHILIP ROSE helped produce a 1988 Broadway play entitled *Checkmates*. It made headlines when one of his co-producers, Michael Harris, was found to be in prison opening night doing 28 years to life for attempted murder and conspiracy and possession of cocaine with intent to distribute as part of a multimillion-dollar cocaine ring. Rose went on to co-produce and direct a limited run of the old *Shenandoah*. When his memoirs were published a few years back, there was no mention of *Late Nite Comic*.

RITA ROSEGARTEN died on February 19, 1996. I opened up the door to communication with Rory by sending him a condolence note. I was pleasantly surprised to receive a card back thanking me and saying that his mother "was a big fan of my music and played the 'Late Nite Comic' tape years later."

RORY ROSEGARTEN continued to manage comedians, with Ray Romano heading the list. He has become enormously successful as one of the executive producers of Romano's hit television series *Everybody Loves Raymond*. He has never produced another Broadway musical.

JOEL SIEGEL continues as entertainment critic for ABC television. He got cancer at age 57...but beat it.

JORDAN TINSLEY died of AIDS on January 5, 1996 at the age of 31.

TERESA TRACY moved back to California and rejoined her husband, whom she later divorced. Her last known appearance was in an episode of a series on the Playboy channel in 1992. She married again and became the mother of two children. She has remained friendly with their father, but has married for the third time and became an assistant to a wedding photographer.

JANET is married and the mother of two daughters. For her birthday a few years back, I sent her the CD of *Late Nite Comic*. It was returned with a note that read "Enclosed are the materials you sent. Do not communicate with me anymore. Janet." It was not her handwriting.

Brian Gari Discography

Bright Spectrum of Colors/The Unusual We/Pulsar Records 1969 (LP cut)
Bicycle Ride/Silent Celebration/Don Marley/Metromedia Records 1972 (45)
The Ashville Untion Recue Mission/Sleepy/Brian Gari/Vanguard Records 1975(45)
Better Than Average/Just Who Am I Sitting Here/Brian Gari/Vanguard 1976(45)
Late Nite Comic/Brian Gari/Improvisation 1980 (LP cut)
Late Nite Comic (Studio Cast) Original Cast Records1988 (LP)
Late Nite Comic/Original Cast Records 1988 (CD)
A Hard Time to Be Single/Original Cast Records 1990
Face to Face/Jana Robbins (all songs BG)/Original Cast Records 1991
Songs for Future Musicals/Brian Gari/Original Cast Records 1992
Love Online/Brian Gari/Original Cast Records 1997
I Can't Make You Free/Brian Gari/Original Cast Records 1999
The Very Best of Brian Gari (Japan) EM Records 2000
Brian Sings Wilson/Brian Gari/Original Cast Records 2002
The Man With All the Toys/Brian Gari/Original Cast Records 2002
Previously Unreleased/Brian Gari/Original Cast Records 2003
New in New York/Yvonne Roome(all songs BG)/Original Cast Records 2003
Here I Come Brazil/Brian Gari/Original Cast Records 2004
Brian Gari Sings Roger Nichols & Paul Williams/Brian Gari/Original Cast Records 2005

Website: www.BrianGari.com
E-mail: BrianGari@BrianGari.com

Index

205

·

Printed in Great Britain
by Amazon